SCENES FROM A SISTAH

SCENES FROM A SISTAH

LOLITA FILES

WARNER BOOKS

A Time Warner Company

This book is a work of fiction. Names, characters, places and incidents are either the product of the author's imagination or are used fictitiously, and any resemblance to actual per-
sons, living or dead, events, or locales is entirely coincidental.

Warner Books, Inc., 1271 Avenue of the Americas, New York, NY 10020

 A Time Warner Company

Printed in the United States of America
First Printing: April 1997
10 9 8 7 6 5 4 3 2 1

Library of Congress Cataloging-in-Publication Data

Files, Lolita.
    Scenes from a sistah / Lolita Files.
       p. cm.
    ISBN 0-446-52100-0
    1. Afro-American women—Fiction. I. Title.
PS3556.I4257S34 1997
813'.54—dc20   96-26372
                                       CIP

Book design and composition by L&G McRee

ACKNOWLEDGMENTS

My deepest thanks to the following people:

Mary Pittman, Renee Stone, and Debby Ryan for making me believe years ago that I was somehow born to do this. Bryan Keith Ayer ("Beav") for being one of my best friends and biggest fans. Eric Brackett, the coolest of cousins, and world's best partner-in-crime and hanging buddy. Rhonda German Ware, my sister, whom I miss dearly and will forever love.

My parents, Lillie and Arthur, and my brother, Arthur Jr., for their constancy and acceptance. The Brackett and Files families for the heritage and traditions. All those years of growing up and listening to my father and my uncles, particularly Jim Brackett, tell outrageous jokes and funny stories have blessed me with the gift of gab and the ability to weave a wickedly mean tale.

Nancy Coffey, my agent, for making me feel so talented. Your support, encouragement, and understanding, especially during my occasional crazed moments of self-doubt, are priceless. I'm glad I can call you my friend. Caryn Karmatz, my editor, for making this first experience totally painless and wonderful. Your support makes me feel like I can do anything.

Troy Mathis, for the initial push. Jacquatte Rolle, my friend, my sister, my mirror. No matter whatever happens in our lives, I love you and I know you love me back. Brenda Alexander, for being the earth mother, sister, friend, and assistant that I've always looked for and needed. Give me a little time. I need you in my camp, girlfriend. Frank Jenkins, my mentor, personal ego-booster, and dear, dear friend.

All my friends, lifelong and new. Even though I can't mention you by name, I cherish your friendship, much more than I can say.

CONTENTS

SCENES FROM A SISTAH

NOCTURNAL ADMISSIONS

I was at O'Hara's on Las Olas Boulevard in Fort Lauderdale. As usual, I was waiting for my best friend, Reesy.

O'Hara's was pretty cool. A dark, enchanting jazzy indoor/outdoor bar, it was a place we stopped in regularly for drinks and eats.

Sometimes, depending on the mood, we went next door to Cafe Europa, a quaint little cafe with an international motif, where the beautiful, and not-so-beautiful, people stopped to have dessert, cappuccino, and the occasional pizza or calzone. To see and be seen.

Often referred to as just Las Olas, like the area itself, this was the Rodeo Drive of Fort Lauderdale. It was a place to feel important and still be able to find places to dine for cheap. Or expensively, if that was your pleasure.

Reesy and I hung out there often. It was adjacent to downtown, which worked well for both of us. My office was only a block over.

I worked as a property manager for a large regional firm and handled several commercial and residential sites in the South

Florida area. I had been doing property management since I left college. The first two years after I graduated, I lived in New Orleans. Then I came back home to Lauderdale, still following the same career path. I had an eye for it. I was consistently one of the best in my company.

As I sat in O'Hara's, I realized it was places like Las Olas that made me realize why I loved my hometown so much.

I also loved being home because Reesy was here.

She was one of those interesting people that you kind of wished you were and weren't at the same time.

Reesy worked a mile away, near the corner of Andrews and Broward at Summit Bank. She was a microfiche clerk, which bothered the hell out of not only me but her parents as well. They wanted her to go to law school. Which she flat-out refused to do. She was probably talking to her mother that particular afternoon, listening to one of the weekly lectures they gave her about what to do with her life.

I sat there waiting patiently for Reesy, drinking Amaretto Sour after Amaretto Sour. More than an hour had passed. Reesy was usually pretty punctual, and ordinarily it would have bothered me to be sitting there alone for so long. But I'd been so stressed that day, the first thing I did when I got to O'Hara's was order a drink.

I sucked down quite a few while I waited. After the hour of waiting came and went, I wasn't even thinking about Reesy.

I caught a glimpse of myself in a mirror at the bar.

My hair was loose, hanging around my shoulders. Usually thick and difficult, a fresh perm had rendered it momentarily tame and manageable.

I liked the way my hair framed my cocoa-brown skin. I actually looked quite attractive as I studied myself in the mirror. My eyes had a gentle brush of bronze shadow across the lids. Almond-shaped, they were sparkling and seductive. A direct reflection of what I was feeling after all those drinks.

The dark brown beauty mark on my upper left cheek was

visible even from where I sat at the bar. I loved my beauty mark. It gave my face an exotic flair.

The jazz combo on stage was sounding real good, and I was seductively sucking on a straw in time to their cover of Stevie Wonder's "Too High."

"That's some lucky straw," a sexy, basso profundo, Barry White–esque voice droned close to my ear.

I cocked one eye to scrutinize the offending intruder. Only to find him not so offending at all.

Alongside me stood a brother.

Not just any brother.

A good solid six-foot-five piece of brother, tight and buff in a cobalt-blue Hugo Boss suit that fit him to a Tee. He was *extremely* handsome. A smooth milk-chocolatey brown with caramel-colored eyes and a sexy head of naturally curly hair trimmed into a neat, flattering, businesslike fade.

It was all I could do to keep my tongue in my mouth. This was a straight-up lollipop in front of me.

Waiting to be licked.

Now, if anybody else (i.e., anybody ugly) had said what he did to me, he would have suddenly found himself wearing Amaretto Sour cologne. But this brother was *three* fine. So instead of showering him with my drink, I gave my straw a long, slow suck, parted my lips deliberately, and pulled my mouth away.

"Is that your best pickup line?" I asked, my lips moist and still parted.

"Is it working?" he asked, his mustachioed upper lip curling in a come-hither smile.

Hell yeah it's working, I thought to myself. *Reach inside my skirt, and you'll see just how well.*

"Hmmm," I responded. "I refuse to answer that on the grounds I may incriminate myself."

"So you're taking the Fifth." He smiled, flashing a fabulous set of perfect white teeth. "Very smart. I advise that of all my clients, especially if what they say may place them in a potentially dangerous predicament."

Good Lord! Ummph! Ummph! Ummph! Ummph! Ummph!

I scanned his body quickly from head to toe, the straw once again in my mouth rushing liquor to my lips.

It didn't make any sense for a man to be this fine!

"I gather you're an attorney," I mumbled around my straw with feigned nonchalance.

"Stefan Adams, attorney at law," he beamed, proffering his hand.

"Nice to meet you," I replied, still nonchalant, offering my hand in return.

"And you are . . . ?" he probed, making my failure to reciprocate with my own name seem conspicuous and rude.

"Armistice Fine," I said.

I saw his left brow shoot up, but I didn't feel like going into the long and drawn-out explanation of how I got my name and why.

"I guess that would make you Misty," he said with relief, "and if so, you're just who I've been looking for."

It was my turn to shoot a brow up.

"You've been looking for *me?"* I asked incredulously.

How the hell did I get so lucky?

"Yes, ma'am." He grinned. "Teresa described you to a Tee. Only she didn't tell me you were *this* beautiful."

Damn. This was some trick of Reesy's. She knew I was putty when it came to good-looking men. Good-looking *black* men.

She also knew I hadn't had none in a while.

Reesy was one of those sistahs who was brash and straightforward. She had no mercy on anybody who was mentally weak when it came to men. Like myself. She was always on my case. I figured she was in the bar somewhere, and she'd sent this bait over to see if I would be my usual alley-cat self.

"All right, where is she?" I asked, turning around on my stool, wobbly and somewhat drunk, scanning the room for her braided head and high-yellow face.

"She's at Snowden & Snowden," he replied. "That's where I work."

I focused my attention on him again, my eyes narrowed with suspicion.

"No, really," he chuckled, touching me on the arm.

Sparks shot out from his fingers, up through my arm, and down my spine.

Right to my cat.

"I stopped into her mother's office to say good-bye for the weekend and invited them here to have a few drinks. Teresa told me she was supposed to meet you and was running late. She and her mom seemed to be having some sort of serious conference. She asked me if I would tell you that you didn't have to wait."

"Umph," I muttered, waving to the bartender for another Amaretto Sour. I turned my attention back to Stefan.

"I come here all the time," I said, my gaze now brazen and free, "why is it I've never seen you before?"

A brother like you would be impossible to miss.

"I've been with the firm three years. I've been working on a huge, pain-in-the-ass, long drawn-out case since last summer, and I didn't get out much. But I closed that puppy today. Our client was awarded one of the largest damage settlements in Florida history. You're looking at one liberated, happy camper right now."

"Congratulations." I smiled.

"Thank you," he beamed. "That's why I stuck my head in to invite Tyrene and Teresa out. But I guess it worked out well after all."

"What do you mean?" I asked with fake ignorance.

I knew damn well what he meant.

"Now that I've met you, I don't know if I should deliver Teresa's message," he said, his eyes scouring my body, making me sizzle with lust from the intensity.

"And why is that?" I asked, my tone dry and phony.

"Because, Armistice . . . ," he began.

"Misty, *please,*" I corrected.

"Because, *Misty,*" he obliged, "I don't think I want you to leave just yet."

The bartender sat the fresh drink down in front of me. Stefan quickly placed his gold American Express card on the counter.

"I've got a tab," I said.

"Not anymore," he returned.

Over the next three years, Stefan and I drifted into a fairly serious relationship. The foundation was sound, but there were times when, no matter what, we couldn't come to terms. Just when things appeared to be going well, something would happen to throw them off kilter. We found ourselves falling into an on-again, off-again pattern that always seemed to lead back to the same argument.

I wanted marriage, Stefan wanted a career. I wanted a career, too, and while I flourished in mine, he languished in a kind of funky corporate limbo.

He kept telling me to hold on a little while longer until they made him a partner. I waited and waited, really believing he wanted to get married.

My parents seemed to like him. In fact, Stefan and Daddy got along quite well. Mama was impressed that he was a lawyer.

During our first year together, I took Stefan to the small town in Mississippi my parents had moved back to after I'd grown up. They came to Fort Lauderdale right after they were married, denouncing Mississippi as backwoods and deplorable. As they got older, in their minds Mississippi lost its bitter edge, and they began to long for the "good old days" when they could sit on the porch and stare out at the cotton fields. When the longing became too strong to resist, Mama and Daddy packed up and went back, like two moths drawn to an overpowering flame.

Stefan seemed to fit right in as he sat on the porch with my parents on his first visit. He even went fishing with Daddy in that hot, cruel Mississippi summer sun. I never saw my father so happy as he was driving off with Stefan that afternoon, cane fishing poles, like Goliath's toothpicks, sticking out the back window of their mud-covered Pontiac.

"He's so mannerable," Mama said to me that day, as if that's all that was needed to qualify a man.

What did that have to do with anything? I wondered. Hell, Ted Bundy was mannerable.

Mama never asked if and when we were getting married. She knew it made me uneasy to be put on the spot like that. Every now and then, though, she and Daddy would drop lines here and there about getting old and hoping they lived to see grandchildren someday.

Needless to say, that made Stefan even more resistant.

I probably would have been less tolerant of him if he wasn't so damn fine. I still had a hard time believing he belonged exclusively to me. There was no way I wanted to give this man up. I might not *ever* get a man this handsome again. It almost made up for not having Denzel Washington, the man of my dreams.

"How is he in bed?" Reesy asked me one day.

We were sitting in a dark corner in O'Hara's, three deep in drinks.

"None of your business!" I snapped.

"That must mean he can't fuck. 'Cause if he could, you'd be breaking your neck to tell me 'bout all the good sex you're having. I've never heard you talk about sex with him once. After three years. And I know how you are, Miss Divine. You'll talk about sex in a heartbeat if it's good. I'd hardly be able to shut your ass up."

Miss Divine was Reesy's pet name for me—it was what she used to call me when we were little kids.

On the first day of second grade, when I first met Teresa Snowden, she walked up to me on the playground, matter-of-factly pronounced herself to be Reesy, and asked, rather *demanded*, of me what my name was.

"Armistice Fine," I said proudly. "I was born on Armistice Day."

"What?" the little yellow girl with cornrows asked, looking at me like I'd said my name was Doo-Doo or something.

"It's Armistice. But nobody calls me that 'cept my grandaddy. You can call me Misty. Misty Fine."

"Okay," she said, smiling, putting her hands on my shoulders. "Miss Divine is easy. You're gonna be my best friend."

Miss Divine. She said it again now, giving me that fake I-don't-mean-no-harm smile.

Reesy had a really pretty face that made it hard to get mad at her. Her skin was a smooth golden hue, and she had deep dimples that men had been crazy over for years.

The ubiquitous braids were tumbling around her face in a cascade of curls.

I glared at her. Calling me Miss Divine was her way of trying to subtly soften the blow of what she was saying. Too late. I was already angry.

"Leave it alone, Reesy," I said firmly. "Stefan is fine in bed."

"No he's not," she said matter-of-factly. "Stefan is just *fine.* That's *all* he is. He's a mediocre lover and a mediocre lawyer. It'll probably be years before my parents offer him a partnership, if ever. There's way too many other people that are better than him."

"Is that true?" I asked, shocked and worried.

How long would he make me wait for him to become partner? Suppose it never came?

"Yeah," she said. "I mean, sure he's won some good cases, but they had to ride him to make him stay aggressive. Stefan requires a lot of hand-holding. You know that. My folks aren't looking for that in the people they make partners. They want leaders, not babies."

"That's not fair, Reesy," I defended. "He *is* my boyfriend. You don't have to talk about him like that."

Reesy laughed a sharp, ruthless, unsympathetic laugh.

"Come off it, please, Misty!" she sneered. "You've been going with Stefan now for three years, and he can't even decide if he wants to marry you or not. I mean, *get real!* Even

8

you've had second thoughts. And third and fourth ones. Look how many times you've broken up with him!"

I swear, she made me so mad sometimes, because she was always dead-on about how I felt, even though I would never admit to those feelings openly.

"That's not true, Reesy. Stefan's going to marry me."

"Yeah, right, Misty! Did he officially say to you he wanted to marry you?"

My blood was boiling.

"No!"

"*See!* That's how sistahs like you end up getting fucked over. It's your own damn fault! That man ain't said shit to you 'bout marriage, and you're sitting around waiting on an assumption. How do you know he even *wants* to marry your ass?"

"He *has* discussed marriage with me, Reesy," I said through gritted teeth. "We've talked about marriage lots of times."

"Has he said he wants to marry *you*? I mean, has he ever said 'I want to marry you, Misty'?"

I didn't say anything. I *couldn't* say anything. Stefan had never said he wanted to marry *me*. Marriage was just this sort of nebulous, already-determined thing between us. Or so it seemed. I was always the one who brought it up. The only time he ever alluded to it was when I threatened to quit him.

"I guess I can take your silence as a no?" Reesy said.

My eyes filled up with tears. She reached over and touched my hand.

"Misty," her voice and expression were softer now, "I didn't say this to make you cry . . ."

"I'm not crying," I cut in.

"Oh, I'm sorry," she said, her tone slightly sarcastic.

I could see a gentle smile forming around the corners of her mouth.

"I thought those were tears in your eyes," she said in a soft voice. "I guess they're just glazed over with love for me."

I pulled my hand away from her. She reached over and snatched it back.

"Look, Miss Divine," she snapped, "I'm not your enemy. I love you."

"You have a fine way of showing it," I mumbled.

"Well, that's me. You've known that for years. I'm not gon' dress things up just to make you feel better."

"Yeah," I said softly, looking everywhere but her face.

I was angry. But I wasn't angry at her so much as I was at myself for always being so stupid about men. Especially one that I should have long broken up with for good.

She grabbed my chin and forced my eyes to look into hers.

"I love you, Misty. You're the sister I never had. You deserve better than this, and you know it. You're beautiful, sophisticated, and you've got a head for business that women and men would kill for. Don't let some half-assed nigga like Stefan keep you down with all this break-up-to-make-up shit. It's not worth it. I mean, he's fine and all. But even that shit gets old after a while."

"I wish it did," I mumbled. "I wish it did."

"Child please," she replied, clucking her tongue and waving her hand.

"Child please, *what?*" I asked.

"Fineness ain't the most important thing in the world, let me tell you," she said.

"Oh really?" I returned. "And what is?"

Her face took on a wicked turn, her brows raised. She didn't say anything for a few seconds. Then she leaned in toward me.

"He still can't fuck," she whispered.

I glared at her, then, surprising myself, nodded my head.

We both burst out laughing, as heads turned in O'Hara's at the two of us cackling in the corner.

One of the largest and most successful law firms in Fort Lauderdale, Snowden & Snowden happened to be owned by Reesy's parents. Reesy, which is what I'd called her from the first day we met well over twenty years before, was a tough-as-nails kind of girl, and she was a chip off the old blocks if there ever was one.

10

Her parents, Tyrone and Tyrene Snowden, were two of the baddest black folks you'd *never* want to meet. Straight out of the mean streets of Chicago, they'd gotten married fresh out of law school, handled some pretty high-profile cases involving the Black Panthers, then came to Lauderdale.

They started a small law practice during the seventies and now, over two decades later, had carved out a pretty serious name for themselves.

These days, with a firm of two hundred-plus attorneys, the majority of whom were African-American as well, the Snowdens were some of the most respected and feared people in town. Their firm specialized in representing high-profile African-American cases.

I remember when I was a kid, they were radical, dashiki-wearing, afro-puffed, Ungawa/Black Power–spouting people. Everything was a racial issue with them.

Before I met the Snowdens, I thought all parents were pretty much like my own. Both my parents were working-class, middle-American black folks. We went on vacations every summer and did normal things, like go to the beach on weekends and barbecue on the Fourth.

To my knowledge, my parents were never racially sensitive, even though they had a right to be, coming from the heart of Mississippi. I certainly don't remember them seriously fighting for any causes or wearing any dashikis. We all had afros in the seventies. But for us, it was more of a fashion statement than an ethnic declaration.

We were a regular family. Now that I was grown, they treated me, for the most part, like an adult. I talked to them once a week, usually on Sunday, and visited them twice a year, in the summer and at Thanksgiving. They were always glad to see me. And they never got in my business or tried to tell me what to do.

I had never known parents like the Snowdens. I didn't know whether to envy Reesy or pray for her. Tyrone and Tyrene were a tough act to please.

They were both high-yellow, just like Reesy, and were two

of the most ethnocentric people I had ever met in my life, giving much credence to a personal theory of mine regarding the militant yellow negro.

I figured there was such a high incidence of radical light-skinned folks because they figured they had something to prove. Like maybe us darker blacks thought a lack of melanin meant a lack of soul, and the light-skinned ones were determined to prove otherwise.

Reesy and her parents definitely had soul. They were a living testament to the phrase "the lighter the berry, the meaner the juice."

The Snowdens were on everybody's A-list. Mostly because people were afraid *not* to put them there. Any hint of exclusion or race-related slighting saw the Snowdens making a public outcry and successfully crucifying the perceived offender.

They had run many an ill-advised rich white person out of town and into bankruptcy, charged with counts of racism in their business practices and social preferences.

The social elite of Fort Lauderdale learned quick: invite them to everything, put them on the boards of whatever, and act damned glad to see them when they came.

This overt duress on the part of the Snowdens paved the way for a proud and popular life, not to mention an incredibly rich one. They resided in a lush and sprawling mansion, not far from that of the heirs of the Anheuser-Busch fortune.

The house was replete with a full-time live-in maid, a live-in chef, and an assortment of other on-site personnel. All of whom were black.

There was a ten-million-dollar yacht docked out back that sailed annually to Africa, sometimes with guests in the likes of the most famous of the black community, both domestic and abroad. Reesy told me that Denzel and his wife Pauletta had sailed with her parents the year before.

"How did he look? Did you see him?" I asked with desperation. I'd been in constant awe of Reesy's life from the moment we'd met. I'd been in constant awe of Denzel since I saw his

fine butt working the sandy beaches of Jamaica in *The Mighty Quinn*.

"Girl, he's fine," she said with boredom, waving her hand like it was nothing. "His body's got it going on, and he looks even better in person, if you can believe that. But he loves his wife. He was pushed up on her like she was an oxygen tank and he needed her to breathe."

"For real?" I said weakly. Damn. I guess he was never gonna be free. A girl could hope though. Ain't nothing wrong with hoping.

"Quit dreaming," she said to me, reading my expression and thoughts without even looking up. "He's never leaving her. He loves her to death. Plus, they got a buncha kids. He *has* to stay with her. That many kids would eat a stepmother alive."

I still remember vividly what she was doing as she said all this to me. She was filing her perfectly manicured nails with a broad, flat, dark gray emory board.

I remember that emory board most of all because I couldn't understand how anybody, even someone as nonchalant as Reesy, could be focused enough to file her nails so casually while she as much as uttered the name *Denzel*.

Just thinking about him upset all my physical apple carts. I wondered if she was lying to me about him being on the yacht. But with her parents, who the hell knew? Anything was possible.

That big house her folks lived in was nestled in the lush isles of Las Olas, the most exclusive area in the city, a maze of islands swimming in intracoastal waterways, a mere stone's throw away from the golden beaches of what was once the premier Spring Break heaven. Las Olas was a place many a poor or middle-class person, present company included, found occasion to drive through, long-eyed and wanting, fantasizing about champagne wishes and caviar dreams.

The Snowdens were truly something else. And the daughter they'd produced didn't fall too far from their tough-trunked tree. While she openly rejected all the spoils of wealth and opportunity they constantly tried to press upon her, she was as much like them as a child could possibly be.

She was an intimidating, aggressive, *in-your-face* sistah with attitude to burn.

Tyrone and Tyrene were very generous with their only child. They tried to give her money, even setting up a quarterly stipend that was automatically issued whether Reesy wanted it or not.

Reesy refused to use the money. Every three months when the check came in the mail, she immediately invested it. That way, she said, her parents were not responsible for her making her own living. Reesy took pride in knowing that she paid her own way for her own existence.

I personally thought this was a bunch of bullshit. It's not like the money wasn't there. If she ever fell flat on her face, she could just use one of those stipends, or she could call her folks.

I also found it ridiculous that they mailed the checks to her. Especially with her living right there in the same city with them. I think Reesy had psyched herself into believing that if her parents didn't hand her the check directly, then she wasn't really volunteering to accept it.

Obviously, that didn't make a difference. She still invested it posthaste as soon as she got it in the mail.

Ironically, she accepted non-monetary gifts from them without the slightest consideration. Reesy had been to Africa four times since we graduated from college, compliments of Christmas tickets from her parents every two years or so. They gave her a new TV, a bedroom set, and all sorts of black art that made my collection look almost paltry in comparison.

But she swore she was paying her own way in life.

I secretly wondered if that was why Reesy never had a serious job that she settled into. I personally don't think she really wanted one.

Reesy had a master's in business. She only got it to appease her parents, who insisted she pursue postgraduate studies.

After that, she stopped bending to the constant pressure from them about what she should do with her life. All she ever took were lightweight jobs, no matter how much Tyrone and Tyrene nagged and protested.

She was a classically trained dancer, having started when she was three years old. She also had one of the most brilliant minds I've ever encountered.

I think, when it got right down to it, Reesy was looking for Mr. Goodbar, just like I was.

Only she wanted Mr. Goodbar to be the real breadwinner and take care of her, just like her parents always did.

Me, on the other hand, I was willing to share the load.

I sat in my office the next day after my talk with Reesy, reviewing cash flow statements with my boss, Tony.

"These look pretty good, Misty," he nodded, his hand on his chin as he flipped through the pages. "You're running Mariner Way like a tight ship. That property was sucking wind when we got it."

"I still have to ride it," I said. "But I think we finally put together a good team over there. Andrea's a great manager. She's keeping the tenant profile top-notch. She'll evict in a heartbeat."

"If that's what it takes to keep the folks in Atlanta happy," he said, referring to our most important client. "They bought that site for cheap, and they want to show a big profit. Looks like you're giving 'em what they want."

I thought I saw a smile tugging at the corner of his mouth.

In response, my lips formed a tight, smug, well-disguised smile. I worked hard, and hustled to keep my portfolio one of the best. It felt good to hear Tony recognizing my efforts. It felt damn good.

Tony wasn't one for gratuitous smiles. Nor did he dole out praise too readily. But he knew my hard work meant larger commissions for the company, on top of the standard management fee. He knew he'd better encourage my efforts, because he damn sure couldn't afford to have me feel unappreciated.

He pushed his chair back from my desk without warning, as he always did, and walked away. When he reached the doorway, he turned toward me, his dark-haired, New Yorky, olive frame imposing and strong.

"Good job, Misty. Good job. Looks like there'll be a big fat bonus behind this one."

I let my smile run wild at that.

"What do you consider 'big and fat'?" I asked unabashedly.

Tony grinned at the question.

"We'll see." He smiled. "From the looks of those statements, I'd say at least five grand."

"Hot damn!" I squealed with glee.

"You earned it," he said.

Then, in his usual fashion, he abruptly turned and walked away.

I leaned back in my chair, basking in the glow of a job well done. I felt invincible. Like I was strong enough to do anything.

I picked up the phone and dialed.

"Hey, girl, whatcha doin'?" I asked when Reesy answered the phone.

"Nuttin' much," she droned, the rustle of papers evident in the background.

I tried to picture what it was she did all day. Copy stuff? Copy stuff onto transparencies? Take photographs of copies and copy them onto transparencies? What the hell was microfiche anyway? I never really saw what she did, I just knew it was way too monotonous for me to even comprehend.

"What are you all giddy about?" she asked, totally devoid of enthusiasm.

"Bonus, girl," I chirped.

"What else is new?" she said.

"C'mon now, I worked hard for this. This money's going to come in handy."

"Don't be stupid and spend it on that hardhead," Reesy threw in.

I ignored the comment.

"Why don't you let me treat you to some Sours?" I asked, my spirits animated and undauntable.

"That's fine with me," she replied, her voice finally sounding upbeat.

"O'Hara's at five-fifteen? Five-thirty?"

"Five-thirty," Reesy said.

"All right. Tonight's on me."

"You got that bonus check in your hand?"

"No," I laughed, "but it's coming. It's coming."

She chuckled.

"All right then, Miss Moneybags. Let's spend that phantom check."

She lowered her voice.

"Gotta go," she whispered. "I'm in the cornfield."

"All right, girl," I said, chuckling at her reference to the ears around her listening.

"I'll see you there," she said.

"Bye, girl."

I hung up the phone and leaned back in my chair, hugging my arms tightly together in a self-embrace. My spirits were still high, full of conviction and decision.

I could do anything, dammit. I was a superwoman. A black superwoman. A *sistah*.

I had a five-thousand-dollar check coming to prove it.

I sat there, smiling to myself, and made up my mind about what I was going to do.

I pushed myself up from my chair and strutted out of the office like a peahen.

I felt so proud. You couldn't tell me nothing.

I was a sistah, after all.

Shiiiiitttt.

A long time ago, I came to the conclusion that men are psychic. Especially calculating men. They seem to have this sixth sense when it comes to women. They know just how far they can push us, and they know when it's okay to ignore us and our threats.

More than that, they know exactly when to say the thing we most want to hear. It usually coincides exactly with the moment we've decided to kick their useless asses out of our lives. It's like they have some sort of radar. They know when we've been talking to our girlfriends, and they know when it's safe to relax and not worry about us taking the advice of our girlfriends.

Conversely, they know precisely the moment we will.

I met Reesy as planned at five-thirty in O'Hara's. I was anxious to celebrate my forthcoming bonus and the fact that it was Hump Day. Most importantly, I wanted to celebrate the decision I had reached about Stefan's tired ass.

A few hours later, having swallowed ten drinks too many, I was secure in the fact that Stefan had no intentions of marrying me.

I was also certain that our relationship, like his career, would always be this floundering thing that I, like Reesy's parents with him at work, would continually have to encourage him to get aggressive about.

So, earlier that day, and, with even more conviction, that night, I made up my mind to kiss his fine ass good-bye.

I knew it was going to hurt. That's why I got so zooted. If I were drunk, it would be harder for me to focus, literally, and I wouldn't be so aware of just how fine his ass was. Nothing was going to make me change my mind. Stefan had to go. That's all there was to it.

I was sitting on my couch drinking a Foster's from the fridge, trying to keep the buzz going until Stefan showed up at my apartment like he usually did. He lived in a townhouse near Holiday Park. Every night he jogged six miles, took a shower, then came over to my place, which was right off Broward near the Las Olas area. Stefan's townhouse was very nice, very spacious. But we spent most of our time at my place. No particular reason. It just worked out that way.

The doorbell rang three times before I noticed it was ringing. Stefan had a key, but he always rang out of politeness. He knew just walking in would scare the hell out of me. When I finally became conscious of the bell, I struggled up from the couch, took a deep breath, and, full of conviction, padded over in stockinged feet to the door.

He was holding roses and a bottle of Perrier Jouet. He looked like a big Snickers bar standing in the doorway like that. Obviously I wasn't drunk enough, because my focus was still clear enough to make out just how fine he was.

"Hey, baby!" he exclaimed, sweeping me into his arms. He kissed me soundly on the lips. He pulled away, a puzzled look on his face.

"Someone's been drinking Amaretto Sours and beer," he smiled. "One of those days at work, huh?"

Before I could answer, he closed the door behind him, took my hand, and pulled me over to the couch.

He stood above me, placed the champagne on the table, and stared down at me with a painfully sweet look on his face.

"Baby," he began, "I know you've had to put up with a lot lately."

I just stared at him. My heart was racing, but I didn't know if it was from confusion or alcohol.

Stefan kneeled down in front of me.

Oh my God! I *knew* he wasn't getting ready to do what I thought he was. My head suddenly began to hurt. At the same time, I felt a nervous glee at the fact that, for once, Reesy was wrong.

"Misty, you've tolerated me pushing you away while I've been trying to get things in order at work, and I know that's been hard for you. I know you want a future. I've been doing some thinking, some long, hard thinking, and I know now that's what I want, too."

My eyes were wet.

He handed me the roses.

"Baby, we've been dating now for three years. I think it's time we took the next step."

I couldn't contain myself.

"Oh, Stefan!" I was crying. "Stefan, I can't believe this! Is this really what you want?"

"Absolutely," he declared, his voice as full of conviction as I've ever heard it be.

I covered my face with my hands, the tears and liquor overwhelming my ability to speak.

"Yep, baby," he said again. "I'm definitely ready."

He popped the cork on the Perrier Jouet.

"It's time you and I lived together."

When the words hit me, they landed like bricks. My face still in my hands, I sat there for a few loaded seconds and made a decision.

This is a step. He never mentioned wanting to live together before. The next logical step will be marriage. You have to crawl before you walk.

All right, I thought to myself. It wasn't what I thought it was. But it was better than I'd expected. I wondered what my parents would think.

As Stefan returned from the kitchen with champagne glasses, handed me one, and clinked it against his in a toast, I was happy. Really happy.

At least I thought I was.

As it turned out, my parents were actually pleased when Stefan and I began living together. They never liked the fact that I lived alone.

Reesy was another story. She was pretty mad at me about the whole thing. She didn't say much about it. Just one dismissive sentence that was vintage her.

"Just don't come crying to me 'bout no more shit that has to do with him. You deserve everything that happens to your weak silly ass."

• • •

Things were fine those first few months we lived together. I gave up my apartment and moved into his townhouse. It annoyed me at first that Stefan wouldn't let me hang any of my black art.

I had a large collection that I was particularly fond of, especially my Frank Fraziers, which were my favorites. They were gifts to me from the artist himself. He had turned out to be one of the nicest people I'd ever met.

"We really don't have room for this stuff, honey," Stefan said.

"Come on, Stefan," I protested, "just let me hang one of them."

"Misty," he said firmly, holding his ground. "You know I hate it when you whine. It's not becoming."

I was totally frustrated.

"What about the masks?" I persisted, referring to my collection of African masks, which most people found quite impressive.

He shook his head.

"Can I at least put up my villagers?"

I also had a collection of African villagers that had been handcrafted in Senegal.

"Fine," he said, walking away.

He was about to get mad, but, as though some advising spirit had suddenly whispered to him words of wisdom, he turned toward me, his face softening.

"Look, honey," he said sweetly. "It's not that I don't want your stuff in here. We just don't have the room."

Yeah right, I thought. *Is that why I can't bring my bed here either?*

I was still sulking, until he casually tossed out the next statement.

"When we buy our house, we'll make sure we get one big enough to hold everything we both have. What do you say about that?"

A broad grin spread across my face.

"Okay," I beamed.

Our house.

Things were definitely looking good for the future.

Our ways of doing things were not that different, but I did notice some patterns with Stefan that I was never privy to when we weren't living together. For instance, he talked to himself a lot around the house.

"Now see, that's *exactly* what I'm talking about. The Bulls are a way better team than the Lakers or the Seventy-Sixers ever were."

"I'm sorry, honey, what was that?" I'd ask.

"Nothing," he'd say absently. Then he'd wander off into another room, in full-blown conversation with whomever it was he was talking to.

That didn't bother me. I mean, it was unnerving sometimes, especially when I walked into a room and he was already deep in conversation with himself. But for the most part, the talking to himself was no big deal. I did it myself sometimes.

Stefan also had a meticulous way of doing everything. His townhouse was immaculate, especially the way he had his little watches, neckties, and colognes laid out. These were things I had noticed in passing over the course of three years, but I'd never really given them much thought. I mean, he was a gorgeous brother. I guess meticulousness was a trait that came with that territory.

It was also a good thing that Stefan's townhouse had two-and-a-half bathrooms, because if there had only been one, I would have been up shit's creek. Stefan spent more time in the mirror than I did. He did more primping and preening before eight in the morning than an Ebony Fashion Fair model.

But this didn't bother me. Again, I attributed it to being part of the baggage of having a good-looking man.

He also loved titty bars. Yeah. Titty bars. But that was something he was into long before we moved in together. He used to go to all the area clubs in Fort Lauderdale and Miami with his buddies. Club Rolex. The Mint. Ecstasy. He went to them all. Not enough to bother me. But I knew he went. And he spent quite a bit of money when he did.

One other thing: his mother called a lot. A whole lot. Like I said, I talked to Mama and Daddy once a week, on Sundays. They weren't the type to pick up the phone and call every five minutes. But not Mrs. Adams. She called at exactly 5 A.M. every morning, and several times during the course of the evening. Starting with as soon as we got home. He always went into another room to talk to her. Even when she called as early as she did in the morning.

At first, I wondered if this was why Stefan had spent so much time at my place before we started living together. I thought that maybe he'd been trying to get away from his mother's kung fu grip. Then I realized that he loved it. He lived for those calls. So much so, that I once made a flip remark about her calling so often, and he damn near ate me alive.

"Your mom must lead a pretty boring life, hon," I said casually one evening after he'd gotten off the phone with her.

"What do you mean?" he said, voice sharp, eyes narrowed.

"Nothing in particular. But, you know, she never even gives you a chance to miss her before she's picking up the phone calling you."

"Is that a problem?" he snapped, his attention completely focused on me.

I felt uneasy, as if I had entered a domain I had absolutely no business in. Like Bosnia.

"No, honey. I like your mother," I lied. "It doesn't bother me when she calls."

Stefan didn't say anything, but his eyes were blazing with anger. In bed that night, he wouldn't even look at me. It felt like I was sleeping with a slab of ice.

When the phone rang at 5 A.M. the next morning, he abruptly reached over me and grabbed it before I was even conscious it was ringing. He didn't get up and go into another room, but I could barely make out what he was saying.

His voice was sweet and syrupy.

"No, Mommy, I've got money," I thought I heard him whisper. I must have been dreaming. No way would a grown man call his mother *Mommy*.

He proceeded to talk to her for a few more minutes, then hung up the phone and went back to sleep.

When we got up a couple of hours later, it was as though nothing had happened.

I never said anything to him about his mother again.

Don't get me wrong. I mean, I had noticed these things on a subtle, much smaller level before we lived together. I'm not blind. The talking to himself, the constant preening, the close relationship with his mother in Tampa were all there before. But now that we were always in each other's faces, they were glaring. And the sex didn't get any better either, but I was already resigned to that.

Nope. None of those things bothered me enough to make a real difference.

It wasn't until a good six to eight months into our cohabitation that I began to get a little bothered. Actually more than just a little. Things began to get really strained between us.

The culmination of all these events, I guess, was the talking in his sleep. I still vividly remember the talking being presaged by the gnashing of his teeth and the shrill, whining moans and grunts. I can't recall which came first, the grunts or the gnashing.

All I do know is that it was when these things began that I became most alarmed at just what it was I was living with.

As I mentioned, the talking in his sleep was prefaced by a series of equally odd events. Things started getting rough for Stefan at work.

"I don't think they plan to make me partner anytime soon," he lamented one day, his tone bitter and resentful. "I don't understand it. I work my ass off for the Snowdens. The least they could do is hook a brother up."

"They can't just 'hook you up,' Stefan," I replied. "You have to *earn* a partnership with them. If that wasn't the case, they'd have over two hundred partners in their firm."

"What the *hell* does that mean?" he snapped. "You don't think I've earned a partnership with them? Is that what you've heard? Did Reesy tell you that?"

"Cool out, baby," I said. "Don't be so touchy. That's not what I'm saying."

He stared at me.

"Just what the hell *are* you saying, Misty?"

This wasn't going well at all. I figured I'd take an alternate route to try and calm him down.

"Baby, you know how the Snowdens are," I said. "They hold black folks to higher standards than white people ever would, because they know what we're capable of. It's not a sign of them being too tough. It's a sign of them knowing the positive potential of a people who once built pyramids and ruled the earth."

He glared at me.

"Shut the fuck up, Misty," he hissed. "Don't give me that Afrocentric bullshit. I don't need to hear it right now."

He turned and stormed upstairs into the bedroom.

From that point forward, things were never, ever, the same.

Suddenly, nothing I could do for Stefan was good enough.

"What's wrong with this cornbread?" he frowned one evening.

I tasted mine. It was fine.

"Nothing. Why? It's the same as it always is when I make it."

"Something's different," he mumbled, getting up from the table and throwing it in the trash.

As if its mere presence on his plate produced toxicity.

The next day I made cornbread again. The response was the same.

"What's wrong with this cornbread?" he asked, getting up to throw it away.

When he came back, I confronted him.

"What's wrong, Stefan?" I demanded. "This is the same cornbread I've been making for years. You always scarfed it up before. What's the big deal?"

"It just doesn't taste right. Something is missing. And it's too heavy."

I glared at him in silence, obviously not satisfied with this response.

"Just don't make any more cornbread. It's too risky to know if I'll like it or not. And if I don't, you've wasted money on the ingredients just to have it be thrown away."

So what about if I like it? I thought. *You're not the only one here eating.*

I didn't cook any more cornbread after that. But it didn't matter. Two days later, Saturday morning, a package arrived for Stefan from Tampa.

I signed for it at the door.

"What is it?" I asked suspiciously.

He was grinning, breaking into the box like a schoolkid.

"It's from Mama," he beamed.

He finally pried open the box and produced one of several tins of what looked like yellow layer cakes.

"What is that?" I asked.

"Cornbread," he replied. "Mama made some and sent them to us to freeze. She used to do this before you moved in. I guess I got spoiled eating her cooking. Her cornbread is the only one I like."

I couldn't believe what I was hearing.

"His mother actually baked cornbread and *shipped* it to y'all?" Reesy laughed.

"Yeah," I said, still shocked and puzzled by it all.

"Girl," she said, waving her hand at me. "I told you not to tell me nothin' else 'bout you and that goofy man. That's what you get for movin' in with him. And his mama."

She laughed hysterically. I laughed nervously along with her.

But it bothered me. In a really big way.

The next surprise was his laundry.

"What happened to this shirt?" he asked, standing over me with what looked like a perfectly fine, crisply starched, white button-down.

I was watching *Jeopardy!*, my favorite show. He seemed to appear out of nowhere, scaring the hell out of me.

"What?" I said in alarm, looking up at him. "I don't see anything wrong with this shirt."

I reached out and touched it, turning it over in my hand.

"It's got a yellowish hue to it. Like it was bleached."

It *had* been bleached. He knew I used bleach. He'd seen me do it a thousand times.

"The shirt looks fine, Stefan. You're making a big deal out of nothing."

"What do you mean, *nothing?*" he demanded. "I have to wear these shirts. I've been noticing this for a while. I just haven't said anything about it because I didn't want to hurt your feelings."

"Oh," I replied, "so now that the novelty is gone, you feel free to hurt me?"

"That's not my point," he snapped.

"Just what *is* your point, Stefan?" I returned.

I had completely turned away from *Jeopardy!* by now, which pissed me off in itself. Stefan knew I loved that show, and he'd probably deliberately picked this time to start a fight. My guard would be lowest because my true attention was focused somewhere else.

"I don't think you need to be bleaching my shirts," he said in a flat tone.

"Then take them to the cleaners," I said with finality, and turned back toward Alex Trebek.

"It costs too much to take all this stuff to the cleaners. As it is, I'm going to have to buy new shirts."

I kept watching TV.

At that point, the phone rang.

"I'll get it," he grumbled, walking over to pick it up.

Which was fine with me. I had no intentions of paying any more attention to him or his nonsense.

Oddly enough, Reesy's words from a few months before came back to me: *He's fine and all, but even that shit gets old after a while.*

I had to agree: at that particular moment, his fineness was the last thing on my mind.

When Stefan answered the phone, his voice took on a whole new timbre.

"Hello," he grunted at first. Then, *"Hi!"*

His tone changed completely. I knew it was his mother.

He headed upstairs with the portable phone.

"I was *just* thinking about you," I heard him whine as he disappeared into the shadows of the second-floor hall.

This pissed me off even more, but I was especially unprepared for what happened the very next day.

That Friday evening, while we were eating dinner (complete with Stefan's mother's unthawed cornbread), the doorbell rang.

Stefan gave me a sheepish look as I rose from the table to answer the door. I didn't understand the look at first, but it became crystal clear when I opened the door.

There stood a beautiful fair-skinned woman, in her mid-forties I'd guess, a thick mane of auburn curls tumbling over her shoulders. Her caramel-colored eyes made a quick, obvious appraisal of me as I stood there in a dingy pair of gray sweatpants and an old Miles Davis T-shirt, my hair in a ponytail, the edges all nappy and in need of a touch-up.

I might have been jealous, thinking this was one of Stefan's former (or, God forbid, present) women, but I immediately noticed the strong family resemblance.

"Yes?" I asked.

"Hi," the woman smiled, trying to look around me into the house. "I'm Gretchen Adams, Stefan's mother. I guess you must be Misty."

My heart was racing. Within seconds, Stefan was behind me in the doorway. He quickly shoved me aside.

"Mommy!" he cried, embracing her tightly.

Mommy?

I stood back and let the twosome pass.

"What are you doing here?" he gushed. "You didn't tell me you were coming right away when I talked to you last night."

Right away?

She placed her peach-colored Coach bag on the sofa and walked over to the dining table, examining the contents of the serving dishes and our plates with dainty disdain.

"You sounded a little troubled, honey," she said absently as she picked through the food. "I thought I'd come down here as soon as possible and give you all a hand. Just with the little stuff, like cooking and laundry. Looks like you could use it."

She lifted the lid on a casserole dish and sniffed, her nose wrinkled tightly.

"What *is* this?" she asked with disgust.

"Chicken casserole," I answered sharply.

"Oh," she replied, rolling her eyes as she replaced the lid. "That's a lot of cheese. Is that healthy?"

Before I could respond, she had moved on to something else.

I noticed her abundant, perfectly formed breasts and wasp waist. It did much to explain Stefan's affinity for titty bars. And for his attraction to my own healthy bosom.

Stefan scampered around her like a puppy that had to pee.

"So how long are you going to stay for?" he asked.

She walked over to the couch, reached down, and swept off the cushion before she took a seat.

"Just till Sunday," she said. "I figured I'd do your shirts and any other clothes you were having problems with, and make a few meals the two of you could freeze for the week."

Furious, I walked over to the table, picked up my plate, and headed upstairs with it.

"Don't mind her," I heard Stefan whisper. "I'm so glad you're here."

"I'm glad I'm here too, honey. This place is a sty."

"I told you not to tell me any more," Reesy laughed. "You deserve exactly what you get."

"But this is ridiculous," I sighed. "She's supposed to be coming back for the next few weekends."

"All I can tell you is make room for her. Looks like you got yourself a big grown-ass mama's boy. I guess it don't help that Mommy looks like Vanessa Williams. Are you sure she's really his mother? She sounds so young. How old is Stefan?"

"Thirty," I said. "She had him when she was sixteen."

"*Damn!*" Reesy laughed. "She's probably still out there freakin' the streets."

"Well, I wish she'd get *back* out there and out of our house," I replied with frustration.

"I wouldn't count on it, girl. Now that you've let Mama in the door, ol' boy ain't gon' let you push her out so easily."

The very next Monday, after Mommy Gretchen left, I encountered the first episode of Stefan talking in his sleep.

I was in a deep slumber, facing him. We hadn't had sex that night because he wasn't feeling very well. I wasn't sure if it was because his mother had gone back to Tampa or what, but I really didn't mind that we didn't have sex. It's not like it was something I was dying to have with him anyway. Not any-more, that is. Sex had long since become dull.

I remember the crunching sound incorporating itself into my dream (I don't quite remember what the dream was), but it became so oppressive, I began to squirm in my sleep. The grinding and crunching were soon accompanied by a shrill whining sound, soon followed by guttural grunts.

My eyes popped open when the noise became so loud that it woke me from my sleep. I stared at Stefan, his face twisting and contorting as he ground his teeth and grunted. The grunts quickly turned into whiny words.

"Mommy," he whimpered. "Mommy, I've got to pee."

I stared at him in shock.

"Mommy?" he called, his arms groping, reaching out for me.

"Mommy!"

My man looked so pitiful laying over there. I had been angry at him more than usual recently, but looking at his cute little, well, big face so tortured on the pillow across from me, I reached out for him in return.

When he felt me touch him, he snuggled closer toward the warmth, nestling deep within my bosom. At this point, it is necessary to interject a relevant piece of information: I sleep naked. I guess I'm just primal like that. Anyway, when I say Stefan nestled deep within my bosom, I mean he was *literally* nestled deep within my bosom.

I rubbed him on the back as he burrowed deeper. The rubbing seemed to exacerbate his pleas.

"Mommy, I'm scared," he moaned. "They're gonna get me. Don't let them get me. I have to pee."

Remember, now, Stefan is a good six-foot-five piece of man. Imagine six-foot-five inches of man crawling up inside *your* chest begging for his mama. *Exactly.* It's not a pretty sight. It was a startling thing for me to witness, but I just wanted to hold him and help dispel whatever demons were flying around inside his head and troubling him.

"Mommy's right here," I murmured instinctively, still rubbing his back.

"You're here, Mommy?" he whined. "You're here?"

"Right here, baby," I cooed.

He burrowed deeper, one of his massive hands clasping my breast desperately.

"There, there," I kept on, thinking he was becoming aroused at the sensation of flesh against flesh, warmth against warmth. The touch of his hand against the swell of my oversized bosom was definitely turning me on. I leaned in closer to him as he took my breast into his mouth.

The sucking was fast and furious at first, then settled down into a rhythmic tugging of his tongue against the nipple.

Very aroused, I began to rub his butt as well as his back. This usually turned him on. I rubbed and rubbed, my back arching toward him with excitement, waiting to feel the huge erection I knew was imminent.

Stefan sucked at my breast for a long time. *A real long time.* Until I realized that he wasn't sucking. He was *suckling.*

Embarrassment and anxiety washed over me all at once. Stefan didn't have anything close to an erection. At the moment, he thought he was nursing on his mama's teat. I didn't know what to do. For all intents and purposes, I was all hot and bothered and ready for sex with what amounted to a two-hundred-and-fifty-pound baby.

To make matters worse, as I lay there, confused and humiliated (at myself and what my man had become), I felt something warm coursing over my thigh and spreading on the sheet beneath me.

I reached down and touched my hand against it, bringing my fingers back up to my nose.

It was pee.

The fucked-up part about it is that it all gathered in a pool under me. The sheet under his big ass stayed dry as a bone.

I lay there in a stupor, Stefan suckling my tit for a good half hour, until he finally fell asleep.

When morning opened her eyes, mine had already been wide for a good five hours.

As soon as he got up and disappeared into the shower, I

snatched the sheets off the bed, balled them up, dashed down-stairs, and threw them in the washer.

Stefan never even noticed the stain. He always got up in the morning and stumbled into the bathroom, oblivious of every-thing until the hot water woke him up. This was usually a cou-ple of hours after his mother had called at 5 A.M. We always slept until seven.

I dumped in some soap powder and turned the washer on and, on my way back to the bedroom, grabbed some fresh sheets from the linen closet. While he was in the shower, I changed the sheets and made the bed. We had long stopped taking morning showers together, so I had that time alone to cover up what had happened in the night. I don't know why I felt like I had to do so.

Part of me felt embarrassed that it had even happened at all. I didn't know if he knew about it and was trying to 'flage. It would have been hard for him to notice the stain in the bed because it was all gathered under me. Still, how he missed that pissy smell, I'll never know.

At breakfast, Stefan said nothing. He munched on a toast-ed bagel with cream cheese and studied the paper. I stared at him, looking for some indication of what had gone on the night before.

"How you feelin', sweetie?" I asked quietly as I sipped my orange juice.

"Fine," he said. He looked up from the paper, puzzled at my question. "How do you feel?"

"Oh, I'm fine," I replied, studying his face.

"Good," he said, and dove back into the paper.

Five minutes later, he jumped up, kissed me good-bye, and dashed out of the house. I had to go, too. I had an important meeting at work with my boss, Tony, regarding something to do with one of the companies we fee-managed for.

Our clients were always calling, or dropping into town, to see just what we were really doing with their properties. One of the asset managers from our biggest corporate client was in town for the meeting. I figured it was a heavy meeting, but I didn't think it would be that big a deal.

I sat my empty juice glass in the sink, picked up my briefcase, and stood in the kitchen, frozen, for a moment.

I needed to talk to Stefan about what had happened. *That* I knew.

I just didn't know how to go about doing it.

"Misty, you remember Rich Landey," Tony said, reintroducing the vice president of Corporate Holdings for the firm we did the most business with.

"Yes, Mr. Landey, how are you?" I smiled, extending my hand.

"Good to see you again, Miss Fine," he beamed in return.

I had met Rich Landey once on a visit to their corporate office in Atlanta to meet with him and the asset manager assigned to the properties we handled. We hit it off right away. An older, attractive white man, he was interested in my opinion, and very impressed with my business acumen.

"Why don't we go into the conference room?" Tony said, waving us inside. "Anybody want coffee?"

I found that interesting. Tony had never offered to get coffee for me. If anything, he usually did something stupid like say *Misty, tell Pam to bring us all some coffee.*

He shut the door to the conference room. Everyone took a seat.

"This is a little unusual, Misty," Tony began. "But this is a request from Mr. Landey, so I thought it best if he came here and extended it to you directly."

I looked from Rich Landey, to Tony, back to Rich Landey again.

"What's this about?" I asked. "Does this have anything to do with the way I'm running the properties? They're all full. And this is an oversaturated market. The cash flow statements have reflected us keeping them consistently in the black."

I thought back to the big fat five-thousand-dollar bonus

check I got just before Stefan and I moved in together, and all the ones I'd gotten since then. Things were going great. Those checks were proof of that.

"Those properties are in excellent shape, Mr. Landey," I protested. "And I'd beg to differ with anyone who'd dare say otherwise."

Off to the side of me, Tony cleared his throat uneasily.

"Actually," Rich Landey smiled, "that's exactly what this is about."

I was confused.

"Look, Misty—" Tony began.

Rich Landey cut him off.

"Let me do this, Tony. It's why I flew here, after all."

"Do what?" I persisted.

"We want to offer you a job with us as an asset manager, Misty," Rich said.

"*What?*" I exclaimed. I looked at Tony to gauge how I should respond to this. He nodded, indicating it was okay to be excited. He even smiled. Something, as I mentioned, he didn't do a whole hell of a lot.

"Misty, you're one of our best, if not *the best*," Tony said, the all-too-rare smile plastered to his face like somebody had slapped it there. This was something that I always knew. It was just something Tony didn't go around saying a lot.

"We know how good you are," he kept on. "And we know we can't keep you here forever."

I sat there, trying to follow all of this.

"Why would you guys want to hire me?" I asked Rich. "My experience isn't in asset management."

Rich smiled.

"We're willing to take a chance, that's why," he replied. "You're good at what you do. You've got what it takes to produce, and produce big."

I glanced over at Tony.

"I'll be honest," Rich said. "This is not a new position we're adding just to get you in the company. We recently terminated an asset manager who just wasn't cutting it. This is a job that requires drive and commitment to see results, and he had neither. I can't afford to fill the position with another weak manager. I wanted a sure thing."

"A sure thing?"

"Yes, Misty. I've been working with you for a while now, and I like what I see. I always knew that, if the opportunity presented itself, I wanted to have you as a part of our in-house team. We'll spend the time and money giving you the proper training. You'd be working for me directly. I'm confident you'd adapt as well to it as you have to what you're doing now."

I nodded, totally floored that all of this was taking place. It felt oddly surreal.

"Would this job be local?" I asked, already knowing the answer.

"It's in our Atlanta headquarters," Rich Landey responded. He gave Tony a quick glance. "Tony mentioned that you're a native of this area, and that your boyfriend is an attorney here."

"Yes," I confirmed.

"Would it be a problem for you to relocate? We'll do as much as we can to accommodate the move and help make a smooth transition for you."

Wow. This was really too much. I sat there, my body feeling limp in that conference room chair. Pleased and perplexed at the same time.

They waited for me to answer. But I sat there in silence, unsure of what to say.

"You don't have to give us an answer right away," Rich Landey said, much to my relief. "Just give it some thought. The offer stands for a while, if you feel it's something worth your consideration. I'll just wait to hear from you whenever you make a decision."

He stood from his chair, offering his hand.

I stood, offering mine as well. Tony stood across from both

of us, grinning awkwardly like some proud father watching his child accept an award.

"I hope to hear from you soon, Misty," Rich said.

"You will." I smiled. "One way or another."

"So what are you gonna do?" Reesy asked as she sipped her Corona. We were in O'Hara's, nestled in our usual dark corner.

"I don't know," I said.

"You want to take it, don't you?"

"I don't know."

"I do," she insisted. "I can tell by the look on your face." She took a hearty swig of her beer.

"Do what's best for *you*, girl. Don't worry 'bout what Stefan says. He ain't married to you. I personally doubt that he ever will be."

"Reesy."

I didn't even want her to get started. I had planned on telling her about the incident with Stefan the night before, but this thing with Rich Landey had come up. It was a good thing. Reesy would have definitely ripped Stefan to me if I told her what happened. She would have ripped him for sure.

That night, before I could tell Stefan anything about what had transpired at work that day, he came in snarling and growling about Tyrene and Tyrone.

"They just put me on this complicated-ass case, and they expect me to pull off a victory for the firm. They acted like they were so confident in my ability. So I asked them."

"Asked them what?" I queried with apprehension.

I knew he *hadn't*.

He knitted his brows indignantly.

"When they planned on making me a partner."

Oh, boy.

"What did they say?" I asked, unsure if I wanted to hear what the answer was, or open this can of worms any wider than it was.

"That bitch Tyrene had the nerve to say I was still a little too green to be a partner yet. After all the fucking shit I've done! All the money I've made!"

I stared at him. I could see the blind fury raging over him, making his facial muscles twitch.

"So I quit," he said flatly.

"You *what?*"

"I quit," he repeated. "I don't need their shit. I can get much further at a white firm. I should have done that anyway. I would have been a partner a long time ago if I had."

I sat there in silence. No way was I going to tell him about my day at work. In fact, I didn't know how I would even be able to broach the subject at all.

We ate dinner. His mother called and he told her about quitting his job. We watched the news. And we watched *Jeopardy!* without me as much as even guessing an answer.

Then we went to bed.

By 8:30 that night, both Stefan and I were dead asleep.

"Mommy!" he cried. *"Mommy!"*

I was awakened abruptly by Stefan's frantic screams and clutches at my breast.

He plopped my nipple into his mouth, sucking it with frenzied desperation. Bringing his body as close to mine as possible, he folded himself into my bosom. Within minutes, I could feel the pee gathering under me on the freshly changed sheets.

I tried to wake him.

"Stefan. Stefan."

I was very careful. I had heard lots of things about being careful of how you wake a sleeping person, especially a frightened one. I proceeded with caution.

"Stefan," I whispered, shaking him gently. *"Stefan!"*

I shook him repeatedly, calling his name over and over again, until he finally responded.

"WHAT?" he snapped, releasing my breast and sitting up in

the bed, his eyes glazed, blood-red, and angry. "What? Why are you shaking me like that?"

"You were dreaming," I whispered. "You were having a bad dream."

"Oh," he grumbled, still angry.

He pressed his palms down onto the bed, leaning back against his pillow. The pressure of his heavy palm near my thigh caused some of the pee to seep his way. He lifted his hand.

"Why is the bed wet? Was I sweating?"

Oh boy. How to answer this one.

"It's urine," I said softly. "You wet the bed. You did the same thing last night."

He sprang from the bed in a rage.

"*Bitch!* I did *not* wet the bed!" he screamed. "Why you wanna tell a lie on me like that?"

"Yes you did, Stefan," I said. "Why would I lie about it? Look at the bed."

I turned on the light and moved over on the bed. Beneath me, the white sheets were stained with a fresh yellow circle that was rapidly widening.

"Something must have scared you," I sympathized, trying to make him feel better.

He stormed around the room.

"I can't believe this shit," he bellowed. "This has never happened before in my life. *You* caused all this."

He glared at me.

"*Me?*" I asked, completely caught off guard. "How did I have anything to do with this?"

"All that fucking pressure. Marriage this, marriage that. I can't even concentrate at work for thinking about the pressure I get when I come home to you!"

"That's not fair, and that's not true, Stefan," I returned. "I haven't talked to you about marriage since we moved in together. I haven't said one single word about it."

"But it's *hanging* there," he screamed. "It's hanging there like a fucking noose that you're just itching to slip around my neck as soon as you find the proper opening!"

"Well, I'm sorry it feels like a noose to you. I thought you asked me to live with you because you wanted to be with me. Not because it was something you felt *condemned* to do."

I sat naked in the bed, Stefan's pee following me to where I had moved and gathering around my bottom, its ammonia stench enveloping me.

"Get up and change that fucking sheet!" he yelled.

I looked over at him, sure that I was not hearing him demand that I do his bidding. Especially since it was *his* pissy ass that had soaked the bed.

"Excuse me?" I asked rhetorically, my neck twisted and curling in a sistah-girl pose.

"You heard me!" he repeated. "Get up and change that fucking sheet! Get that shit outta here!"

I stared at him in sheer disbelief. He had to be crazy. He just had to be out of his fucking mind.

"You change it!" I snapped.

"What?" he asked, his face twisting even tighter. "*What* did you say?"

For a minute, I got scared. But this was Stefan. I'd known him for more than three years. He had his damn nerve, telling me what to do.

"I said *you* change the sheets. It's *your* funky piss."

During the next few seconds, I saw a large brown blur dive toward me, a sudden flash of light, and felt a fierce, blinding pain in my left eye.

Then the lights went out.

"I oughta kill that motherfucka!" Reesy exclaimed, storming around her bedroom.

I was in her bed, the left side of my face swollen, my eye sealed shut. The phone was ringing off the hook. I guess Stefan had figured I would definitely be here.

"You oughta have his black ass arrested!" she kept on.

I watched her. She was in more of a rage than I was, talking all ghetto and hard, like she did so often. Even though she had a formal upbringing and serious college education, she liked talking like that. It was yet another way of defying her parents' conventions.

She paced to and fro like a cheetah. If Stefan had been within a mile of Reesy, I believe she would have torn him to pieces.

The phone was still ringing.

Stefan had taken me to the emergency room, scared to death that I wouldn't come to. I don't know what cocka-mamie story he told them at the hospital about what happened, but I made sure they didn't let him come into the room with me once I became conscious.

They asked me if I wanted to talk about what happened. I told them no. They asked me if I wanted to press charges or see their counselor on spousal abuse. I told them I didn't want to talk about it.

I didn't even want my parents to know about this. It would scare them to death. They were so afraid of something happening to me, all alone in Fort Lauderdale. They were relieved that I had Stefan to protect me.

Mama and Daddy would have had a double heart attack if they knew he was the one I needed to be protected from. Daddy would probably take one of those cane fishing poles and introduce Stefan to a new type of enema.

Reesy was the only person I knew I could talk to. Aside from my parents, she was my family. She was my real protector.

The nurse called Reesy for me, and she came to the hospital and picked me up. She took me back to her apartment, where she had been pacing and ranting ever since. I told her about what Stefan had done. I even told her about him peeing in the bed and sucking my breasts.

"Wait until my folks hear about this!" she screamed, her arms flailing about in the air. "It's a good thing he quit, because they damn sure would have fired him. You can sue him for this, you know."

I sat back against the pillows, frustrated, listening to the ringing phone.

"Don't tell your parents about this, Reesy." My voice was barely a whisper. "I don't want anybody but you to know."

She stopped pacing and looked at me. I noticed her eyes were filled with angry tears.

"This is a bunch of bullshit," she said. "You know, you should have left this bastard a long time ago. He didn't wanna marry you, and all this freaky shit with him talking to himself, staying in the mirror so much, and being so tight with his mother. We should have seen this coming."

I was quiet.

She rubbed me on the back.

"Look, girl. I know the last thing you need is me yelling and rehashing the whole thing over again with you. I'm just *so* mad, I could kill him. *Look at your face!* Nobody deserves to go through shit like this!"

I started crying. The tears stung my left eye something fierce. The phone rang and rang and rang.

"Don't cry, Misty. Not over that bastard. He's not worth it."

I nodded.

"If anything, cry happy tears over the fact that at least now you know what to do."

"What do you mean?" I whimpered.

"I mean you can take that job in Atlanta now."

I had forgotten about that in all of this.

"You hear what I'm saying?" she continued.

"Uh-huh," I sniffled.

"Good, Get away from this nigga. Pursue your career. There's bigger and better things out there for you, Miss Divine. Just finding some nigga to marry you ain't gon' be the answer to all your problems."

She brushed a stray hair off my forehead.

"I'd hate to see you go, but I think the world has something better than this shit out there for you."

The phone was still ringing.

Reesy snatched the receiver off the hook, bringing it up to her ear.

"Look, motherfucka, you call here one more time, and I'm gonna give you something to pee in the bed about for real!"

She was quiet for a moment. Then a sheepish smile crept over her face.

"Hi, Ma."

Two days later, I called Rich Landey and accepted his job offer. Tony gave me the rest of the week off. He didn't know why he was giving it to me. I said I needed the time. I planned to move to Atlanta within the next three weeks, after tying up a few loose ends.

I never had any real contact with Stefan again after that night at the hospital. I got an immediate restraining order against him, and Reesy arranged to go to the townhouse to gather up my things.

I told my parents that the reason I broke up with Stefan was that our relationship wasn't going anywhere. I never told them about the fight. When I told them about the new job, they were proud, but I could tell they didn't want me to move to a strange city where I didn't know anyone. Who was going to protect me? Daddy wanted to know.

"God looks out for fools," I joked with him on the phone.

He had no idea how foolish I really felt, sitting there with a swollen eye and a hole in my heart.

A few times, I saw Stefan's car parked down the street, just far enough out of range of the restraining order to not be in violation. He knew I saw him. He parked outside of Reesy's apartment and sometimes near my job.

But he had sense enough not to call me.

If he had, I would have had his ass sent straight to jail.

I should have done that from the very beginning. But I guess when it came to men, I was kinda stupid. A part of me felt sorry for him.

And I truly believed he was suffering now. Jail probably wouldn't have made a difference.

I stayed at Reesy's until it was time for me to go to Atlanta. During my stay, I found it very easy to live with her, a fact that I would have never believed had this whole thing not happened.

We hung out at O'Hara's, cooked together, and she helped me pack up my things for the move.

Before I left, I had actually begun to relax.

I was sleeping much better. No one was pissing on me now. And I didn't have to worry about anybody sucking my breasts.

Unless I wanted them to.

THE 'LANTA OPPORTUNITY

It took me a little bit of time to adjust to Atlanta once I made the move.

Getting situated was kind of hard without Reesy around every day. I'd grown accustomed to having her to talk to and help me with things. I even found myself missing Stefan after having lived with him for almost a year.

But all I had to do was think about him clocking me in the eye, and the thought of missing him fled with a quickness.

I found a nice apartment in Stone Mountain, in one of the Treehills apartment communities. My new boss, Rich Landey, had referred me to several different areas, and this was the one I found I liked best.

The apartment was huge, like a house, and, I swear, the entire complex seemed to be filled with up-and-coming African-Americans. It was visually powerful to see so many of us living together in such a positive light. Something the media swears just ain't possible.

In my former job as a property manager, I had been over several communities with a large number of units. Treehills was incredible. It must have been a twelve-hundred-plus-unit apartment complex, landscaped beautifully, as if it were a national park.

My apartment was a big, spacious two-bedroomer with a washer/dryer, a huge living room with a patio just outside, an eat-in kitchen, dining room, two bathrooms, a fireplace, *and* a sunroom. And the rent was a couple hundred dollars cheaper than I had been paying in Fort Lauderdale.

I converted one of the bedrooms into an office. I didn't anticipate that I'd have much need for a second bedroom.

I loved being able to sprawl around again in my big four-poster bed. When Stefan and I lived together, I had had to put it in storage. He said it was way too big to fit in his townhouse.

Which was a lie, of course. He just wanted us to sleep in *his* bed.

I hung my black art all around the apartment in strategic places where it would face me whenever I sat down. I put my collection of African villagers on the mantel over the fireplace. I hung my African masks in a clever collage in the hallway.

But, by far, my favorite room in the apartment was the sunroom.

I loved the feeling of solitude and peace that washed over me when I sat in that sunroom in the afternoons. In the evenings, the lamplight outside filtered in and blended with the light of the moon to give the room an intimate glow. This is where I hung the majority of my collection of Frank Fraziers. His *Aisha* series gave the room a distinctly inspiring flavor.

In the midst of those beautiful hangings, I would curl up on my futon, sip hot spiced tea, and listen to the sounds of some old Stevie Wonder while I read.

It was wonderful. The only thing missing was Reesy.

And a good man.

Oh well. At least I had a great job to go to.

A great job I couldn't wait to get started with.

• • •

Everyone was so friendly the first day at work. Rich Landey had someone waiting for me at the front desk when I arrived.

"Misty?" asked an elegantly tailored sistah, mid-forties or so.

"Yes." I smiled, pleased at the pervasiveness of the power-ful images of black folk in Atlanta.

She extended a slender, graceful hand.

"I'm Rebecca," she smiled, "Rich's assistant. He wanted me to personally show you around and help you get situated."

Hmmmm. Interesting. Rich Landey had a sistah for a secre-tary. I figured this must be the *new* South.

"Thank you." I smiled. "I'm really excited about being here."

Rebecca smiled warmly in return, her face radiant when she did so. It seemed truly genuine.

"We're excited to have you here. I'm always excited to see good things happen for one of our own."

We both smiled, conspiratorially, at each other.

I felt proud and stealthy at the same time, like I was now part of some secret order that all of African-American Atlanta belonged to. A feeling I never quite got in Fort Lauderdale, despite my networking efforts there. The black middle class there was much too cocooned and private about who they let into their circles.

I assumed that when Rebecca said "we," she meant black folks. Perhaps I was being too assumptive. Maybe her "we" meant the company.

Nah. That couldn't be the case, because I had not been a part of the company until now. It must have been a black thang. That had to be what it was.

She signaled for me to follow her.

"Have you gotten yourself situated okay?" she asked, run-ning her hand casually across her closely cropped hair.

"Um-hm," I nodded. "I really like where I live. I can't believe how inexpensive it is. Everything is inexpensive here. I actually bought some gas for seventy-seven cents a gallon."

"Yeah," Rebecca replied. "It is a beautiful city, and it's surprisingly affordable. Most people don't realize that until they get here. Finding a job can be kind of hard, though. You have to know where to go. Or be persistent."

We turned down a marble corridor to a bank of elevators. Rebecca pressed the UP button.

"So where did you move?"

"Stone Mountain," I returned.

"Oh really?" she smiled. "I live out that way, too. It's a bit of a trek, but it's worth it. I'm pretty close to where you are. I live in Lithonia."

"Oh," I nodded, like I knew where that was.

"I guess that means nothing to you right now." Rebecca laughed.

We got on the elevator.

"You still have to get your bearings, I guess."

We were on the elevator alone. I had come to work early. It was only seven-thirty. But Rich had planned on being there, and I guess he'd arranged for Rebecca to be there, too.

"Where exactly do you live in Stone Mountain?" she asked.

"Treehills Apartments."

"Girl!" she exclaimed, "you're right next to where I live! That's just off Hairston. I'm over on Panola."

I nodded. "Good. Perhaps we can get together sometimes. I don't know anybody here. I need to make some friends."

Rebecca waved her hand. "Girl, trust me, you have friends here. You just don't know it. Probably people you grew up with, went to school with, something. Everybody and their mama's moving to Atlanta. It's the Chocolate City for the nineties. It's becoming our people's cultural center."

Yep. Rebecca was definitely on the Afrocentric trip. I liked that. I liked that a lot.

"Don't worry," she continued. "You'll run into some of your friends eventually. In the Underground or the malls. Or the clubs. Do you like to go out much?"

"Not really," I said, scrunching up my nose. The party scene had long since lost its luster for me.

"Well, that's all right. There's plenty of places for you to run into people you know. At concerts and picnics in the park. Freaknik. Juneteenth. Everything."

"I think I'm a little too old for Freaknik," I said, referring to the annual picnic that drew millions of young African-Americans to Atlanta.

"I don't know," she chuckled. "Everybody goes to Freaknik. It's a spectacle. And it's kinda fun."

We rode up to the fifteenth floor.

"I'll introduce you to some people," she said. "My husband and I entertain quite a bit. He's head of the InterCounty Minority Economic Development Board."

I was impressed. I stole a quick glance at her left hand. Perched happily on her ring finger was what had to be the biggest rock I'd ever seen. Several smaller diamonds were in orbit around the giant of a stone, shimmering like little moons.

"Hugh is always bringing someone new to our house or dragging me out to some kind of function. Maybe you'd like to come along. You seem pretty down to earth. You'll make friends fast."

"That would be nice." I smiled.

Perhaps it would give me the opportunity to meet some quality people. I wanted to be a part of the positive energy I felt pulsating all around me.

"Are there a lot of us in the building?" I asked with hesitation, wondering if this was okay to say.

"Oh, yeah, honey," Rebecca replied. "We're all over the place. This is Atlanta. You can relax. We are *highly* visible here."

The elevator doors opened. We exited onto a beautiful floor with an array of spacious offices.

"Rich is really excited about you being here."

"I still can't believe he gave me this opportunity," I conceded.

We walked through a series of thresholds and turned a few corners.

"Rich is a great guy to work for. He's been talking about you since he first met you. More so since your portfolio was performing so well."

"How long have you worked for him?" I asked.

"Collectively, about ten years. I worked for him before at another company. I went on to do some other things, but he sought me out and brought me here."

She leaned a little closer to me.

"One thing I can say about the man: he's brand loyal. You do a good job for him, he'll support you to the ends of the earth."

I listened, nodding.

"I think he's got big plans for you," she added.

"You think so?"

"Oh yeah," Rebecca said matter-of-factly. "He's been eyeing you as a potential employee for this company for a long time. After the performances and profits we saw in the past year, he just knew he had to get you on board here."

I liked Rebecca. I really did. It felt good to be in the presence of another sistah, an impressive one at that, and not feel so competitive or have her feel threatened by my presence.

Of course, maybe Rebecca didn't have anything to feel threatened about to begin with. I didn't know how much money she was making. She did work for the big guy, after all, and her husband was obviously well paid. That outfit of hers was pretty sharp, her nails were well manicured, and her coif was laid. No need to even discuss the ring.

We stopped in front of a beautifully carved cherrywood door.

"All right, girl," she whispered, "good luck. And if you need anything, I'm right here, one door down the hall."

"Thank you," I smiled. "I appreciate everything."

"No problem. Just holler when you need help."

She opened the door and waved me in.

"Misty!" Rich boomed, grinning broadly.

"Hi, Rich." I grinned in return.

I looked over my shoulder to see Rebecca discreetly closing the door to leave Rich and me to talk.

She mouthed the words *good luck*, and then her beautifully coiffed head disappeared behind the dark red of the cherrywood door.

Rich worked with me exclusively that first week. He came in early in the mornings and went over company goals and objectives. He took me on a tour of sites in the Atlanta area that would be included in the portfolio of properties I would be responsible for.

He told me that my portfolio would ultimately include several sites in other states. I gushed with pride over that. I was beginning to feel like one of the big dogs.

Rich took me to lunch with him everyday, and he had me sit in on meetings with other asset managers. He made me feel at ease and that this was definitely a place that I could call home.

I had thought that the transition from property manager to asset manager would be a tough one, but I saw that it was merely a role reversal. I was now the client.

The real estate management companies would now be working for *me* and licking *my* boots. They'd be jumping for *me* when they knew I was coming to town.

Other than that, in both jobs I had the same primary objective: to make the properties, now termed *assets*, as profitable as possible. It'd be a breeze. It was something I already knew I was good at.

Rich assigned me to shadow another asset manager, Jeremy, for my first month. Jeremy was to share a portfolio with me for the first ninety days, then eventually segue all of the responsibility to me completely. In order to free himself up to be able to do this, he had to assign some of his own portfolio to another manger. I don't think he was too happy about having to do this.

Jeremy, diminutive and nerdy, with designer eyeglasses that

didn't quite suit him and a shock of blond hair that made him look like Dennis the Menace, was a hot-shot Wharton grad who didn't have time to be training a newcomer. He was pleasantly resistant when first told of his pairing with me.

"Jeremy," Rich boomed, slapping him on the back, "I want you to take good care of Misty for me. Show her how you do it. It won't take her long to get a grasp of what we do around here."

Jeremy glanced up at me from his desk, his smile forced and wan.

"Sure, Boss," he said, "but who's going to make sure Waukegan is staying on track?"

Jeremy looked over at me as if to say *No offense, but I've got work to do.*

"Don't worry about Waukegan," Rich replied. "I just want you to take care of Misty."

I stood there awkwardly, not wanting to create any problems for anyone. I knew how I would feel if some newcomer got dumped on me.

"But what about—" Jeremy began again.

Rich raised his finger in an amused admonishment that Jeremy recognized as a serious demand to shut the fuck up.

"Don't worry about *any* of your assignments, Jeremy," Rich repeated. "They'll all be taken care of."

"All right, Boss," Jeremy sighed, shrugging his shoulders in surrender. "You know what's best."

"Good deal!" Rich exclaimed.

He turned toward me, his hand on my back.

"I'm going to leave you with Jeremy, but I'll be checking in on you daily."

"Okay." I smiled. "I appreciate all the attention, Rich. I really do."

"I just want to make sure we give you the tools you need to be a success here. If there's anything I can do for you during your training or even after you become well situated, you let me know. You understand?"

I grinned.

"Absolutely."

"Good deal," he said, slapping me gently on the back. "She's all yours, Jeremy. Take good care of her."

"Yeah, Boss," Jeremy whined.

Rich walked away, leaving me to take a seat in the vacant chair in Jeremy's office.

I leaned forward on his desk, my elbows resting on the hard wood surface, my face in my hands.

"Look," I began. "I'm sorry about this. I didn't mean to have you get saddled with me for three months. I know how it is to have work to do."

Jeremy's brow had been knitted in frustration, but slowly the furrows began to fall away. Like I had shamed him into liking me or something.

"It's all right," he said, his voice taking on a more accommodating tone. "It's just this all caught me off guard, you know."

"I understand," I said.

He leaned toward me.

"So I hear you were a real go-getter down there in Fort Lauderdale."

"I tried," I laughed.

"I guess you're gonna give me some real competition." He smiled.

"I'm hoping I can learn a few things. Rich has had nothing but high praise for you."

"Well," he said, obviously proud.

We both sat there for a moment, silence hanging over us in a friendly, unobtrusive way.

"I went to Fort Lauderdale once," Jeremy blurted. "My sophomore year in college."

He said this like I was supposed to validate the comment somehow.

"Did you have fun?" I asked.

"I met a lot of girls, and there was a lot of free sex going on."

I studied him as he said this. It was hard for me to imagine tiny little Jeremy with his out-of-place glasses and corny appearance pulling a lot of women.

"But those days are over. Life is way too serious for that kind of thing now. I don't see how I ever did so much crazy stuff back then."

I just nodded. I casually scanned for a glimpse of his left hand. He wore a wedding band. Even *this* geek was married. And I couldn't even manage to get a relationship right.

Jeez. What was my problem? Internally, I sighed.

"College days," he said with a dismissive shrug.

"Yeah," I replied.

I was anxious to get to work. Not sit here and think about what made Jeremy more romantically marketable than I was.

"So . . . ," I began, "what do you say I just fade back here into the woodwork and watch how you structure your day?"

"That'd be good." He smiled. "I've got a few phone calls to make."

"Should I leave?"

He waved his hand.

"No, no, no, no, no. Today is the day I do my weekly harassment of the management accounts. They've come to expect it."

He snickered.

"I actually get a kick out of it. Let me show you how it's done."

Oh brother. A Napoleon complex. I could see right away that the next ninety days with old Jeremy boy were going to be a barrel of fun.

Reesy was miserable in Fort Lauderdale without me. She called me every single day to complain about one thing or another.

Her parents were driving her crazy to conform to their capitalistic, culturally conscious ways. Reesy wasn't biting, even though she was more like them than she cared to acknowledge.

54

She wasn't dating anyone seriously and her job wasn't what she'd exactly define as a career. But that was the story of her life, so far. During our conversations, she began to bounce around the idea of moving to Atlanta herself. She acted as though she was merely thinking out loud, but I knew she had already made up her mind.

Which was fine with me. I wanted her to come. It would really feel like home if she were here.

"It sounds like you're having so much fun up there, girl," she said one night. We had been on the phone for three hours. My phone bills were ridiculous. I'm sure hers were, too.

"I am. I rode over by Morehouse today. Just to see the whole Atlanta University Center. You know, with Clark, Morris Brown, Spelman, and Morehouse?"

"Unh-huh."

"Child, you should see it over there. There's all this construction going on where they're putting up more buildings, and it's nothing but *us* walking around on those campuses looking like the true leaders that we are. It's like that all over this place. Cultural pride is just everywhere you go."

"It's a wonder my parents never moved there," she said.

"Your parents are too content in Las Olas with their nice little mansion," I laughed. "Plus, they've built their own little cultural fiefdom. Their firm looks like a scene out of Eddie Murphy's movie. What was it? The one where the whole building was black, and everybody wore a custom-made suit?"

"*Boomerang.*"

"Yeah, *Boomerang*. Atlanta's like that. You just get that sense of purpose and direction. Guess what I'm doing this weekend?"

"What?"

"I'm going to a lecture," I said.

"What kind of lecture?"

"On Afrocentricity. By the guy who founded the movement itself. His name is, wait, let me look at the ticket."

I groped for my purse, found it, and pulled out my wallet.

"Here it is. His name is . . ."

"Molefi Asante," Reesy said matter-of-factly.

"Yeah," I stammered, amazed. "How did you know that?"

"Remember who my parents are. They made me go to a lecture he gave here a couple of years ago. They belong to a study group that sponsored bringing him in. It was excellent. I just couldn't let my folks know it. They would've had me toting the freedom flag for sure."

"So it was good?" I asked.

"Oh yeah," she said. "You'll definitely enjoy it. It's right up your alley."

"I'm not going to ask you what you mean by that."

"I'm sure you know, Miss Black Art Mammy." She chuckled.

I put my wallet back in my purse. While I was putting my purse away, Reesy went into her spiel.

"I'm getting really tired of this place," she stated, seemingly out of nowhere. "It's no fun without you here. Mama wants me to come over all the time, especially now that she knows I ain't got no local hang-out partner. She wants me to hang with her, like we're sisters or something. And you know, that's definitely *out*."

She sighed loudly.

"She and Daddy are always inviting me to dinner, like they *just* want to see me. The last thing I want to do is sit around and listen to my parents lecture all damn day about what they think I should be doing with my life."

"Where would you go if you moved?" I asked, knowing full well what the answer was.

"I'on know," she said softly. "I just wanna get out of here."

We both knew she would come here. I guess she was just waiting on me to say it. To extend a formal invitation.

"It would sure be nice if you were here."

"You mean that?" she chimed in her sweetest, most innocent voice.

"Oh, come off it, Reesy," I laughed. "You know you'd love to come here. I just wish you'd do it and shut the hell up."

"I'm thinking about maybe coming by the beginning of next month."

"Damn! You're not wasting any time!" I choked, still laughing.

"Ain't shit here." She giggled.

"Why don't you fly up next weekend, and I'll show you around? There's quite a few cheapo flights from Fort Lauderdale to Atlanta."

"Then why haven't you been home since you left, nigga?"

"I've been busy, Reesy. You know that."

"Yeah right," she said.

She was quiet a moment, then said, "Why don't I come up this weekend?"

"I'm going to see Molefi Asante, remember?"

"Oh yeah. Never mind. I'll wait."

"Silly," I laughed. "You could come see him if you want."

"Maybe I'll get into that stuff once I'm away from my parents. I'm just not ready for it right now."

"Whatever," I said. "I better get off this phone. You know, I think your moving here is actually an excellent idea."

"Yeah?" she asked gullibly.

"*Hell yeah!* It'll be good to recover the money I spend on phone calls to your ass. Talking to you every other day has been bleeding me dry."

"Bye, bitch," she snapped.

"Love you, too, girl," I giggled.

I hung up the phone, glad to know she would soon be here.

I loved my new job. Like Jeremy, I spent my workday harassing people who had the type of job I used to have when I worked in New Orleans and Fort Lauderdale.

I demanded higher net operating income and lower expenses from the companies who fee-managed our properties. I was taken to lunch by companies who were just dying to manage our real estate.

I took trips to Florida, Texas, Louisiana, Arizona, and New

Mexico to tour properties in my portfolio, which was concentrated primarily in the Sunbelt. I began to build up a fat frequent flyer account.

I was invited to speak at seminars all around town as an on-the-rise representative of the black professional community. I quickly discovered that as an aggressive, savvy African-American woman with an eye for business, I was a commodity, though not a rarity, in Atlanta.

All around me I was surrounded by similar positive black images. African-Americans were everywhere in suits, ties, tailored dresses, and trench coats, carrying briefcases and talking on cellular phones with a sense of purpose. They drove Benzes, Bimmers, Z's, Range Rovers, and Porsches. There were Land Cruisers galore.

I rarely saw a negative example of a black person. Even the burger flippers at McDonald's were neatly attired, with excellent presentation. And everyone's hair was hooked in Atlanta. The more I looked around, the more I felt both proud and inadequate at the same time.

When Reesy finally moved to Atlanta, we spent most of our evenings and weekends together. Her apartment was a little closer to downtown, so sometimes I spent the night over there when I didn't feel like fighting the traffic in to work.

Once again, true to form, Reesy found a menial job way beneath her mental skills and abilities, as an accounting representative for a vending supply company. I didn't give her any grief about it. I was just glad she was here.

Every weekend there was some big cultural festival going on at Grant, Piedmont, or Chastain Park. When I found Little Five Points, I was in heaven. It was the coolest place I'd ever seen, with all the funky little shops with their funky little retro clothes, Afrocentric boutiques, and record stores with hard-to-find music at easy-to-afford prices. Reesy loved it, too. It was as eccentric as she was.

The interesting thing about Atlanta was that it was chockful of brothers. There were more in Atlanta than I could possibly imagine—clean-cut, dreadlocked, jet-black, high-yellow, cocoa-brown, short, medium, tall, employed, unemployed, or looking for a sugar mama to take care of them.

Whatever your pleasure was, there was a brother there to fill it.

What I *didn't* find out until later was that the majority of them were either married, bisexual, gay, or just plain playing the field for all they could get out of it.

One guy at work, Cleotis from Mississippi, became one of my favorite lunch buddies. Cleotis was a well-packaged, good-looking brother, but he was so country that he never even came remotely near my plane of consideration.

He gave me some interesting perspectives, though, which, in retrospect, I should have heeded more carefully than I actually did.

Over curry goat and oxtails, plantains, and rice and peas from a quaint little Jamaican cafe downtown, Cleotis told me how the brothers had it made in Atlanta, sometimes having women five and ten deep.

Cleotis informed me that the female-to-male ratio was fifteen to one. He said it was easy to have multiple relationships because the women were so desperate for companionship, and more than a few of them were willing to share a man as long as they has access to occasional sex and someone to go out with.

Per Cleotis, these women were willing to settle for not even half a man, just a piece of a person who was living like a fat rat, preying on the fear of being alone that runs so rampant among black women.

These men never had to spend their own money, and sometimes didn't even have their own place. They lived with women who were content to let them come and go as they pleased.

According to Cleotis, even some sistahs had multiple relationships going on, dating more than one man who was dating more than one woman. On any given day, these "smart women," as Cleotis proudly referred to them, always had a date, a man, and more than their fill of exotic sex.

He said he was dating three women who were doing this very thing. It made it easy on him. He had his fun, they had theirs. Cleotis said it was the best thing that had ever happened to him.

It sounded like one big nasty orgy to me.

I told him I didn't believe it was like that all over Atlanta, just in the funky little circles he traveled in. That something like this could never, in a million years, happen to me because I could spot a cheating man a mile away. Cleotis told me I was far too naive.

WAX BE NIMBLE

One brisk Saturday, as dusk changed the light from bright to dim, I lay back on my futon in the sunroom, sipping a mug of hot spiced tea and rifling through the pages of *Cosmo*. I had been living in the city for over a year now, and it had long felt like home for me.

A few pages into the magazine, I spotted an article on wax strips that completely captured my attention.

The phone rang. I picked it up absently.

"Hello?"

"Hey, girl," Reesy piped. "Whatcha doin'?"

I kept reading, completely engrossed by the details of the article. I was so involved in what I read that I didn't even answer her.

"Misty!" she shouted. "Girl, what's up?"

"Stop yelling in my ear!" I snapped.

"What's wrong with you?"

"Let me call you right back," I said.

"Right back?"

"Yeah," I lied. "I'll call you in a few minutes."

I put the phone down and dove back into the magazine. The wheels in my head were turning with a keen intensity.

I guess I need to back up a little bit to give an explanation of why I would become obsessed about an article on wax strips. And actually, it was not really an obsession with wax strips.

I had a horrid hangup about body hair. On women, anyway. (It was perfectly welcome on men, as long as it was not so nappy that it cut). I mean, seeing a woman with body hair is the most revolting, repulsive, make-my-stomach-lurch thing I can think of.

I knew it was irrational of me to think this way, but I'm making no excuses for my reasonings or idiosyncrasies. I found body hair on women to be nasty, and when I saw it on myself, I was absolutely grossed.

Thus, needless to say, one of my daily (and nightly) pursuits involved ridding myself of body hair.

Let me make one clarification: body hair in every place *except one*. I found the absence of hair *there* to be alternative and blatant. And far too much upkeep.

I believed it sent a message to men that a woman who did not have hair *there* was wild and adventurous (read, a *freak*).

While that may have been inherently true about me, I didn't prefer to announce it. I felt that part of my mystique lay in the gentle unfolding of my kinkiness, not in the announcing of it by shaving the hair *there*.

Which moves me closer to explaining why the wax strips were so necessary.

I had been shaving my legs and underarms with disposable razors ever since I was twelve. I think that was when my underarm hair first appeared. I was proud but repulsed at the same time. I was glad to be growing up, but I found the appearance of hair under my arms to be primal and dirty. So I shaved it, and my legs, daily.

I got to the point where I could not even bear the thought

of stubble, so I shaved the hair (legs and underarms) twice a day: during the morning shower and the evening bath.

The hair *there* I left alone, to grow in a wild thatch any way it chose. But the bikini line hair disturbed me a great deal because it marred the flawless expanse of hairless skin I saw when I wore my bra and panties.

The hair that grew wildly along my bikini line was a source of much grief for me because I had deemed it a necessary evil that I had to live with.

You see, I tried shaving it. That usually lasted about a half a day, and then the entire bikini line area I had shaved would bump.

You know what I mean by bump, right? It's what happens to black men around their chins and neck sometimes when they shave with a razor.

When the hair began to grow back, it doubled up inside the follicle, forming a bump, sometimes with nasty white stuff in it. When the bump dried up, it left a little scar. I think the medical term for it is pseudofolliculitis, or something.

Anyway, that's what happened when I shaved my bikini line with a razor. The bumps would be everywhere. And they would be huge. And they would itch. *Like crazy.*

Like most proud, upwardly mobile women with a healthy sense of professional self-esteem, I had a vanity streak. Not that I had the best-looking body in the world (which I didn't). My butt was not very big. I did have a nice full bosom that I wore with pride. And I was constantly battling my stomach in the war against fat.

I considered myself *slim, but.* I was *slim, but* I had problem areas. Areas that I'd probably struggle with for the rest of my life. So if someone (most likely a man) who had never met me asked me over the phone what size I was, I always said *slim, but* and left it at that. No one ever asked any further. I guess the response sounded so stupid, what more could you say?

Regardless of the *slim, but* thing, I was very proud of my good skin. I had a very even complexion. My face never had pimples and managed to maintain a youthful buoyancy without me having to do much to it. My body was similarly very evenly complected.

So you could imagine the visual torment I experienced when I saw those bumps along my bikini line after I shaved. When the bumps flattened, they left little scars, which eventually went away, but for at least a three-week period, it was a living hell.

Which is why I had resigned myself to living with bikini hair. It was less painful, and visually not as unpleasant as the bumps.

I know you're thinking, What about hair removal lotion, like Nair? Well, I tried that, too. And though I managed to be smooth and silky, the very next day I'd still start to bump as the hair began to grow back. It was just as unpleasant an experience as shaving.

And alphahydroxy products helped dry up the bumps, but the scarring was still there. Which I hated most of all.

So this *Cosmo* had special significance for me.

The only time wax strips came to the front of my mind was when I began dating someone and the prospect of sleeping with him became imminent. Usually, the time to sleep with him came upon me before I could plan the waxing (as in, it was a spontaneous decision).

So I would jump up quickly from a hot and heavy session of making out, having decided that the man of the moment and I were definitely going to hit the sheets.

I would pretend to have to pee, rush to the bathroom, get out the razor, pull down my drawers and do a quickie shave of the bikini line. By the time I began to bump, it would be time for him to leave the next morning.

During the three-week period that ensued, during which I bumped, scarred, itched, and then it all faded away, I would make sure he and I did it in the dark (if the relationship lasted that long), and he never saw the bumps. I made sure his hands didn't wander lingeringly in that area. I definitely made sure he never went *down there*.

I would also make sure he never saw me in my underwear. He could see me in a bra or topless, but he didn't see my lower half unclothed during the light of day. (Me topless was usually enough of a temporary diversion anyway; at least until I could turn the lights off.)

When the bikini hair had grown back after three weeks, if he and I were still together, I didn't bother to shave it anymore. After three weeks, I usually dropped all pretenses at being cute. My attitude was *Love me, love my bikini hair.*

I hadn't had a real man in my life for quite some time. Only the two I worked with, Rich Landey and country ass Cleotis. But by luck, I had begun to cultivate a wonderful relationship with a man whom I found very attractive, very bright, and very funny. He worked in a building not too far from my office.

Usually Cleotis and I would go to the Underground or somewhere downtown for lunch. One day Cleotis was out sick, so I went to Hooters by myself. I know it sounds crazy. Normally, I don't seek out places where men are encouraged to openly ogle big-breasted waitresses. But Hooters had some damn good chicken wings, and that day, I had an insatiable craving for wings and a basket of curly fries.

It didn't matter that I was alone. I took a newspaper with me to tune out the girls in their skimpy neon shorts and the bold stares of the sundry men nearby.

"Miss, would you mind if we seated someone else at the table with you?"

The sistah smiled at me, her breasts bound tightly in a knotted Hooters T-shirt.

"We're having a major lunch rush, and occasionally we ask people if it's okay for them to share a table. It's no big deal if you don't want to."

She gave me the most gracious of gracious grins.

I didn't really feel like sharing a space with someone, but there were three free stools at the big table where I was sitting. I looked around. The crowd was certainly getting thick. I hadn't even noticed.

"Sure," I said pleasantly.

Damn, I said inside.

"Hi. Thanks," said the handsome brother sitting down at the table.

He seemed to appear out of nowhere. The waitress must have had him hiding behind her back.

"I'm kind of in a rush, so I appreciate you letting me join you," he said. "I just had to have some chicken wings today."

I smiled. He seemed nice. I was suddenly reminded of how I met Stefan at O'Hara's during happy hour a few years back. Definitely a bad experience.

A sharp, riveting pain ripped through me at the unwanted memory.

"Roman Frazier," he said, extending his hand.

"Misty Fine," I replied.

We proceeded to have a nice talk, exchanged work numbers, and parted fast lunch buddies.

I met Roman again, at Hooters, the next day for lunch.

"So, Misty," he began, "are you a single girl here in Atlanta?"

"You got it," I said. "I'm kinda enjoying it, too. The last relationship was a bit much. Left a bad taste in my mouth."

"I know how that is," he returned, a serious, empathetic look on his face.

"Why? Are you single?" I asked.

"As single as they come," he replied.

He was so damn handsome. I knew Hooters was a place for men to gape at women, but I was the one doing all the gaping. I couldn't take my eyes off him.

We had a good lunch that day. A good lunch indeed.

Roman made me laugh hysterically, and I found this to be remarkably sexy. After quite a few casual conversations, ours started taking a turn for the comfortable and familiar, and we began talking about all the things we liked and disliked.

Somehow, our conversations found their way to sex. I don't

know *how* it came up, but he mentioned that he found the absence of hair *there* to be an incredible turn-on. I refrained from comment on this, as *there* was the one place I never considered shaving. Too much upkeep, remember? Too alternative and blatant. Adventurous and wild. So I kind of chuckled ambiguously, and went on to the next topic.

As time passed on, Roman and I developed the most passionate and sensuous conversations and occasionally started seeing each other for dinner and movies, but I wasn't quite ready to consummate the relationship.

The day (i.e., night) finally came around when we had reached the limit of our discussions. There was nothing left to talk about. The only thing left was to *do it*. We had a date planned on a Thursday evening. I was cooking him a gourmet dinner, and we were going to watch rented movies in front of my fireplace.

Consummation was inevitable. I could hardly work that day. Roman called several times to make sure the plans were still on. He was excited, and I was even more so at the prospect of what sex was going to be like between us, since we had already practically had sex with each other in our minds and through our exchanges.

We each knew what the other liked, what to do, what to say, where to go.

I left work early to prepare dinner and the atmosphere to be *just so*. He was due at seven, so at five-thirty I ran a long hot bath, jumped in, and pored over my body with loofahs and gels, slathering every sensual cream and oil at my disposal over me.

As I stood (on the toilet) and assessed myself in the bathroom mirror, there it was, jutting out at me: the bikini hair. And I hadn't bought wax strips yet. And he was due in less than an hour, since it was now almost six-thirty. I couldn't let him see the bikini hair. He wouldn't find it sexy at all.

So I whipped out the razor and did a quickie shave. I shaved all around the unruly thicket of hair growing in the middle, stooping and bending, squatting and flexing to get every iota of hair and stubble around my panty line.

And then, I don't know what possessed me, but I did it. I decided to be alternative and blatant. Adventurous and wild. And in five crazy strokes, I shaved off all the hair from *there*.

I slathered the area with a sweet-smelling sesame oil and examined it quizzically, pondering over the strangeness of its appearance.

It was smooth as silk, soft as satin, an unfamiliar mound and delicate folds I had not seen uncovered for more than half my life. And I was quite full of myself as I pulled on a pair of black bikinis over my now totally hairless, scrubbed, oiled, and invigorated body. I knew he would be pleasantly surprised. And sex was gonna be, oh honey, *so good* that night.

By seven, I was seductively cute and comfortable in a pair of camel-colored leggings and an oversized camel cableknit sweater. My hair was coiffed, yet slightly tousled, and I smelled faintly of sweet citrus and sesame.

The weather outside was nothing short of bitter, but my place was toasty, candlelit, fragrant, and had a soft glow that was conducive to romance. Mellow music chimed through the speakers, and the aroma of good food excited the senses.

I was walking through the apartment, a glass of chablis in my hand, when the doorbell rang. I took a quick swig, set the glass on the counter, walked to the door, and looked through the peephole. It was Roman, with his fine self. I paused, readied my pose, and casually flung the door open.

He was cold, but I could see the warmth wash over him as he looked at me standing in the doorway. I must have looked pretty damn good, because he smiled broadly as I rushed him inside. I took his coat, sat him down, gave him a glass of chablis, and we dove right into conversation.

Somehow, Roman managed to kiss me, and we wound up entangled on the couch. I knew we had better eat, so we sat down to dinner, and finished it off with another bottle of wine. I put on a movie, and we cuddled in front of the fireplace.

Soon, the movie was watching us, and the petting became very heated, very heavy.

Just as he began to lift my sweater over my head, I heard a distant, muffled chirping that became increasingly loud. Roman groaned, looked down at his hipside, and pressed the pager for a readout. He asked to use my phone, called his voice mail, retrieved a message, made another call, mumbled some words frantically into the phone, groaned again, and gave me *the look*.

You know *the look*. The *damn baby, I wanna be with you so bad, but I gotta go* look.

He explained the dilemma, thanked me for dinner, moaned "Misty, I'm sorry," with the most supplicating puppydog look he could muster, said we'd try it again on the weekend, kissed me passionately, sucked on my neck helplessly, groaned again for good measure, opened the door, and in a *whoosh* of cold air that rushed into my apartment and blew out the candles, he was gone.

I flopped down on the couch, dumbstruck. In front of me on the table was my half-empty glass of chablis and his almost full glass. I downed them both, washed the dishes, and made my drunken way to bed, peeling off clothes as I wove unsteadily through the hallway.

I fell into bed naked, head spinning, too drunk to be angry, too tired to care. I don't even know when sleep hit me. I think I was asleep before I fell into bed.

I woke up the next morning scratching furiously, unconsciously. As my eyes opened I stretched wildly, trying to get my bearings. I lay in bed weak, body groggy and sluggish. My blood felt toxic.

And as thoughts recalled the events of the night before, I found myself scratching again. I lazily glanced down at my hand in motion, and sat up, horror-stricken.

Down there was covered with bumps. Thousands of them. *Millions* of them. Little bitty bumps with little white heads that itched like crazy on the hairless mound and around the bikini line.

In my panic, I raced to the bathroom, two-fisted scratching all the way, stood on the toilet, and examined the bumps. They were hideous. It was a horrific sight. There would be no sex for me this weekend. Or the next. Or the next or the next. Not for another twenty-one days or so.

I was mortified. At my stupidity for rending my body through such torture, just to get some dick. Even breaking my cardinal rule of never shaving the hair *there*. Just to get some dick. I was repulsed. Indignant. And ashamed. I decided I would not be seeing Roman again.

That was three months ago. The hair *there* had since grown back. An untamed flourish of thickness twice as unruly as it was before. Shaving it must have doubled the follicle density or something.

The hair took a very long time to grow back, and the stubble and bumps tormented me for many nights on end.

I pawed, clawed, and scratched my way through those weeks, avoided looking in the mirror, and was razor-shy (except for my legs and underarms) for a long time.

I declared the area sacred ground, like some national park or wildlife preserve. It was protected from all threat and free to grow as helter-skelter as it chose.

But time did tend to dull the senses and soften the remembrance of particularly intense events.

Lying on my futon that Saturday, reading that *Cosmo* article, I found myself once again entertaining thoughts of conquering my bikini hair, and the wax strips reared their head as the last resort. The last hurrah. If they didn't work, I would surrender and forfeit all future battle.

I didn't call Reesy back. Instead, I jumped into my car and drove to the nearest beauty supply store.

As always, whenever I am in one of these stores, I left with far more than my intended purchase. I wandered around the store and gathered bath creams, body gels, glycerine soaps, loofahs, and colossal bottles of never-before-tried sale-priced shampoos (which the saleslady assured me would make my hair like silk).

My handbasket almost full, I finally meandered my way over to the depilatory section. I could see from afar that a full-scale area of the store had been devoted to hair removal. None of those tiny clusters of Nair, Neet, and Bikini Bare that you found at the grocery store either.

This place had everything a girl needed to remove hair from every possible skin surface and orifice (if necessary).

I studied the various creams and waxes, and then, as I turned to the right, my gaze fell upon them: hair removal strips (for the body). $9.99. A box of twenty-four. More than enough for me to experiment and test their effectiveness. I was *muy* excited at the prospect of waxing the night away.

Driving back home, I could feel the presence of the wax strips in the bag beside me, and I sensed that success, nay, victory was just a few short minutes away.

Out of nowhere, while I was in the store, it had turned into a nasty, rainy, chilly evening, and as I pulled up in front of my apartment, the rain was coming down in torrents. I grabbed the bag (a very big bag) and raced through the rain and cold, uncovered, upstairs into the apartment.

I went straight back to the bedroom, into the bathroom, and put away all my goodies, except for the wax strips. I stepped out of my clothes, sat down on the toilet, and read the directions.

The box had a patchwork picture on the front of a naked woman with satiny smooth skin. Sure . . . she was white, but in my mind's eye I imagined that my skin, too, would be that satiny once I applied the wax strips.

I found it amusing that they were called hair removal strips *for the body*. (As opposed to being for where else, I couldn't imagine.)

There were actually two strips per sheet, stuck together. They had to be peeled apart. The instructions said to pull my skin back tightly, press the wax strip on, and snatch it off.

I did.

I snatched hard. It stung a little, but the hair came off. I actually went through about five sheets (yes, ten wax strips), before I realized that one could be used over and over again, as long as it had a sticky surface.

Duh.

So I kept reusing the ten strips over and over until I had snatched (pun intended) off all semblance of bikini-line hair. The stinging lasted only a few seconds after I pulled the strips off, and miraculously, *the hair was gone!*

I stood up on the toilet and examined the hairline. The areas on both sides of my thighs were beet red from all the snatching and pulling.

Then, right before my eyes, as I watched, patches of bumps rose in legions in the flushed areas on my thighs! I started, renewed with the horror from the experience of three months before.

But, just as quickly, before I could even fully react, they dissipated. I mean, *they laid flat down!*

The areas were still beet red, but the skin was smooth and supple. I was suspicious, but other than the redness, it looked pretty good. I knew the test would be overnight, though.

I went about my business for the rest of the evening, did some work, watched some TV, read a book. I dozed off full of anticipation of what the morning would bring.

I awakened fully conscious of the wax strip test. I ran my hands over the bikini area, and felt . . . *nothing*. I didn't want to get excited just yet, though.

I jumped up, rushed to the bathroom, and stood on the stool for confirmation. No bumps. No redness. Just smoothness. No itch. No nothing.

Pure-dee unadulterated, satin-silk smoothness. Just like the lady's on the box (only brown).

I wanted to be elated. I secretly was. But I didn't want to show it for fear the bumps would rear their ugly white heads again. I had never used a product where I didn't bump.

Ever.

It was simply too good to be true. I knew time would tell. But inside, I was very, very pleased.

At work the next day, I sat across from Rich Landey in one of the conference rooms. He and I had been working all day long, papers and sandwiches spread out across the table, reviewing the profit margins of sites in my portfolio.

I had kicked off my shoes and was redlining a cash flow statement that had been sent to us by one of the management companies.

"Excuse me for a minute, Misty," Rich said. "I'm going to run to the head."

I chuckled.

"Sure thing, Boss," I replied.

I really liked Rich. He treated me with respect. Like I was his equal. Just one of the guys.

As soon as the door shut behind him, I slipped my hand under my skirt. I had on a pair of thigh-high stockings, so I had easy access to my bikini line.

The skin was still silky smooth.

I smiled to myself.

Victory was mine.

Two weeks passed, and the bumps still had not returned. There was no stubble, and the area was still as smooth as that very first day of pulling and snatching.

Since then, I'd bought eight more boxes of the wax strips (just in case there was a run on wax strips and I couldn't find any more in town).

Okay, maybe that's a bit much, but I figured I'd wasted too many years of torment. I deserved as many boxes of my salvation as I chose to buy. I could apply the wax strips for my own satisfaction, not just because of the spontaneous prospect of sex.

I felt very good about myself. I was not indignant, ashamed, or repulsed at my actions anymore.

I do have one confession to make, though. I had a very hot date with Roman. I know I said I'd never be seeing him again, but "never" doesn't mean what it used to years ago. Anyhow, at that crucial moment before my sweater came off, I excused myself to go use the bathroom.

I whipped out the strips, pressed one to each thigh, and snatched simultaneously. As I silenced a scream, I caught a glimpse of my image in the mirror. Panties down, legs astraddle, a beet-red streak down either side of the inside of my thighs, I smiled sheepishly to myself. I guess some things never change.

I'd still do anything.

Just to get some dick.

TOUCH ME IN THE MORNING

I grabbed my purse and keys from my desk, turned the lights off in my office, and pulled the door together.

"Good night, girl," I said, waving to Rebecca.

"See ya, Misty." Rebecca smiled, brushing her hand across her always-together hair.

I rushed toward the elevators, managing to dash inside one just as the doors were closing. It was already full, but I squeezed on in.

I stood up front, panting.

"Where you going in such a rush?" a voice from the back asked.

It was my friend Cleotis.

"I gotta run a few errands and get home," I said between gasps.

"Why you breathin' so hard?" he asked. "You getting outta shape, girl."

"I know, I know."

The other people in the elevator stared forward, as though they didn't even hear us talking.

"You must have a hot date with you-know-who," he smirked.
I grinned sheepishly.

I had been seeing Roman consistently since we met a year
ago. I even told Mama about him. Not the gory details. Just
that I was seeing someone and that it was kind of serious.

I knew if all those people hadn't been in the elevator,
Cleotis would have said *that nigga*, which was how he normally referred to Roman. *You-know-who*, however, was the
more appropriate thing to say at the time.

"You just put me down," he continued. "Don't even have
lunch with me no more."

I felt bad. Cleotis was the one who'd hipped me to all the
cool downtown eateries, especially the holes-in-the-wall where
the best food could be found.

"I know. I'm sorry," I said.

A short, plump white woman with freckles and a mane of
thick red hair pulled back into a bun glanced over at me accusingly. Like she was on Cleotis's side. I quickly averted my eyes
from her.

"How 'bout tomorrow?" I asked.

"Naw," he protested. "That's all right. I don't want no pity
lunch."

"Cleotis!"

"I'm serious, Misty," he said. "But ain't no hard feelings.
You know where to find me when old boy falls off."

The elevator doors sprang open and people spilled out into
the parking garage.

I dashed away, waving at him over my shoulder as I raced
out to my car.

"See ya, sweetie!" I called.

"Bye, girl! Don't have no accident tryna get to that man!"

I stopped by the store and picked up a couple of porter-
house steaks, some baking potatoes, a head of escarole, and a
loaf of crusty sourdough bread.

I rushed through traffic, maneuvering my way through all the holes between cars and speeding through all the yellow lights.

I pulled up in front of my apartment, snatched the bag from the car, and dashed upstairs.

I flipped on the lights, dropped my purse and keys on the table, and went straight to the kitchen. I glanced at the clock on the microwave over the oven. It was 6:15 P.M.

I took everything out of the bag, set it on the counter, and washed my hands. I prepared the steaks and slid them into the oven. I placed the potatoes on a plate and put them in the microwave. And I quickly made a Caesar salad and put it in the refrigerator. I left the loaf of bread on the counter. I would stick it in the warm oven when Roman arrived.

I picked up my keys and purse from the table and took them to the back. I turned on the shower and let it run while I peeled out of my work clothes.

Inside of fifteen minutes, I was freshly showered, had lotioned and oiled my body, spritzed on some of Roman's favorite, a pineapple-mango body spray from Bath and Body Works, freshened my makeup and hair, and was back in the kitchen checking the steaks.

It was 7:30 P.M. I gingerly bent the blinds back and peered from my bedroom window, anxiously watching for his car. Roman drove one of those very nineties, responsibly sporty jobs, a black Acura Vigor, and from where I stood, I could furtively watch for him, my constant angst a secret shared only by me, the four walls, and my oft-pinched miniblinds.

This happened every time Roman came over. I'd rush from work, run to the store whenever necessary (I usually kept my place stocked with food), shower, then stand there clutching the blinds, my heart racing in semi-anticipation/expectation of some mishap or foiling of plans, and watch for his car as it turned into the parking lot.

When I'd finally see his car pull up, I'd dash into the bath-room, give my hair a quick tousle, check my face and lipstick again, then rush to the sunroom and casually sit on the futon.

With my heart rate skyrocketing from excitement, nervous-ness, and needless bursts of energy from all the sudden dash-ing around, I'd sit there calmly flipping the pages of some cerebral or ethnically correct journal (*Architectural Digest, Upscale, Essence, Vibe,* etc.), my television strategically placed on *Jeopardy!, Crossfire,* or *Kids in the Hall* (especially since Roman always came over in the early evening after work).

(Not that I didn't really read these magazines or watch these shows. I just felt there was no harm in flaunting how lit-erate, politically conscious, and comically in-tune I was.)

Roman would walk up the sidewalk and see me upstairs through the light of the sunroom, sitting on my futon looking as nonchalant as nonchalant could be, flipping through my magazine and nodding intently at the exchanges on *Crossfire* on the TV in the living room.

Sometimes he would climb onto the railing that led to the patio outside my living room, and be standing outside the slid-ing glass door. He would tap softly to surprise me. I always pre-tended not to hear the first tap (we women can be so full of shit). Then he'd tap again and press his gorgeous chocolate face against the glass, teeth bared in a sexy grin.

I'd act startled, put on a fake admonishing face, and let him in.

My heart racing, stern expression in place, I'd open the door.

"Boy, you better quit sneaking up on me like that! One day you're gonna get shot!"

Roman would be standing there, smiling all sly, sexy as hell in a snug golf shirt that showed off his ample chest, and tight stonewashed jeans that hugged the strong curves of his mus-cular thighs, or a cotton buttondown and a crisp pair of chinos that draped the high roundness of his perfect butt.

"You ain't shootin' nobody, girl. If anybody's gonna be doing some shootin', it's gon' be me, and it ain't gon' be no bullets."

Roman would casually circle my nipple with his fingers as he said this, sending shocks of electricity through me. I'd push his hand away and cluck my tongue, opening the door wide enough for him to enter.

"You better stop, before you start something you have to finish," I'd say.

"That's the goal," he'd smile, patting my butt as he walked into my apartment.

Next thing you know, my dress, shorts, jeans, *whatever*, would be up, down, or off, and we'd be doing it right there on my living room floor. Sometimes right in front of the sliding glass door and my curious neighbors in the building just across the way, the sounds of Alex Trebek's perfect intonations as he posed answers to contestants competing with my moans of pleasure and cries for *more, deeper, faster, harder.*

Roman would then get up, peel off the condom he'd donned, tie it in a knot and drop it on the floor, zip his fly, and head to the kitchen.

I'd get up and dash down the hallway into my bedroom, away from the fishbowl view of the sliding glass door, and wash up in the bathroom. When I came back, Roman would be on the couch, remote in hand, munching on steak and Caesar salad, or whatever gourmet dinner I had whipped up.

I'd go over to the sliding glass door and close the blinds, pick up the condom wrapper and the dirtied condom from the middle of the floor, toss them in the trash, and plop down on the couch beside him.

I hardly ever ate. I was usually so happy he was there that I barely had any appetite at all. We'd watch TV for the rest of the night (typically whatever it was that Roman wanted to watch), get into bed around eleven or twelve, get it on for another hour or so, then fall asleep.

He'd leave around three or four in the morning.

"I like to get to the gym by no later than five so I can get in a good workout and a quick game of racketball."

"Sure, honey. I want you to keep that body fine for me."

Roman would do me again before he left. Really. This man had the most incredible sex drive of any man I had ever known. He left me feeling satiated and insatiable at the same time. He did things to me that I had only read about in *Cosmo* or *The Hite Report*. Things that were definitely missing during my last relationship, with Stefan, who was gorgeous, but sucked (and I mean literally, in more ways than one) in bed. With Roman, my G-spot and multiple orgasms were regular items on the menu. I think that's why he had me so excited to see him all the time.

Every morning, he would pat me on the butt as he climbed out of bed, slide into his clothes, and leave me in the pitch darkness of my apartment. I could always hear his car as he cranked it up and pulled away, leaving me to doze back off to sleep, fucked-out, sexually intoxicated, wondering why he never asked me to go to the gym with him to play a little rack-etball or get in a good workout as well.

This do-si-do went on almost every night. Except for on the weekends. Roman spent his weekends with an inner-city kid as a part of the Big Brother program.

They'd go to the park and play ball, he'd cook for the boy, and they'd go to movies. The boy (whose name was Jimmy or Timmy—I wasn't sure which it was; I think Roman called him both names at one time or another) would stay over at Roman's place from Friday night until late Sunday afternoon.

On Sundays, Roman took him to church and tutored him. Usually, by the time he took Jimmy/Timmy back to the inner city, he was so tired that he spent the night catching up on his sleep at home.

I didn't talk to Roman on the weekends at all. I knew how much his work with Jimmy/Timmy meant to him. He even told me he'd like me to meet Jimmy/Timmy one day, once their relationship was a little more solid.

Like clockwork on Monday, though, he always showed up at my place at 7:30 P.M. for quick sex, dinner, TV, more sex, sleep, and sex.

I was so sprung on Roman and the sex that it was all I could think of, day in and day out.

Against my better wishes, I'd been keeping my cat hair off with wax strips ever since Roman and I began seeing each other on a regular basis.

Just to make him happy.

Snatching it off with wax strips hurt like a mug, but I only had to do it every few weeks.

I was in love with Roman. I knew it. It had to be love. Otherwise, why would I think about him all the time? I was obsessed with him. The way his hands caressed my body, the feel of his supple thighs, how he looked poised above me in bed.

I thought about him incessantly, and I knew I wanted to spend the rest of my life with him. He must have been feeling something similar for me. He *had* to be, since he went out of his way to see me almost every day, and shared so many of his hopes, dreams, and fears with me. We talked about everything.

He must have loved me. I mean hell, I was a regular fixture in his life.

The issue of Roman's feelings seemed to be constant fodder for confrontations between Reesy and me.

One Sunday afternoon we were kicking around, doing something close to nothing in her roomy apartment. Bob Marley's *Could You Be Loved* was playing, and the sun was beaming brightly through the sliding glass door.

I was curled up on her couch sipping a Pepsi and half-reading the latest issue of *Essence*. Reesy was painting her nails a bright, hoochie-mama red. It looked damn good against the backdrop of her yellow skin.

We had been talking about work, and I don't know how, but Reesy had managed to maneuver the conversation to me and Roman.

"Jeremy and I are supposed to fly to Albuquerque next week," I said.

"Who's Jeremy?"

"You know, the little nerdy guy who works with me."

"Oh," she mumbled, her attention focused on her nails. "I thought you guys weren't working on the same stuff anymore. Didn't he help you when you first started?"

"Yeah. We don't share a portfolio anymore. There's a site the company's interested in buying, and this is a sort of recon trip to check it out."

"Nice," she muttered.

I could tell that she was not interested in the slightest about what I was talking about.

I sipped my Pepsi and flipped through the magazine, barely noticing the pictures. I wondered what Roman was doing right then.

"So how's your job coming?" I asked with boredom.

"Same old same old," she replied.

"How long are you gonna do that?"

"What?" she asked, looking up. "Paint my nails? Till they're done."

"No, silly," I returned, "your job. I mean, is there any growth potential there for you?"

She went back to her nails.

"I'on know," she mumbled. "It's just a job. No big deal. I'm thinking of getting a night job."

"Oh yeah?" I asked, my curiosity piqued. "Doing what?"

"Nothing critical," she said. "Just to make some extra money."

"Umph," I said, absently.

She looked up, her eyes narrowing to catch the meaning of my grunt. I ignored her, continuing to flip through the magazine. I turned to the back, to the horoscope section.

"So where's Roman today?" Reesy asked.

"I don't know," I replied.

"What do you mean, you don't know? Isn't he your man?"

She blew on her fingernails.

"I'm not his keeper, Reesy."

I kept reading my horoscope.

"Why are you getting so flip? I didn't say you were."

I glanced over at her. The corner of her lip was curled upward in an interesting smirk. I returned my attention to *Essence*.

"How come you never see him on the weekends?" Reesy persisted. "He must be hiding something from you."

"He's with Jimmy on the weekends," I defended, pretending to read. I couldn't even concentrate. "Why would I want to interfere with that? In fact, I admire him for it. More brothers need to make a conscious contribution to our people. I feel bad for not doing the same."

Reesy waved her hand with its bright red nails, dismissing my comment as the bullshit she felt it was.

"I thought you said the boy's name was Timmy."

"Timmy, Jimmy, I can't remember."

"You should," she clucked. "You better make sure it's not *Jenny*."

"See, Reesy, that's what's wrong with you. Sistahs like you have no faith in our black brothers, and that's what's driving them away from us," I snapped. "If we'd stop being so suspicious of them and give them our support, maybe they'd give us our props instead of rushing off to white women. Brothers like white women 'cause they don't give them no grief. Maybe we can learn a lesson from that."

Reesy stared at me, shaking her head.

"Do you hear how you sound?"

"What do you mean?" I asked.

"You sound like a fool, Misty," she said. "Sistahs like *you* are making it easy for niggas to have their cake and eat it, too. First of all, white women let brothers dog 'em out, that's why the brothers keep running to 'em.

"Ain't no right-minded sistahs gon' let a nigga come and go as he please, have sex with any and everybody, then roll back up in the house like it ain't nothin'. Most real brothers don't have no respect for white women. They just run to 'em 'cause they know they can get all the kinky strange they can't get from us. Ain't no sistah gon' be lickin' a nigga's asshole and shit like that. But white girls'll lick a ass in a minute. I'm sorry, but that's some nasty shit, and ain't that much love in the world to make me do some mess like that."

I had closed the magazine and was now quite angry.

"Reesy, you know you got a foul mouth."

"I'm sorry, but I'm tellin' it like it is. I know how brothers are, and I thought you was old enough and done been through enough shit to know how they are, too. You need to find out what that nigga be doin' on the weekends. If he's just so-called bonding with his little brother Ji—Timmy, or whatever the hell his name is, like you say he is, ain't no reason you can't hang out with them. You need to speak up for yourself, Misty. 'Cause he damn shole ain't gon' speak up for you. I thought you learned that from your fiasco with Stefan."

Reesy made me so mad sometimes. Especially when she brought up shit from my past that I couldn't refute. Like my failed relationship with Stefan.

"Roman comes to my house every night, like clockwork. If he was up to no good, like you imply, I doubt he would appear with such consistency."

Reesy clucked her tongue, shaking her head again.

"Girl, you sound like a spokesperson for *Sistahs Hoping It Turns Out Nice*."

"What the hell is that?" I asked.

"Maybe you know it better by it's acronym: *SHIT ON*."

"Is that a real organization?" I asked incredulously.

"It may as well be," she smirked. "There's legions of y'all out there hopin' things are gonna turn out right, but y'all ain't holding these brothers up to no levels of accountability. People treat you how you let them, Misty. That's Relationship 101."

"Roman doesn't treat me bad. He treats me like a queen."

"When was the last time he took you to dinner or a movie?" she fired.

I thought about it, and quickly rushed to his defense.

"He doesn't have to. I love cooking, so I usually make dinner for him. He picks up rented movies all the time."

"Exactly. That brother's got it made. He don't have to do shit but spend a few bucks at Blockbuster, and for that he gets all the free food and coochie he can eat, and a free night's sleep to boot. You're like a walking Marriott for this nigga."

"That's nasty, Reesy."

"But it's true, I'll bet," she quipped. "I hope you're at least using condoms."

She blew on her nails again.

"Of course I'm using condoms," I snapped at her. "You know how scared I get."

"Well, I hope you're telling the truth and not just lying like some women I know," she said.

I was thoroughly annoyed at her by now.

"'Cause you ain't hurtin' nobody but yourself if you're lying. The least you can do is look after your body, even if your mind is gone."

"I'm using condoms, Reesy."

"All right, girl," she said. I don't know if she believed me or not. I wasn't going to try to convince her. Condoms were pretty much a permanent fixture in my sex life, and had been for years. I admit, there had been times when I slipped up. Times when the moment was too intense for me. I had let Stefan and Roman both talk me into not using condoms a few times in the past. They both used the same line.

Come on baby, let's do it natural, just this once. So I can feel you better.

Yeah. Sure.

Reesy waved her bright red nails in front of her and smiled at me sweetly.

"Look, girl, you know I love you, right?"

Her tone was softer. I searched her face. When I saw what I knew were good intentions, I softened my expression as well and nodded.

"Yeah, I guess so."

"You *know* so. You know you're the closest thing I have to a sister. I know you realize how much it hurt me to see you after Stefan battered you like he did."

I nodded. I had to give it to her for that. She held my hand through everything that happened with Stefan. During the time I stayed with her after the breakup, she made sure, even more than the courts, that the restraining order I got against him was enforced.

"You also know I don't like seeing someone as smart and as beautiful as you let someone as slick as Roman sounds slide in and out with no accountability."

"You've never even met Roman," I said plainly.

"That's 'cause the brother ain't never around during normal hours for me to see." She laughed.

I didn't see anything funny.

"Is he still jetting out at the crack of the crack of dawn to go to the gym?" she asked.

"Yeah."

"Now you're tryna tell me that *that* doesn't bother you at all?" Reesy asked, making sure she watched her tone.

"No, it doesn't," I lied.

"You know you're a lying heffah, Miss Divine." She chuckled softly.

Miss Divine. She always resorted to calling me that to make me feel good.

As a child she'd done it all the time. I always laughed then, and as I thought of it now, it seemed so innocent and sweet.

And here we were now, laying around doing nothing, just like we used to do when we were kids, and she was calling me that silly name, making me feel like I was the best friend she had in the world.

Which I knew I was. Otherwise, I wouldn't be listening to her talk to me like this.

"So you're telling me his leaving you that early in the morning is just fine by you," she continued. "You wouldn't have it any other way?"

"I didn't say all that. But if you saw his body, you wouldn't be challenging me like this right now. It's in perfect condition. He *has* to be working out, and it ain't during the day, because he's at work. I know because he calls me from work all the time. So the morning is the only time that he could be getting that body in shape like that."

Reesy nodded silently, as if she understood. I knew she didn't. She was just patronizing me like she sometimes annoyingly did. She kept waving her nails, and alternately blowing on them.

"All right, girly. If that's cool with you, then fine. Have you ever gone to the gym with him to work out?"

"I don't like getting up that early," I lied again.

"*Umph,*" she grunted.

"What did *that* mean?" I snapped.

"Nothing," she added quickly. "I was just digesting what you said."

"Look, Reesy. Why don't you just let me be the judge of what my relationship with Roman is."

"*Relationship?*" she asked sarcastically.

"Yes, my *relationship*. Because, regardless of what you think, Roman and I *do* have a *relationship*. It may not follow the dictates of what *you* think it should be, but it *is* a relationship. He shares his hopes and dreams with me, and he talks about all the things he wants out of life."

"Does he ever include you in those hopes and dreams?"

"We never talk about them that way. We talk about what we want to accomplish in life, not so much about whom we want to accomplish it with."

"*Umph,*" she grunted.

"And you can just stop with your little judgmental grunts, Reesy. I have no complaints with Roman. I see him twenty-some days out of the month, almost every night out of the week, all night long, and that's more than some wives see their husbands."

"All night long?" she challenged.

87

"For the most part, yes," I retorted. "The part of the night that matters."

I paused for a moment, and then, for evil no-good measure, I added, "I'm probably more satisfied right now than you'll ever be in your whole life."

Reesy went ballistic. Her hands froze in midair and she started working her neck. The official, I'm-about-to-read-your-ass, sistah-girl gesture.

"*See?* That's what's *wrong* with you and all the rest of your *SHIT ON* friends. Y'all confuse sex with love. Just because that man's giving you good sex . . ."

"*Great* sex," I corrected.

". . . Well, *great* sex then, don't mean shit. There could be another bitch on the other side of town just like you having the same conversation with her friend about all the *great* sex she's getting on the weekends and in the morning when her man comes in from his late night job."

"Fuck you, Reesy."

"No, fuck *you*, Misty! If you're too stupid to see that something is up with a motherfucka who leaves you every morning 'fore the sun comes up and don't *nevah* call your ass on the weekends, then you keep on. I hope he takes your ass for a fucking ride, 'cause you deserve it. Stupid bitch!"

I was furious. Reesy and I called each other names all the time, usually in jest, but she was crossing the line this time. I wanted to blow up, but instead I jumped up from the couch, picked up my keys, grabbed my purse, and walked away.

When I reached the front door, I heard her call out to me.

"Misty."

I thought maybe she was going to apologize. I was livid, but an apology from her would have taken away the edge, just a little.

I turned around and looked at her, my face expectant.

"At least make the motherfucka buy the condoms. That is, if you use them. Don't let him ride your ass for free."

I nearly snatched her door off the hinges as I stormed off to my car.

• • •

But, you know, in the privacy of my mind I often gave audience to the things Reesy said to me.

I wasn't too happy with how things were going. I wanted better. I wanted more.

I stood at the window now, pulling back the miniblinds to watch for his black Acura Vigor. I hadn't talked to him on the phone today, but I didn't worry. I had been running around at the office all day, so I really hadn't had a chance to think about it.

What I had been thinking about, though, was what Reesy had said to me. I knew she spoke the truth, even though she was a little harsh and insensitive in her delivery. She had asked questions about Roman and what he did on weekends and why he left so early in the mornings that I didn't really allow myself to entertain.

I just sort of repressed them, in the hopes that if I didn't think about them, they would eventually go away.

Instead, I lavished love and attention upon him, making sure he always had his favorite foods, a receptive home to relax in, and a welcoming body that was eager to please him sexually.

I had turned into a manic, obsessed woman who was waiting for acceptance, giving 300 percent to a man whom I never even had a conversation with between the hours of 5:00 P.M. Friday and 8:00 A.M. Monday.

The fact that I only saw Roman during limited hours bothered me a lot. Early during our relationship, when I was still emotionally confident enough to confront him about things, I had tried to make an issue of it.

"Why don't you ever bring Jimmy over here on the weekends?" I asked.

"It's Timmy," he said, his voice short and clipped. "We discussed this before. That's my time to bond with him. I'm not sharing those moments with anybody other than him."

"But this is every weekend, Roman. It doesn't make any sense. It's almost like you've got something to hide."

"What are you saying, Misty?" he said, his face hard and serious. "Get to the point."

I was trying to be tough. Trying to prove that I wouldn't let anyone else ever do me the way that Stefan had done.

"I'm saying this weekend thing isn't good enough for me, Roman. We have to spend more time together. I'm not going to accept this. This is bullshit."

"So you're tryna tell me what to do, Misty?" he said, angry.

"I'm telling you what I'm *not* gon' let you do," I replied, standing firm.

"Then fine. I can't give you any more time than you're getting. I work all day. I give you my nights. My weekends are dedicated to Timmy. If you can't accept that, too bad. That's the way things are gonna be."

He picked up his keys, slammed the door, and drove off.

I didn't see him the next day.

I spent the night alone, in my bed, shaking in the darkness. I didn't like being alone. And I was in love with Roman. There was something about him that validated me. Something that I needed to make me feel like I could sustain a relationship. Especially after Stefan.

The next day, I called Roman and begged him to come back. I told him the weekends weren't important. That I didn't want to give up the time I already had with him.

I was humiliated, having to break down and call him like that. But in my mind, I needed him. When I saw him that night, I forgot all about feeling humiliated. I was happy he came back.

I lost something that day. I lost confidence, and I lost position. Roman knew he was in control of our relationship.

Reesy never knew about me breaking down to Roman the way I did. I would never admit to her that I had been that weak.

But I stood there now at that window deciding again that I was going to take a stand. Snatches of time with Roman here and there weren't good enough for me anymore. As spineless as I knew I had become, I was willing to take another wild stab at demanding more.

I had deliberated at length about what I was going to say to him. I was going to ask Roman to let me come with him to pick up Jimmy/Timmy on Friday.

I was going to lie and tell him we had a program at our church on Sunday (Lord, forgive me) where they were going to talk about the importance of strong African-American male role models in the lives of young black males.

I was going to tell him I thought it would be good for him and Jimmy/Timmy to attend it together. I knew I could always feign surprise if Reverend Jenkins preached on something else.

If Roman said no, I was going to confront him. It wasn't what I wanted to do, but I was going to do it. I was going to demand to know what he really did on the weekends, and ask him where he thought our relationship was going.

If that didn't work, then I would have to use Plan B.

I didn't know what Plan B was, but I was crazed at this point. Plans were coming to me like visions to a prophet.

By 9:30 P.M., I was silently hysterical. I ran from the living room to the bedroom, to the window, to the sunroom, to the bathroom. I beeped him, but I didn't get an answer. I didn't dial his house because he told me that at night he kept that number turned over to his pager. So it would have dialed his pager again. I called his office, but his voice mail came on.

The food was in the oven, still warm, but drying out pathetically. My heart was pounding, and I almost tore one of the miniblinds as I pulled it back and peered into the darkness for a sign of his headlights entering the parking lot.

I wondered if he'd gotten into an accident. I prayed forgiveness as I thought of how I had been plotting to entrap him, when all along he was probably totally innocent, and perhaps lying dead or severely injured on the highway. I called 911.

"911."

"Yes, how can I find out if you have any reports of car accidents?"

"Ma'am, you'd have to call the police department directly," the vaguely female voice stated in a monotone. "911 is used to report emergencies in need of assistance."

"This is an emergency."

"Ma'am, what is your situation?" the voice droned unenthusiastically.

"I need to find out if my boyfriend has been in an accident. He's a few hours late, and I'm concerned that something may have happened to him."

"Ma'am, that would be classified as a missing-persons report. The police department cannot pursue a report for a missing person until at least twenty-four hours have elapsed since his or her disappearance."

"How can I find out if he's been in an accident? Don't you all track car wrecks and calls that come in for police and ambulances?"

"Ma'am, you're going to have to call the police department directly for that," the voice droned on.

"What good are you people?" I screamed, slamming the phone down.

I paced around the room maniacally, rushing to the window when I heard a car pull up outside.

I looked out. It was an old blue Monte Carlo. My voyeur neighbor who watched me and my man get it on every night.

My man. Yeah. Roman was my man, no matter what Reesy or anybody said. And right now my man was missing. I felt sick and helpless. I wanted to cry, but was so used to repressing my emotions that I didn't know how to.

I found myself suddenly not caring if he had another woman on the other side of town. I wanted my man back. I wanted my Roman.

I just prayed to God he wasn't dead.

MANIC REPRESSION

Three days passed. I thought I was going to lose my mind. Roman didn't call.

I couldn't even concentrate at work. I must have picked up my phone a hundred times, calling his job. All I got was his voice mail. I didn't know what gym he went to, otherwise I would have showed up there at 5 A.M. each morning to confirm that he was, in fact, okay. I filed a missing-persons report, but nothing had come of it yet.

I still couldn't cry, but I was so anxious and upset that I couldn't even eat. Every time the phone rang at work, I lunged for it, hoping it was Roman.

Rich Landey stuck his head in my door.

"What are you doing for lunch?" he asked.

"I have an appointment," I lied.

"Okay." He smiled brightly and turned away.

Before I could bring my hand to my mouth to chaw on my fingernails as I had been nervously doing, he stuck his head in the door again.

"Are you all right?" he asked.

"Yeah," I said in an obviously artificial voice.

"You sure?"

"Mmm-hmm," I nodded.

"Good deal," he said, and disappeared.

At night, I wandered around the apartment with my hair pulled back, no makeup, looking all scrungy in a pair of sweats that I slipped into when I got home.

I even slept in the sweats. I didn't wash them for three days straight. I cried hysterically, wiping my nose on my sleeves. The sweats became crusted and grungy, but they were my security blanket.

I didn't wash my hair for three days. It was a tangled, natty mess that I brushed back into a pathetic bun every morning when I went to work.

I hadn't been this miserable after my breakup with Stefan. Not even close.

I must have called Roman's pager a thousand times. Nothing. I was convinced he was dead.

By Friday, I was experiencing stomach cramps and dry heaves.

Late Friday night, not long after I managed to drift off fitfully to sleep, the phone rang.

I practically snatched it off the hook.

"Hello?" my voice was desperate.

"Hey, girl," the voice said softly. "Whatcha doin'?"

It was Reesy.

"Nothing," I said shortly. "I was asleep."

She was quiet for a minute.

"What are you doing home?" I asked, my tone abrupt.

Reesy had recently gotten a night job, in addition to her day one as an account rep for a vending company. I didn't know what she did at her night job, but she worked real late, especially on the weekends. I figured she was moonlighting as a waitress, and she just didn't want to tell me about it.

"I took the night off," she said. "I felt like playing hooky."

"Oh," I said. And nothing else.

"You still mad at me, Miss Divine?" Reesy asked.

"Don't call me that," I said. "You were unnecessarily evil to me the other day."

She sighed deeply.

"I know, honey. I'm sorry. I've been agonizing over that conversation ever since it happened."

"Well, it's good to hear you have a conscience."

"Yes, Misty, I do have a conscience. I just get so mad sometimes when I see how brothers treat us. I mean, we'll give them our right arm if they'd just treat us right, but they don't see us as their partners. We're just something for them to get over on."

I cut her off.

"Reesy, I don't feel like having this conversation again."

"I know, girl. I didn't call to get you upset."

"Really? That's a switch."

She sighed again.

"Look, Misty. I mean, just because I can be an ass sometimes and speak my mind without moderation doesn't mean I have bad intentions. I just love you so much. I only want the best for you."

"Well, I have a mother who wants the same thing, but even she doesn't talk to me the way you did."

"I know, honey, but you and I share a closeness that you know can never be compared to a mother/daughter relationship. We're sistahs, girl. In heart, soul, and spirit, if not blood."

"Yeah," I said blankly.

"Misty."

I said nothing.

"Misty."

"*What*, Reesy?"

"Listen. I'm sorry about what I said about Roman. If he's making you happy, fine. It's your life. I don't want you to go through what you did with Stefan. I just want you to be happy. Okay?"

95

I felt a lump in my throat.

"Are you happy?" she asked.

The lump felt big as a golfball.

"Misty," she asked again, "are you happy?"

I couldn't breathe for the golfball.

"Misty, are you there?"

By the time the tears finally began to fall, Reesy had hung up the phone and was on her way over.

I let her bang on the front door for a few minutes before I let her in.

At first, when I heard the car pull up into the parking lot, I'd looked out the window in the hopes that it might miraculously be Roman. When I saw her black Montero, I released the blinds and plopped back down on the bed.

She rang the doorbell furiously and banged on the door like a fool. The only reason I opened it was so the neighbors wouldn't report a disturbance. Right now, Reesy was the last person I wanted to see.

I opened the door, my face puffy from crying, my eyes blood red.

"Girl, you look like shit!" she shrieked.

"And so it begins . . . ," I muttered.

I shut the door behind her and shuffled off to the kitchen. I reached into the refrigerator and grabbed a bottle of Gatorade. Citrus Cooler. Michael Jordan's favorite. That's what the bottle said anyway.

Reesy was right behind me.

"What is wrong with you?" she pressed. "Did that nigga do something to hurt you? Come on, you can tell me!"

I glared at her. Still clutching my bottle of Citrus Cooler, I padded down the hall back to my bedroom.

When I climbed into bed, Reesy got a glimpse of my socks. They were black on the bottom.

She looked at me like I was crazy. She walked over to my

dresser and opened the top drawer. Not finding what she wanted, she opened drawer after drawer until she produced a clean pair of footies.

She came over to the bed, sat down, and pulled the nasty socks off my feet. She didn't say anything as she tenderly slid the clean footies over my feet.

I thought I was going to cry again.

Reesy took her shoes off and climbed into bed. She picked up the remote from the nightstand on her side. The side where Roman usually slept.

She turned on the TV and channel-surfed until she landed on some cheesy T & A movie on Cinemax. Bikini-clad women cavorted across the screen, dropping their tops at random to expose their gargantuan breasts for no reason at all.

Dinosaurs ran around in the background while men in army uniforms had pseudo-sex with the titty-flashing chicks. I found myself chuckling at the stupidity of it all.

"You can always count on *Skine*max for some late night sex and gratuitous nudity," Reesy laughed.

She was handling me perfectly. She didn't even look at me as she spoke. She just eased herself into my environment and quietly relaxed me with her unobtrusive companionship.

We watched the program in silence, both of us chuckling occasionally at the buffoonery of the movie.

My voice broke the silence.

"Roman is missing," I muttered.

Reesy was a champ. She was careful not to raise her voice too high and aggravate my already-aggravated temperament.

"What do you mean, he's missing?" she asked quietly, her voice just as even as mine. She didn't glare at me with her usual penetrating stare. She angled her head just so, so she could hear me clearly without making me feel uneasy in any way.

"I haven't heard from him since he left early Tuesday morning. He never called or came by that night."

I waited for her to say something. But like a true friend, she just listened patiently.

"He always shows up. He's been like clockwork for the last few months. I'm afraid something's happened to him."

Reesy still did not say anything. She kept her gaze fixed on the dinosaur titty-romp.

"I filed a missing-persons report. Maybe something happened to him on the road somewhere."

I heard Reesy sigh softly. I watched her intently as she fingered the remote, her attention now fixed on the rubber buttons. Her finger traced absently around the edges of the mute button.

"Reesy, you can say something. I know a million thoughts must be racing through your mind right now."

I blew my nose loudly.

"Just be careful how you say it to me. Right now I need a friend, not a mother/conscience/feminist/sistah-girl-voice-from-the-pages-of-*Essence* to tell me how to achieve personal happiness by freeing myself from the clutches of the evil black man. The last thing I need right now is to have my feelings hurt."

Reesy sighed again, her finger still playing with the remote buttons.

"I wasn't going to do that, Misty," she said softly. "What have the police told you so far?"

"Nothing," I said. "They have all the information about him, and they said they would keep me posted if they heard anything. I haven't heard from them. I've been calling them before they get a chance to call me."

"What do you think happened to him?" Reesy asked.

"I don't know, Reesy. It's like he just fell off."

I sniffled loudly, still babbling.

"It's like he just . . . *fell off.*" My voice trailed off into a pitiful whine.

"People don't just fall off, Misty," Reesy said. Her voice was still calm and quiet. Matter-of-fact, not judgmental in any way.

I hadn't even realized it, but the remote was now on the bed and her hand was rubbing my back, ever so gently.

My tears dropped noiselessly onto the bed. Reesy kept rubbing my back. It was soothing. The tears soon stopped. I took a few deep breaths and leaned my head on Reesy's shoulder.

Reesy rubbed my head with her other hand and kissed the top of my hair.

"I love you, Miss Divine. You know that, don't you?"

"Mmm-hmm," I sniffled, nodding my head.

"Good. Everything's gonna be all right. Don't you worry."

"You think so?"

I could feel her body moving as she nodded her head vigorously.

"He's gonna call you. That's one guarantee in life I learned a long, long time ago. They always call you. No matter what. Those motherfuckas always call you."

I rested peacefully against her, at ease for the first time in more than three days.

I heard her sniffing above. Was Reesy crying, too?

"Misty?" she asked, her voice barely a whisper.

"Hnnh?"

She spoke hesitantly.

"When . . . was the last time . . . you washed your hair?" she asked.

I burst out laughing. I laughed so hard that I couldn't stop.

"I'm serious, girl," she shrieked, laughing along with me. "It's pretty funky. And what's that all dried up on your sweats?"

I could barely talk for choking with laughter.

"Snot," I choked.

Reesy leapt from the bed and pushed me out of it, into the bathroom. She pulled back the shower curtain and turned on the water, waving me into it. Her expression was fixed into a serious stare.

I looked at her and burst out laughing again.

"I'm for real, girl," she said sternly. Then she burst out

laughing. "You need to get in that shower right now and wash your funky hair."

I stepped out of my clothes and into the shower, still laughing. Reesy bent down, picked up the sweats with her fingers as if they were contaminated, and snatched the curtain shut.

"Where are you taking those?" I asked with alarm.

"To the washer," she called from the hallway.

I heard her lift the lid, and turn on the washing machine. Within a couple of minutes she was back in the room watching TV.

As the warm water washed over my head and coursed over my body, I was glad I had her in my life.

"Reesy!" I called out over the rush of the water.

"What?" she answered.

"I love you, girl."

She was quiet for a moment.

"I love you, too. Stank bitch."

I came out of the shower bundled up in my most comfortable chenille robe, a towel wrapped tightly around my head.

Reesy was sitting on the bed, still channel-surfing. She had put on one of my nightshirts.

"Did you wash your hair thoroughly?" she asked.

"Yeah."

"You want me to dry it for you?"

"Yeah." I smiled. "That would be nice."

Reesy hadn't dried my hair in years. It was something we used to do all the time when we slept over at each other's place. We'd been doing it since we were kids.

I went back into the bathroom and got my blow dryer and a brush. I handed them to her and sat on the bed.

She rubbed the towel into my scalp to remove the excess water. Then she plugged in the dryer and began gently brushing through my hair.

The sensation of the warm air rushing across my scalp and the feel of the brush relaxed and comforted me. I closed my eyes, focusing on the sound of the dryer and the rhythmic strokes of her hand.

"Feeling better?" she asked.

"Much," I said, exhaling deeply.

We both stayed like that for a few quiet moments, enjoying the soothing repetition of her movements, the undulation of my neck in response to her pulling, and the whizz of warm air enveloping us, creating an atmosphere conducive to bonding and confession.

"You know, Reesy, sometimes I wonder if I must be losing my mind," I started.

"That's not good," she replied. "Remember the words of our illustrious former vice president, Mr. Quayle."

"What was that?" I asked, eyes still closed, my body still lulled by the pleasurable feel of having my hair dried.

"You remember him at the United Negro College Fund meeting, quoting their slogan. He said 'the mind is a terrible thing to lose.' It may have been the most prophetic statement ever made by man."

We both laughed.

"You're silly," I said. "Actually, he said 'it would be a terrible thing to lose one's mind.'"

"As if that's any better," she chuckled.

I was quiet, wondering whether I should tell her. Then I decided I would. I could tell my best friend anything.

"I begged him to stay a long time ago," I confessed. "I actually told him I didn't care about not having weekends, as long as I could just have him."

Reesy didn't say anything in response. She just kept up the gentle, rhythmic strokes of brushing, never once increasing the pressure or her pull on the brush.

I waited to see if she would. She didn't. She just listened. I didn't even sense her usual judgmental tone.

"Why would I do something crazy like that?" I asked. "I gave up all rights to anything when I did it."

"Did you mean it?" she asked, her voice soft.

I opened my eyes.

"I don't know," I shrugged, slightly throwing off her rhythm. She gently pushed my shoulders down, suggesting I keep still.

"Sorry," I said. "I don't know if I meant it or not," I kept on, "I mean, part of me said that I would never just sit back and take whatever a man dished out. Not anymore. But another part of me needs what Roman has to offer. I feel like I need it really bad."

"Mmm-hmm," she said. Nonjudgmentally.

"Does that mean I'm crazy?" I asked her. "Have I lost my mind?"

"No, girl," Reesy said, stopping for a moment to stroke my head in reassurance. "It just means you're human. Taking a stand, a strong one, when it comes to men is not one of your strengths. You do other things so well. I guess giving us a tragic flaw is God's way of keeping us in balance."

That sounded so beautiful and powerful as she said it. I actually felt as though she understood me.

"I do believe He gives us opportunities to learn," she continued, "like this one is for you. I think moments like this are times for us to look at what's really important. Who we are inside and what we mean to ourselves. And to our friends. Our true friends. That's what's really important."

We were both quiet.

"Hand me the phone," I said, my voice soft.

"Why?" she asked, reaching for it. "Who are you going to call?"

"Susan Taylor. That quote needs to be in next month's *Essence*, girl. It's too good to just let pass."

"*Girl!*" she laughed, putting the phone back down. "You's a fool!"

"I learned from the best," I said.

We both chuckled as she began drying my hair again. I have thick hair. Like sheep's wool. It's pretty once it's fixed, but it's a mutha to get it to that point.

I closed my eyes again, relaxing.

"Reesy, do you have any secrets?" I asked.

I felt like we could talk about anything that night.

"Mmm-hmm," she replied, her voice low.

"Anything I don't know about?" I asked.

"Mmm-hmm."

I turned my head to look up at her.

"For real?" I asked in surprise. "What secrets would you have from me?"

She twisted her lip in a sardonic smile and turned my head back around with deliberate effort.

"Do you want me to dry your head or not?"

"Yeah," I said, "I just want to know what you're talking about."

"You just focus on keeping yourself still while I do this," she replied. "I can talk to you without you jumping around all over the bed."

I sat there and waited for her to tell me. She kept on brushing my hair.

"Reesy?"

"What?"

"So tell me."

"Tell you *what?*" she laughed.

"Your secrets! I want to know what kind of secrets you have."

"They're not big deals. Not really." She paused for a second. "Well, you might think that one of them is."

"Oh, really?" I asked, ripped with curiosity.

"Yeah," she sighed. "I guess my biggest secret is that I hide things from people. I don't like them knowing every little thing I do because I don't want them telling me whether they approve of it or not. Or that I'm bad or good, or whatever, for doing what I do."

"So you hide things from people like me?" I probed, somewhat hurt because I typically told her so much of what went on with me.

"Yeah," she said, her voice soft. "Not because I don't trust you."

She tried to clarify matters.

"It's just easier for me to listen and give advice than to talk and take it from others. My parents give me too much advice. They're always in my face. It's kinda made me shell-shocked."

I found all this rather amazing. I mean, Reesy was always giving me hard-core, no-holds-barred, humiliating, make-me-cry advice. It was hard to believe that *she* of all people was afraid of having that same kind of talk turned back on herself.

But now that I thought about it, Reesy was a problem-solver for me. She was always saving me. I very rarely, if ever, had opportunities to save her. And it was always me talking, me confessing, me giving up the goods.

I mean, I knew about her life, her boyfriends, her frustrations for the most part. But it usually wasn't because she came to me saying *Girl, I need help*. It was usually because the subject came up during a time when we were discussing something that had to do with me.

"So you said I might think one of your secrets is a big deal," I said. "What is it?"

She chuckled above me.

"What's so funny?" I asked, trying to turn my head.

She gripped it firmly.

"Misty," she admonished.

"Sorry."

She sighed, still brushing my hair.

"It's about my night job."

"Your night job?" I inquired, confused. "I thought you worked at a restaurant."

"Where'd you get that from?"

I shrugged, forgetting to keep still.

"Sorry," I whined, as she sighed in frustration loudly above me. "I thought you were a waitress at a restaurant or a bar. I just figured you were making extra money."

"Hmph. I guess that's close."

"Close how?" I asked.

"Well, it *is* kind of a bar," she chuckled. "And I *do* make quite a bit of extra money."

"All right, Reesy," I said, barely able to keep still, "turn off the dryer, 'cause I have to turn around and look at you on this one."

She did.

"Now. What kind of work do you do?"

Reesy smiled, a sheepish, major confession kind of smile.

"I'm an exotic dancer," she said, her voice matter-of-fact, as if to say *So there. Now you know.*

"WHAT!" I screeched, jumping up from the bed. *"You're kidding me, right?"*

Reesy sat down on the edge of the bed where I'd been sitting.

"No, I'm not," she said flatly.

"Get outta here, Reesy! You are *not* a stripper!! No way! What the hell would you be doing that for? You don't need the money!"

I paced around the room as I said this. She sat calmly on the bed watching me.

I glanced at her over there, looking so collected. I stopped in my tracks and began to giggle.

"You lying heffah!" I sputtered. "Why you playing with me like that?"

"I'm not playing, Misty. I told you that you would think it was a big deal."

Her face was dead serious. Her left eyebrow was raised as if to confirm what she was saying.

I couldn't believe it. I mean, I really couldn't believe it. The *last* thing I would have expected to hear from her was this.

Not that it was incredible. Reesy had an awesome body. She had booty, but not fat-nasty booty like some of the women you saw in all those gangsta rap videos, all small-waisted, wide-assed, and thick-thighed in that gross ghetto kinda way.

I mean, hell, ain't nothing wrong with the Hottentot Venus. That's the black woman's natural physiology—big booty, big thighs, big titties and all. There was just something about seeing it jiggled around and exploited in a vulgar video that made me sick.

Reesy had a tight, physically fit butt. And she had a perfectly sized bustline, not too small, and not too melony.

Not that I'd been checking out her body for any sexual interest on my part. But you know how we women are. If somebody's been your friend practically your whole life, you know exactly what it is about her you hate and love. And if she's got a great body, you've probably spent most of your life wishing *you* had it instead of her. Thinking how things would be better for you if only you had her body.

Another reason it wasn't so hard to believe was Reesy's training as a dancer. She'd been dancing since she was barely able to walk. She took dance classes regularly, jazz, modern, street, ballroom, all kinds of stuff.

But *shit*, there was a big difference in finding something conceivable and knowing it was happening *for real*.

"Swear to God you're not lying to me," I challenged.

"I swear to God," she returned without hesitation.

"No, Reesy, no," I said, grabbing my head with my hands and pacing around the room again. "Say it ain't true. Why would you be doing something like this? I can't believe you would do something like this!"

"Misty," Reesy said, "stop being so dramatic."

I turned toward her, my face twisted in anger.

"What do you mean? I'm as serious as a heart attack!"

I kept walking around the room.

"I can't freaking believe this," I muttered to myself.

"C'mon, girl, and let me finish your hair," Reesy ordered.

"No! This is not funny, Reesy. This is not funny at all."

She let out a deep sigh.

"How come you never told me this?" I demanded.

"Because I knew you'd do just what you're doing now."

"What, freak out?" I laughed with bitter sarcasm. "You're damn right! So would your folks, if they knew about this!"

"This has nothing to do with my folks," she replied, "or *you*, for that matter."

"It sure as hell does! It involves me just as much as my relationship with Roman involves you!"

"I should have never told you. Look at you. You can't even handle it. You've suddenly turned into my mother."

I stopped stomping around the room and stared at her.

"Why are you doing this?" I asked. "Is it money? Do you need money? I've got plenty of money; you could have come to me if you didn't want to go to your folks."

"Misty, just sit your little black ass down," she said. "This ain't got nothing to do with me needing no damn money, so you can just chill with all the drama."

"Do you take your clothes off?" I asked her.

"Of course," she said easily.

I couldn't believe how cool she was about this. She sat on that bed, staring back at me, all level-headed and easy. I was acting like she was being forced into what she was doing. When I saw the beginning of the curl of a smile at the corner of her lips, I realized that this was right up Reesy's crazy ass alley.

I began to laugh uncontrollably.

"You're a stripper? A fucking stripper? I can't believe this shit!"

"Exotic dancer," she calmly corrected.

"Stop it, girl!" I squealed.

She chuckled along with me.

"I'm not lying, Misty. I dance naked several nights a week."

I listened to her, utterly taken aback.

"Reesy . . . ?"

"Yeeess," she grinned.

"How *in the world* did you get involved in exotic dancing?" I asked.

It was her turn to shrug.

"I don't know. It was something I was curious about. You know I love to move my body. It was damn near the only kind of dancing I wasn't doing."

"There's more to it than that," I said, unconvinced.

"Well, yeah," she grinned.

"So . . ."

She sighed, patting the bed for me to come sit down. I took a seat next to her.

"You'll be able to appreciate this, since you know me better than anyone else . . . ," she said, pausing.

"Go ahead," I urged.

"I guess I get kind of a rush out of it," she confided.

I was totally into what she was saying, forgetting my own distress.

"What kind?" I inquired. "A get-naked rush? Like you enjoy being an exhibitionist?"

"Well, yeah, I guess that's part of it. But that's not what I really mean."

She leaned back on the bed, laughing. She rubbed her palm against her forehead.

"I can't believe I'm telling you this stuff," she said, rolling her eyes toward the ceiling. "Man!"

"I can't believe you *never* told me this stuff!" I returned. "I'm your best friend. This has completely blown me away!"

She looked over at me.

"It's not like I've been doing this all my life, Misty," she said defensively. "I've only been doing it since I moved here."

I shook my head.

"This is such a trip," I said. "This is a straight-up trip."

Reesy just smiled.

"So what's the real reason you get a rush out of this?" I asked. "You said it's not just the nudity. What else makes you wanna do it?"

She didn't hesitate to answer.

"The power."

I knitted my brow, trying to understand her answer.

"I don't get it," I said. "What power? Strippers are basically toys for men. They poke and prod and touch your stuff. It seems like it would be really denigrating, which doesn't seem like you at all."

She nodded.

"I can see how it would *seem* that way," she replied, "but it's really not."

"Explain this to me, Reesy."

"Okay," she said, sitting up in the bed. "You know how men are usually the ones who try to manipulate and control our every action?"

"Yes."

"Well," she said, gesturing heavily, "when you're an exotic dancer—which, by the way, I prefer over *stripper*—men are completely at your mercy. You can withhold pleasure from them, dole pleasure out to them, give them attention, take it away, whatever. And the whole time, they are totally helpless. Their actions are reduced to mere reactions. They can only react to whatever it is you do. Like an expectant puppy. Waiting for a snack."

"But don't you *have* to give them attention if they pay for you? I mean, like if they pay to have you give them a table dance, or a lap dance?"

Her brows were raised high in amusement.

"What do you know about table dances and lap dances, Miss Divine?" she asked, laughing.

"I know," I said evasively.

"How?"

"That dog Stefan. He used to go to Club Rolex in Miami all the time. And Ecstasy. And the Mint."

"Umph!" she said, still laughing. "For somebody who couldn't fuck, he shole was looking at a lot of pussy!"

I joined her in laughter.

"Reesy?"

I decided to be slick and try to slide in a question. Since she was being so open and all.

"What?"

"So, um, well, um," I stammered.

"Spit it out, Misty," she said.

"Um. Okay. Do you let them look at your . . . your . . . you know, your *thing*?"

Reesy was amused at my uneasiness.

"My *what*, Misty?"

"You know!" I said in exasperation. "Your cat!"

"Yes."

"Ooh, girl, no you don't!" I giggled, like some silly schoolkid.

"Yes, I do," she replied. "They can *look* at it all they want. But they can't *touch* it unless I give them permission to. That's why I love all this. I'm an instrument, in complete control, working them over. And they're so submissive, girl. I feel like it's a victory for every oppressed woman when I see a man go crazy over some coochie. And they all do it. Every single one of them."

"Wow," I said. It was all I could say. "Wow."

"Wow ain't the word for it."

"So you said they can't touch your cat unless you give them permission. Do you ever give anybody permission?"

"Sure I do," she laughed. "The ones I wanna take home with me. And I've had some excellent pickings from where I work. You'd be amazed at the men that come in. Bankers, doctors, roughnecks, reverends. I've probably seen every politician in Atlanta sitting at some table, a drink in his hand, looking up my cat. It's a trip, girl. And you know their wives are at home just sure their man is out doing business."

I thought about that.

"I don't think so, Reesy," I mused. "I believe they know. They just don't want to think about it. That's how I was with Stefan. I never asked him about all the titty bars. It was just this kind of unspoken thing that he knew I knew about."

"Yeah," she agreed. "You're probably right."

I leaned back against the pillow, not caring about my hair anymore. The shock of all this had probably electrified it into dryness anyway.

"So you're not scared of AIDS, meeting these men in clubs

and taking them home? And being around all those people with your clothes off?"

"Of course I'm scared of AIDS," she stated. That's why I use condoms. And I get tested all the time."

I was impressed. That was more than I could say. I didn't always use condoms with Stefan or Roman. And I was too scared to take an AIDS test. I had never had one, although I was ashamed to admit it.

"That's good," I said quietly.

"And I don't just go rubbing up on people with my cat, like I'm crazy. I wear a thong when I lap dance."

I nodded. This was so wild. Really. It just exceeded the boundaries of my imagination. I would never have the nerve to do something like this. I mean, put me in the business world, and I'll do anything. But take me out of that element, and I'm insecure, easily shaken and deterred, everything. In the face of all this, my respect for Reesy went up at least a good five notches.

"You know what's funny about all this?" I asked.

"What?"

"Look at your parents. They're these big-time lawyers, money for days, and you're a stripper."

"Exotic dancer," she corrected.

"My bad. Exotic dancer."

"So what's so funny about all that?" Reesy asked.

I laughed.

"I just think it's funny how you rich kids are always the ones most out there. Y'all end up being radicals, slackers, prison-bound, cult-seekers, exotic dancers, cross-dressers, you name it. Y'all are a fucked-up bunch."

She laughed.

"You're right. But we're not by ourselves."

"What do you mean?"

"You forget. There's another group out there almost as bad as us."

"Who's that?" I asked, then realized the answer as I asked the question.

"Preacher's daughters!" we both said at once. We burst into laughter.

"So why do you think that is?" I probed.

"I don't know, girl. I guess all the pressure we get from our parents. To be as successful or righteous as they are. It's a heavy burden to bear. You feel like doing something as far removed from them as you can to shake off any possibility of having to meet their expectations."

"Man, Reesy," I whistled. "That's pretty deep."

"It is, ain't it?" she chuckled.

"So where do you work?" I asked.

"The Magic City."

"For real?" I exclaimed. "That's the top spot in town!"

"I know," she smiled.

The Magic City was practically world famous. Brothers from around the country made the trek to Atlanta just to go there. Supposedly the strippers, all of them sistahs, looked like models. Even the waitresses. Rumor had it the waitresses walked around naked, serving customers. The Magic City set the standard that the rest of the African-American exotic dance world tried to emulate. I once heard a commercial on the radio station back in Fort Lauderdale for a club advertising that their dancers were imported from Atlanta. *Imported.* Can you believe that? Like they were animals or something, and these animals were definitely the best.

"You have to be really good to work at the Magic City, don't you?" I asked. "Are you sure this is the first time you've ever done this?"

"I'm sure, Miss Divine. Remember, I *am* a dancer. All I had to learn was the part about taking my clothes off. Which I found kind of instinctive, too."

She grinned at me.

"Wow" was all I could say.

"I know . . . ," she said, her face brightening. "You should come see me dance one night!!"

I let out a loud guffaw.

"Hah! I don't *think* so! No way am I gonna go in there with all those men looking at *me!*"

"Well, hopefully," she chuckled, "if I'm doing my job right, they'll be looking at me."

"I don't know," I replied with much trepidation. "I'd really have to think about that."

"It would be fun," she coaxed. "I could take you back to meet some of the other dancers. You'd be surprised. One of them goes to Spelman. Two others are from Morris Brown. One has three kids, and girl, she looks like her cat is tighter than mine ever thought about being."

"Really," I breathed. This was all so eye-opening.

She stood up and picked up the dryer again.

"Don't worry 'bout it, girl," I said, stopping her. "It dried a long time ago."

She laughed as she unplugged the blow dryer and wrapped the cord around it.

"So," I asked, "do you have a stage name?"

"Yeah," she smiled.

"What is it?"

"Get this: it's Peanut Butter."

"Why?"

"Girl, don't you get it? As in Reese's Peanut Butter cup."

"Oh," I said. "I would have never got that."

"Well, the men do. They love it. They're always asking if they can stick their finger in my peanut butter."

"For real?" I marveled.

"Yeah, girl," she laughed. "This one guy I went out with, a news anchor, used to want me to say 'You've got chocolate in my peanut butter.' Then he would say, 'You've got peanut butter on my chocolate. Lick it off.'"

I laughed hysterically.

"Are you serious?"

"Uh-huh. As a heart attack." She was laughing, too. "Needless to say, I had to let him go."

"Okay," I said, putting my hand over my ears, "that's

enough! I don't want to hear any more about this. It's too crazy for me to digest. We need to take our butts to bed."

"All right," she agreed. "I'm sleepy anyway."

I climbed under the covers on my side.

"Are you gonna do something to your hair, like tie it down?" she asked.

"Oh yeah," I replied. I was so wigged out by our conversation, I had forgotten about my hair, which was all over my head. I must have looked like Chaka Khan. I grabbed a scrungee from the nightstand beside me and pulled it back into a ponytail. Then I turned off the light.

"Good night," Reesy said.

"Good night," I returned.

I lay in the darkness, quiet for a moment.

"Reesy?"

"What."

"Are you sure you didn't make all that up about being a stripper just to divert me from thinking about Roman?"

"Exotic dancer," she corrected. "And no, I didn't. I just shared my most personal secret with you. Nobody else I know knows about it."

"Okay," I sighed.

"Okay then," she replied. "Good night."

I paused, then . . .

"Good night, Peanut Butter," I giggled.

I heard her giggle, too.

"Goodnight, Chocolate."

I woke the next morning to the smell of pancakes, eggs, and bacon. Reesy was in my kitchen cooking up a storm.

I walked in, my T-shirt rumpled from the deep sleep I had finally fallen into after the shower, my face feeling like it was a hundred years old. My mouth was so cottony, it felt like it was lined with fleece.

"You're burning it up in here, huh?" I asked groggily.

Reesy had golden pancakes piled high, and crisp rind bacon

was stacked in a plate on the stove. She was scrambling eggs and stirring grits at the same time.

"Yeah, girly. I figured you needed to eat. I know you probably ain't ate nothin' in three or four days. And I know that confession I made last night must have drained the little bit of energy you had left clean away."

"So that wasn't a dream?" I mumbled.

"No, it wasn't," she said in a singsongy voice.

I picked up a piece of bacon and began munching on it.

"Mmm. This is good," I said. "I needed this."

Reesy glanced over at me as she cooked.

"Misty, you got enough food in that refrigerator to feed an army. And your cabinets are stocked to the gills. I know you always keep food around, but you don't eat enough to have this much food on hand."

"I cook a lot for Roman," I said between munches.

"Shit," said Reesy. "Roman's got it made. He's eating like a king over here."

I opened the refrigerator and grabbed a container of orange juice. I poured myself a tall glass and dropped in a few cubes of ice.

"Pour me one of those, would you?" Reesy asked.

I reached in the cabinet and got a glass.

"Don't fill it up all the way," she added.

I stopped when the glass was halfway full and looked at her.

"That's fine," she said.

I put the juice back into the refrigerator, picked up my glass, and sat down at the dining table.

She put the eggs and grits onto two plates, and brought the pancakes, bacon, and two plates over to the dining table on a tray. I got up to get the syrup and butter, but she motioned me to sit down. She got the syrup from the cabinet and the butter from the fridge and set them both on the table.

I smiled at her. Reesy was all right.

"You must be trying to make up for being so mean to me last week," I said.

Reesy grinned like she was embarrassed.

"I'm just tryna look out for my girl. We're all we've got in this great big city. I don't know how I ever let you trick me into moving here in the first place."

My hand froze in midair, the syrup I was pouring spilling over in a great big glob onto my pancakes.

"*You lying heffah!* You're the one who had to follow me here. I didn't ask you to move to Atlanta. You came traipsing behind me like the lapdog that you are."

Reesy threw a piece of bacon at me.

"You crusty bitch, sitting over there talking shit with all that crud in your eye. I came here 'cause I knew you didn't need to be in no big ass city like this by yourself. You woulda been lost. Just look at you now!"

I laughed, picking up the bacon she threw and eating it.

"*Oh!*" I squealed. "So you're gonna take my adversity, my personal, secret fears that I'm sharing with you, and slap me in the face with it. And you call yourself my best friend? You yellow hoe, the only reason you rushed up here was because you thought you was gon' scoop some fine men. It ain't have nothing to do with me, and you know it!"

"Like that's not why you moved here!" she retorted.

"I moved here because I got offered the job of a lifetime. And there was no way I was gonna turn that opportunity down. Unlike yourself. You come up here claiming you just want to get away from Fort Lauderdale and your mama. Next thing you know, you're shakin' your naked booty at the hottest spot in town."

Reesy smacked her lips as she licked syrup off them, rolling her eyes in mock anger. I crunched on a bacon rind and rolled my eyes back.

It was amazing.

I was feeling so much better. It was as if I had forgotten all about Roman.

Reesy's coming over turned out to be the best thing after all.

• • •

116

"Can I put on these jeans?" Reesy yelled from the closet.

"Which jeans?" I asked, stepping out of the bathroom.

Reesy emerged from my walk-in closet in my favorite pair of jeans. The ones with the slash underneath the right butt cheek. Roman hated those jeans. But they fit Reesy like a glove. She looked fabulous.

"Yeah, girl. They look real good on you. Just don't try to take 'em home on the sly. You know those are my favorite."

"I know, you trick," she snarled playfully. "Quit tryna accuse me of something before I lift 'em for real."

She rooted around through my blouses.

"What kind of top should I wear with this?"

Like I said before, Reesy had an awesome figure. We were about the same height. I was five-seven. She was five-seven-and-a-half. Though my shape was not as chiseled, we could wear a lot of the same clothes, even though I was a little bit bustier than she was. I pulled out my red halter top.

"Here." I proffered the top. "Wear this. It'll look cute on you with those jeans."

Reesy snatched the top and held it up.

"Now, Misty, you know I ain't got enough titties to fill this out like you do."

"Trust me, you're just the right size for it. It'll probably fit you better than it does me anyway."

Reesy slipped into the top. It looked great on her.

"Now go look in the mirror," I said.

She rushed into the bathroom. She smiled in pleasant surprise as she turned and looked at herself from behind.

"Girl, I might have to steal this outfit from you," she chided.

"Don't even think about it," I retorted. "You can wear it out today, but it's coming back home with me tonight."

"Watch me," she challenged.

"All right now. You ain't crazy."

She let out a quick laugh, and looked at me in mock amusement.

"Naw, baby," she said, "you can hang it up. This outfit is mine now."

She put her hands on her hips and shook her booty at me. Just as I was about to come into the bathroom and pretend to take my clothes back, the phone rang.

I froze.

I stared at the phone for a minute, then looked up at Reesy. Both of us were silent. Fear shot through me like a bullet.

"You want me to get it?" she asked, taking a step forward.

"*NO!*" I shrieked, alarmed at my intensity. After a second ring, I lunged for the phone.

"*Hello?*" My voice shook like Jell-o.

"Hello?" a man's deep voice echoed back.

"Roman?" My heart was beating a mile a minute.

"I'm sorry, who?" the voice said.

"Is this Roman?" I asked.

For a moment, there was silence on the phone. Then the man asked, "Is this the Goldberg residence?"

"No, it's not. Who's calling?"

"This is Sy," the voice said, "Sy Horowitz." Suddenly it sounded very white. Very white and very kosher.

"Wrong number," I said dryly, hanging up the phone before he had a chance to respond.

I stood there for a second, my hand still on the receiver, even though it was back on the hook. I stared at the phone, saying nothing. After a while, Reesy broke the stillness.

"You ready, girl? I want to hit the Lenox Mall and show off this hot new outfit of mine."

I looked up at her, my expression blank.

Before the tears had a chance to fall into place, Reesy had picked up both our purses, my keys and hers, and had her arm stuck through mine, hauling me out the door.

By the time we got to the mall, Reesy had been chatting so incessantly that I had no choice but to not think about Roman. She told me ridiculous stories about the people at her job.

"Girl, there's this transsexual, Kenyatta."

She started laughing.

"What?" I asked, curious.

She was cracking up so much, she couldn't even get the story out.

"What?" I persisted, more amused at her than whatever it was she supposedly wanted to say.

She was choking.

"No, girl, listen," she panted. "This fool, Kenyatta . . . child . . . he, she, whatever the *fuck* it is, comes to work every day in full drag, right?"

Tears were rolling down her face. She could barely keep the wheel straight as she drove.

"Yeah?" I asked. "What's so funny about that? I've seen transsexuals before."

She held up her finger.

"No, girl," she interrupted, "what's fucked-up about Kenyatta is that she looks like a straight-up female. I mean, she got booty, *pow*, titties, *pow!*"

She started laughing again.

"She's got way more body than we'll ever have. And her clothes and hair are *hooked*. Kenyatta is damn *gorgeous!*"

"So? And?"

"Kenyatta wants so bad to just meet a nice guy who don't give a shit that she used to be a man. She don't want some gay nigga who just wants another nigga in drag. She truly believes she was always a woman, and now she has the body to prove it. Kenyatta wants a heterosexual brother who's looking for a heterosexual sistah."

"What's wrong with that?" I said in defense of Kenyatta. "There's lots of people who feel they're trapped in the wrong body and gender."

She kept giggling.

"Let me finish." She snickered. "This is terrible. I really shouldn't be making fun of her. Him. *Whatever.*"

I waited.

119

She looked over at me.

"You know what we call Kenyatta?"

"What?"

She burst out laughing again.

"The Gobbler."

"Why?" I asked.

"Girl, she's got an Adam's Apple bigger than your head!"

She couldn't stop laughing.

"I mean, here she is, fine as hell. Brothers come in and see her and make their way over to her desk from clear across the room. Soon as they get up close and see that big gobbler up under her neck, they make like Carl Lewis!"

"That's messed up," I chuckled.

"It really is," she giggled.

"Why won't she just get it removed?" I asked.

"Shit, I guess she ran out of money. All that surgery, and she can't get a man because of that. You should see it. Her neck looks pregnant."

She kept laughing.

"You're crazy," I said.

"Girl, that ain't nothing," she kept on. "You should see my boss. You know I walked in on that bitch sitting in her office eating boogers?"

"Are you serious?" I exclaimed, wrinkling up my nose. "That's disgusting. This was your boss?"

"Yeah, girl. Olivia. She's this prissy white bitch that walks around all day like she's the shit. Then, when no one's looking, she's got her finger stuck up her nose as far as it can go."

"Gross," I groaned. "Did she know you saw her?"

"Yeah!" she laughed. "I had been standing in the doorway for about five minutes, waiting on her to look up. She'd dig, then ball it up on her finger, and eat it."

"Reesy stop!" I screamed. "This is *soooo* nasty."

"Exactly," she agreed. "I just stood there. I couldn't even move."

"When did she notice you?"

120

"She finally realized somebody was standing in her doorway. She looked right at me. Her eyes were bucked, like she had been caught fucking. Girl, her finger just froze, right there in her nose. She couldn't say shit."

"What did you do?"

"I said *Ew!*, and walked out of her office!" Reesy squealed.

"No, you didn't!" I said with alarm. It was such a disgusting image. "Did she ever say anything to you about it?"

"What could she say? I guess she just figures it was our little secret. Child, you know I told everybody in that office!"

This was way too vivid for my tastes. Some things I just didn't need to know about. People eating boogers was definitely one of them.

We cruised the lot for a while in search of a parking space, found one, then made our way into the mall. In no time at all, my concentration was diverted to shoes, jeans, skirts, and CDs. Every now and then, as I made a purchase, I wondered what Roman would think about the thing that I was buying, but Reesy usually rushed the thought away with her endless chatter.

She pulled me around the mall from store to store until, exhausted, I announced to her that I needed to sit down.

"Are you hungry?" she asked. "I could go for some pizza."

"Pizza's fine with me," I said. "Just get me to a table somewhere so I can put these bags down."

We headed for the food court, both of us loaded down with purchases. My feet were hurting from the unstretched pair of block-heeled shoes I was wearing.

Reesy twitched alongside me, shaking her ass like she was Miss It in my outfit. I had to smile at her. She knew she looked good in it, and she wanted everyone else to know it, too. She was getting lots of stares from men and women alike.

As a matter of fact, whenever we were out, men often stopped Reesy in recognition, like they knew her. She usually smiled and waved back at them, then skitted along without much comment.

Armed with her loaded confession from last night, I suddenly understood why.

As we rounded a corner toward the food court, she nudged me with one of her bags.

"Ouch!" I shrieked. "Why'd you hit me like that?"

"Girl, *that's her!*" she hissed, gesturing with her head toward a tall, sophisticated white woman walking toward us.

She looked to be about forty years old, her features very chiseled and regal. She was clutching a little terrier close to her chest. The terrier had no distinguishing features, other than two eyes peering out frightfully from wads of silken hair.

"That's *who?*" I whispered back.

Before Reesy could answer, the woman was upon us.

"Teresa, how are you?" she droned nasally. "Out spending the money you work so hard for, I see."

She scanned the bags we clutched, openly taking inventory of the stores we had purchased from.

"Just trying to catch the sales, Olivia," Reesy cheesed fakely. "I'll be a bargain hunter till the day I die."

Olivia smiled again, her pinched nose sniffing at me ever so subtly. The little dog yelped.

I felt somewhat awkward as Olivia stood in wait, apparently of an introduction from Reesy. I nudged Reesy slightly.

"What? Oh, I'm sorry. Armistice Fine, this is Olivia Bachrodt, my boss. Olivia, this is my best friend, Armistice Fine."

When Olivia offered her hand, I recoiled instinctively. I don't think she noticed it. I shook her hand quickly, and returned my hand wretchedly to my side.

"Armistice," she mused. "What an interesting name. What is the story behind your receiving such a powerful moniker?"

Moniker? What the hell? Who the hell says *moniker?*

Reesy cleared her throat.

"I was born on Armistice Day. My grandfather was a veteran who wanted a permanent remembrance of his service to his country, so my parents let him give me this name."

"It's very beautiful," she whined. "It's so resonant, so sibilant."

The little dog yelped again.

"All right, Marnier, Mommy's leaving soon," she cooed to the ball of hair.

"It was good meeting you, Armistice," she smiled wanly. She turned to Reesy.

"I guess I'll see you on Monday, Teresa," she said, her nose pinching in tightly with each word.

"First thing," Reesy cheeped.

The terrier yelped once more, defiantly.

"All right, Marney," she gurgled, "Mommy's leaving."

The two of them darted off down the hall, Olivia the epitome of elegance, and her little dog, too.

I wiped my hand frantically against my jeans.

"Gross!" I cried.

Reesy burst out laughing hysterically, dropping her bags in the middle of the floor. I glared at her.

"Why didn't you say something?" I snapped.

She was laughing so hard, she could barely speak.

"I tried to warn you, heffah, but she practically popped up on us out of nowhere. How was I to know Booger Bitch was gonna wanna shake your hand?"

She was cracking herself up.

"Wooh!" She laughed. "That was nasty, Misty. You don't know *where* that hand's been."

"Let's go," I said, pissed. "I want to stop by a bathroom before I eat."

"I hope so," Reesy laughed. "Otherwise you might have more toppings on your pizza than you realize."

She laughed uproariously at that. She had gathered up her bags and we began walking toward the food court again.

"I can't believe a woman can be *that* sidity, and eat her own boogers."

"Believe it, girl," Reesy laughed. "I seent it with my own two eyes."

"Does she know about your night job?" I asked.

"Why should she? She's too caught up in herself. Diggin' her nose and totin' that dog all damn day."

"Are you afraid she'll ever find out?"

"No," she replied.

"What if she does?" I kept on.

"Then I guess I'll just cross that bridge when I get to it, won't I?"

I guess that was the end of *that* subject.

When we reached the food court, I headed straight for the bathroom. Reesy came along with me.

The first thing I did was wash my hands. Twice. Had to get those invisible boogers off. Then I used the toilet. While I was in there, I heard someone call Reesy's name.

"Hey, girl!" Reesy screamed, all loud and sistahfied. "Where you been, heffah? I ain't seen you 'round the office in a coon's age!"

I silently hoped the girl was black, and that there were no white people in the bathroom to hear Reesy make such a stupid remark.

"I was in San Diego, child. My sister moved out there, so I flew in to help her get settled into a new house she and her fiancé just had built. She's getting married next weekend."

"Your sister Stacy?" Reesy asked.

"Yeah! I forgot you met Stacy."

"You introduced her to me one time at the office. I remember because she was so pretty. All the brothers in the office were talking about her when she left."

"That's Stacy." The girl laughed. I could tell by the way she talked that she was definitely a sistah.

I was taking my time. I didn't feel like meeting another boogerfied person from Reesy's job.

"So what are you doing back here?" Reesy asked her. "Aren't you in the wedding?"

"Yeah, child, I'm the maid of honor," the girl said. "I came back to pick up the outfit Stacy wanted to wear when she and

Roman leave for their honeymoon. All those stores in California, and she just has to have this outfit from the Lenox Mall. I figured I'd fly in, do some last-minute things for her here, and go right back."

I was immobilized in the bathroom. No way could a coincidence be that uncanny.

Knowing Reesy the way I do, I knew she zoomed right in on everything.

"Roman?" she asked.

"Yeah," the girl said. "I don't think you ever met him. Roman worked so much, he was hardly ever around. He just flew out there this week. He gave up his apartment months ago and was staying at my place. The only time I ever saw him was in the morning when he came home from his night job; then he turned right around to go to a day job. He was off on the weekends, and that child used to sleep all day."

"Is *that* right?" Reesy asked.

"Child yeah. He's been saving money left and right, just so he could build this house and pay for the wedding. Girl, he *loves* himself some Stacy. Now that the house is all finished and the wedding's so close, he shipped the car up, then he flew out and got settled in."

"They're getting married in California?" Reesy asked.

"Yep. In the new house. *Girl, it's so biggg!* I gotta show you pictures when I get back!"

"Oh," Reesy said casually. "So when did he fly out?"

In the bathroom stall, my heart was expanding rapidly inside my rib cage. I thought it was going to burst.

"Tuesday afternoon," she answered. "Why? Did you know Roman?"

My legs began to shake furiously. I could hear Reesy speaking, but the sound seemed kind of muted.

"I'm not sure," she said. She hesitated a moment, then asked the question.

"I think a friend of mine knows him. What's his last name?"

I waited, terrified. It wasn't him. I knew it wasn't. My Roman wouldn't have done this to me.

"Frazier. Roman Frazier," the girl said. "He drives a black Acura Vigor."

I remember the scream as it escaped my body and the sound of running feet to the door of my stall.

I don't remember anything after that.

After that, everything went black.

Reesy knew that I had been sitting in that bathroom stall listening in horror to the truth about Roman. When she heard me scream, she rushed over and banged on the door. When I didn't answer, she crawled under, and was shocked to find me slumped back, unconscious, on the toilet. She slapped my face gently until I began to stir.

When I finally came to, she led me over to a row of chairs against the wall. My chest was tight with pressure and I couldn't stop shaking. She wet a paper towel, sat beside me, and wiped my face.

As she gently stroked my forehead, cheeks, and chin, I drew strength and comfort from the indignance and rage I saw blazing in her eyes. Her yellow face was flushed red, and the corners of her mouth twitched uncontrollably. Reesy, the self-appointed nemesis of all good-for-nothing black men, was livid. And I mean *livid*. She wanted to kill.

"*That motherfucka!*" she shouted. "That black ass *motherfucka!*"

I sat there, shaking, crying, catatonic.

"Just don't call me stupid, okay," I whimpered. "I should have seen this coming. I should have. I guess I'll never learn."

She hugged me tightly, my champion and defender.

"Naw, girl, don't say that. You can't help it that you have a big heart. You just keep giving the wrong niggas a chance."

I was crying uncontrollably. I wondered how I was going to tell my parents that my relationship was over with yet another man. They probably thought I was totally unstable.

Beside me, I could feel the heat from Reesy's anger bubbling deep within.

I kept crying. She held me tightly.

"They're all dogs, Misty. They all are."

She sighed in frustration, shaking her head.

"I love black men. I do. I really do. But I swear to God, they make it so hard for us to love them when they do shit like this."

I sniffled, the sound of her voice comforting me.

"It's not just black men," I said, defensively. "I'm tired of everybody blaming everything on them. Who knows? Maybe it's me. I'm just too fucked up. I can't seem to see the signs."

She lifted my chin and wiped my face gently with her fingers.

"You're just too sweet, baby," Reesy said. "We need to find a way to channel some of your office piranhaism into your relationships."

I nodded, looking down at my hands.

"See, when you meet these men, they're all peaches and cream because they can tell how sweet you are."

I listened to her closely. She was always right.

"Then, once they know they've charmed you to death, they start with the bullshit. By then, it's too late for someone as nice as you to emotionally divorce yourself."

She stroked my head.

"That's all right, though." She chuckled. "We fixed ol' girl."

"Who?" I asked, looking up at her. My voice sounded pathetically weak and weepy.

"Roman's soon-to-be sister-in-law," Reesy smirked.

I winced at the mere sound of his name. And the thought of him getting married to someone else.

"Did she see me?" I asked in alarm. "Does she know why I fainted?"

"I told her everything," Reesy said smugly.

I felt embarrassed, *mortified*. Now the whole world would know how stupid I was. It was bad enough that I had to find out things the way I did. Now, to top it off, the sister of the girl Roman wanted got the satisfaction of witnessing the humiliation of the girl he threw away.

She probably thought I was some crazed fatal attraction who had been chasing after a man who wasn't interested. She had no idea how much Roman had been chasing after me.

I sat there, feeling worse than ever. The thought of it made me sick. Especially the way she told Reesy how Roman was *soooo* crazy about her beautiful sister Stacy.

"What did she say?" I whimpered. "Who did you tell her I was?"

"I told her you were his girlfriend," she said with a smile.

I was stunned at that. Reesy knew damn well she didn't think Roman and I had a relationship. But as I studied her face, I could see that she had gotten a sick satisfaction out of knocking the wind out of the girl's happily-ever-after love story.

Inside, I was glad.

"I told her how that sorry motherfucka's been spending his nights with you for months, having all kinds of crazy sex. That he never once mentioned a Stacy."

"What did she do?" I asked, my spirits lifting.

"She just stood there with her bad weave, mouth all open, looking stupid."

I perked up a little.

"She had a bad weave?" I asked, pleased. "I thought she was pretty."

"*Girl!* Her hair was fucked! Stacy's the one that's cute. And even she ain't all that. She's just light-skinned with good hair. You know how niggas eat that up."

That sounded ironic coming from her, but it made me feel better.

"So how did you know the girl had a weave?"

Reesy rolled her eyes. I knew she was doing all this for my benefit.

"*Please*, Misty! You could see the tracks, and the color didn't even match! Her own hair was sticking up all around the weave."

I giggled with delight. The pressure in my chest began to lessen.

"All these damn hairdressers in Atlanta, and she comes rolling up in the middle of the Lenox Mall with her hair all ate-out! And she ain't light like her sister. She was way too dark to even try to pull off wearing a blond weave!"

We both chuckled at that. I hesitated a moment, then asked Reesy a pointed question.

"Did she say she was going to tell Stacy?"

I don't know why I cared. But I didn't want Roman to get off scot-free for what he had done to me.

"Naw," she said slowly. "I think she got mad at me."

"Why? For telling her about me and Roman?"

Reesy shook her head. There was a wicked smile on her lips.

"No. For calling her sister a stupid bitch."

I gasped.

"*No, you didn't!* What did you say?"

"After I told her about you, she got all flip and said that a man's gonna be a man, but Roman's heart was with Stacy. So I told her I was sorry to hear that her sister was such a stupid bitch."

"When did you say all this to her?"

"When I was trying to get you to open the stall door. Before I got you out, I had to set her straight about what was going on."

"So she left?"

"With a dust behind her," Reesy said with an evil grin.

I leaned over and hugged her tight. In the face of my humiliation, Reesy had managed to handle things for me again.

"Thank you," I whispered.

"It was my pleasure," she replied. "If Stacy's crazy enough to stay with him, she deserves everything she gets. She did you a favor."

I nodded, leaning back.

"One less dog in Atlanta," she said, offering me a comforting smile.

"Yeah," I sighed, halfway meaning it, halfway still wishing it was me that Roman loved. My tears had begun to subside, my nose was a little less runny, and the heaviness in my chest had become almost featherlight. But there was a pain in my heart so sharp and so deep, I seriously wondered if it, or I, would ever truly recover.

Reesy watched me closely, studying my expression. As usual, she could see right through me. She knew that, despite everything, a part of me was longing to have Roman back again.

"Misty, what you need to do is see these motherfuckas in their element. You need to see them for the dogs they really are. Once you do that, once you recognize them at their basest level, it's hard for them to trick you. You'll always be able to see right through it."

"How would I do that?" I asked, sniffling one last time.

"Come on," she said, grabbing my hand and leading me from the mall bathroom.

"Let's go have ourselves a few drinks."

We went to Houston's.

I didn't have any appetite, so I had Amaretto Sours for dinner. About six of them.

"Gon', girl," Reesy encouraged. "Drink up. You need to desensitize yourself to this shit."

In retrospect, I realize that she *wanted* me drunk and desensitized.

She knew that when I got drunk, *really drunk*, I was a bold, straightforward bitch.

As soon as I sucked down a drink, another one was beside me. In my state of imbibition, I went from enraged, to sullen, to giddy. Reesy watched it all, a plan brewing under that braided head of hers.

When she figured I was just toasted enough, she said . . .

"I've got an idea."

"What's that?" I giggled, apropos of nothing.

"I gotta go to work in a little bit," she said. "Why don't you go with me? You can see what I do, and how I do it."

"*Hmmm* . . . ," I mused, actually considering the suggestion.

Reesy recognized my vulnerability. And leapt on it. She knew that since I was drunk, it was *the only way* she could get me to go to the Magic City.

"You can learn a few tricks for the bedroom," she joked.

"*Hmmph!*" I snorted. "Like I'll be using them anytime soon!"

"You will," she encouraged. "Watch, girl. You'll recover in no time."

I smiled. A drunken smile, but a smile nonetheless.

"Plus, Misty," she added, "this'll give you a chance to see how these motherfuckas act. They're all dogs, let me tell you. That's their lowest common denominator."

I didn't know if I believed that or not, but I was willing to check it out and see.

At that point, feeling as hollowed out as I did, I was willing to do anything to make me forget.

REESY'S PIECES

I sat in the Magic City clutching my fourth drink.

A Long Island iced tea. Served in a mason jar.

And I was drinking it with a straw. *Very, very fast.*

This wasn't my fourth drink of the day. It was more like my tenth. I had quaffed quite a few Amaretto Sours before I even got here.

My head was spinning. So was the room.

All around me were naked women, all sistahs. They looked like models from any one of the sundry videos on BET. Some were dancers. Others were waitresses, carrying trays and serving drinks, their parts exposed for all the world to see.

I was served repeatedly. Any other time it would have felt weird to have a naked woman bring me a drink. Any other time it would have bothered me to be gawked at by brothers who probably thought I was some dyke coming in for a piece of the action. Any other time it would have made me self-conscious to see so much perfection in the face of my own physical shortcomings.

Any other time I wouldn't have even *been* here.

But I was so trashed now, I didn't give a shit *where* I was. And the Magic City was just as good a place as any other to make me forget the pain of hearing about Roman earlier that day.

So there I sat, a half-empty iced tea in front of me, damn near drunk out of my gourd.

I didn't know how I was warding off the depressingly heavy thoughts of what had just happened with Roman and me, but I did.

A part of me knew, though, that as soon as the liquor wore off, depression was going to hit me.

Like a ten ton pile of bricks.

"Somebody sitting here with you?" a fine brother asked, practically shouting over the loud music.

He was wearing a suit. He looked like he could have been a doctor, all neat and trimmed and important looking.

I stared at him directly, my face completely uninviting.

"Actually, I'd prefer to be alone."

He persisted. "You sure 'bout that? Let me buy you a drink."

His eyes drank me in hungrily.

I was totally repulsed by his vulgarity.

"I'm absolutely sure," I snapped. "Why don't you get lost?"

"All right then." He laughed, raising his hands, giving me a strange look. "To each his own."

On stage, a dark-skinned woman, and I mean she was *really* dark-skinned, almost blue, was dancing. She was writhing and gyrating, and the men were throwing money at her like it was going out of style.

"It's Your Birthday" by Luther Campbell was playing.

"Go, Hershey, it's your birthday!" the men chanted.

Hershey (how appropriate) wiggled her torso downward until she was practically squatting, whirling her pelvis like a pro. She worked her way to the edge of the stage, her body

133

still lowered in a squatted position, and undulated her hips close to the hands waving money.

The men hungrily stuffed it inside her G-string, the only place where they could put money on her.

Hershey didn't have on a bra.

I had never seen *black* nipples before. I mean black, for real. Asphalt black.

Hershey worked her stuff into the faces of the men.

"Go! Go! Go!" they chanted.

Hershey took off her G-string.

I sat there, sipping my iced tea, watching another girl wave her coochie in the faces of what appeared, on the surface, to be a group of distinguished men.

When Hershey took off her G-string, the crowd went crazy. They went absolutely wild.

But let me tell you: this girl was so black . . .

(*How black was she?*)

. . . This Hershey was so black, I couldn't distinguish where her cat hair ended and her skin began.

Not that I was looking at her cat or anything.

Yep.

She was mighty black.

I watched her working her stuff, the men completely out of control. It actually looked like fun. I figured, hell, I can do that. I can gyrate and move my hips around like that. And I've got better breasts, too. With nice, cafe au lait nipples. I could turn these men on, no problem.

A man held a dollar toward Hershey's cat. He held the dollar very close to the lips.

And I don't know how the hell she did it . . .

. . . but Hershey's cat lips *caught hold of that dollar and took it out of the hand of the man.*

Maybe I *couldn't* do what she was doing after all.

I think Hershey's been practicing her Kegel exercises, that's what I think.

I ordered another iced tea.

Hershey ended her set and left the stage, the men squealing and howling with delight at her performance.

I saw one guy say something to a freckle-faced, freckle-bodied waitress, who went over to Hershey and whispered something in return.

A few seconds later, Hershey was over at the man's side. He handed her money, and she began dancing naked on the table. Doing a slow grind in front of his face.

The man stared up at her, grinning from ear to ear, his eyes bright like beacons.

This was a damn shame. The man, who appeared very respectable and upstanding, could have very well been my father. He probably *was* somebody's father. Somebody who had no idea their father liked to look up into snatch.

The music in this place was incredibly loud. So loud, you could barely hear anyone speak.

Not that it mattered.

Talking was the last thing anybody in there was thinking about anyway.

The music changed up. The deejay put on "Brown Sugar" by D'Angelo, which I really liked. I was feeling mellow and relaxed. I didn't give a fuck about anything. I was flat-out drunk.

I started moving my body to the music, my eyes closed.

When I opened them, I noticed I was getting a few interesting stares from some of the men.

I looked up on stage, my eyes opening wide.

Reesy had come out, and she was up there wiggling around seductively to the music, all slow and sexy.

"YEAH!" one older man shouted. "Work that pussy, baby!"

Reesy had on a black sequined thong.

That was it.

Her body was perfect.

I mean, it always had been. And I'm no lesbian. Never have been. Never will be.

But Reesy was gorgeous up there.

And from the way she was moving her body, she knew it.

She saw me watching her, and winked.

I smiled, rocking my head in beat to the music.

She made this circling motion with her body, turning it around very slowly, until her back was to the audience.

Then she bent over, her legs spread wide apart, and looked between her legs at the screaming men. She smiled her best smile. Her breasts weren't even hanging. Even with her head upside down, her breasts remained perfectly in place.

Reesy grabbed her butt cheeks and pulled them apart.

A man reached up and stuck a dollar there.

I burst out laughing, drawing attention from a good many men.

"You like that, huh, baby?" said a bright-skinned brother at the table beside me. "You like that dollar up the ass?"

"Yeah," I replied, a wicked smile on my face. "That shit turns me on."

Like I said, I was drunk out of my mind.

Reesy stood up there on that stage, pumping, bumping, grinding, and hunching her body into poles, palms, whatever.

She slid down front and let a fine ass brother pull her G-string off.

He pulled her cat toward him, like he was going to lick it. Just when he got close enough to do so, Reesy wriggled her hips, cleverly slithering and maneuvering away.

She did a split in the middle of the stage, her long legs stretched out damn near over the entire floor. She grabbed one of her breasts and licked it.

The entire club went wild. Reesy was obviously a favorite. The men were flinging twice as much money as they had doled out to Hershey.

"I want some of your Peanut Butter!" a man up front sang to her, bastardizing the lyrics of the song playing.

Reesy was definitely a pro.

She impressed the hell out of me.

I remembered the little yellow-faced, braided-head girl I

played patty-cake and double Dutch with as a child. Never, in my wildest imaginings, would I have pictured her doing *this*.

I wondered what Tyrone and Tyrene would think if they saw her now.

I wondered if Tyrone Snowden would be here, just like these men, watching now, if Reesy was not his daughter.

Probably so.

The song ended, the stage filled with money.

Reesy gathered up the money, then disappeared from the stage.

The music came up again, and another dancer appeared.

I sipped on my drink, my body moving rhythmically to the sound.

The liquor was working wonders. Thoughts of Roman were far, far away.

Reesy appeared beside me. Topless. And bottomless.

Any other time, I would have been uncomfortable. But this was my girl. She took a seat at my table.

The men beside us were abuzz with excitement.

"How you doing, girl?" she asked. "You having a good time?"

I grinned.

"You're a little freak, ain't you?"

She laughed.

"What do you think?" she said.

I giggled, sucking down more of my iced tea.

A man walked by and touched Reesy on the booty. She rolled her eyes, a twisted grin around her lips.

"I'm only doing one set tonight," she said. "We can get out of here in a minute."

"Okay." I smiled, my back still hunching up and down to the music.

"Look at you, girl," she chuckled. "You're having a good time! I told you you would. You've forgotten all about that asshole, haven't you?"

"Yep," I said, still grooving to the music.

"Told you so."

The freckled waitress walked up to Reesy.

"Girl, that man over there wants a lap dance from you," she said.

"Uh-uh," Reesy replied, shaking her head. "I'm about to get outta here."

"He's paying two hundred dollars," the waitress said. "Don't you see who that is?"

She nodded discreetly.

Reesy and I both looked across the room.

We both recognized the man immediately. He was a popular congressman. Very well respected in the Atlanta community. A fine upstanding alumnus of Morehouse. A gentleman. And a scholar.

Who happened to like lap dances.

Reesy looked at me, her eyebrows raised.

"See what I mean?" she said. "They're all dogs. Even the good ones."

"Are you gonna do it?" the waitress asked.

"What the hell," she said. "Misty, I'll be ready right after this."

Reesy stepped into the thong, which she was holding in her hand, and sashayed over to the table, men whistling and howling at her the whole way over.

She walked up to the congressman, his face one big grin. I saw him hand her money.

Then she lifted her leg over his and climbed onto his lap.

I watched her rub him up and down, her crotch grinding into his.

Occasionally, he ran his hands along her breasts. She would push them out of the way, teasing him, her crotch grinding deeper and deeper into his.

The man, who was stocky and yellow, turned redder and redder as she moved her bottom around on his crotch.

How could she do this without getting turned on? It

couldn't be me. I'd have to bring some closure to the act. Somehow.

The congressman looked like he was about to pop. As I sat there in amazement, staring at her working her crotch, watching him get all excited and crazy, I became angry.

That congressman had a wife that he appeared with on TV and all around Atlanta. And there he was now, bumping and grinding a stranger.

It made me think of Roman. And what he had done to me.

I was furious. I wanted to kill Roman. As I glanced around the room, I wanted to kill every brother in there.

"Go! Go! Go! Go!" they shouted at the dancer-du-moment on stage.

She worked her stuff all around, enchanting them with the power of pussy.

I felt sick. I wanted to get out of there.

A few minutes later, Reesy appeared by my side.

"His dick was sticking me like a dagger," she whispered. "Horny fucker."

"Get me outta here," I hissed.

Reesy looked over at me.

"I guess you see how they are, huh?" she asked.

"Yeah," I replied, so mad that my eyes were filled with tears.

"All right, girl," she said. "Let me get dressed. We'll be outta here in less than five minutes."

I couldn't get the image of that congressman groping all over Reesy out of my head.

"How can you do that?" I asked, sickened at the thought of all those apparently decent brothers in there doing such indecent things.

"It's actually kinda fun," she replied. "And it's a great way to maintain control."

She pulled out of the parking lot and onto the street.

"I feel sick," I moaned.

She looked over at me, concerned.

"What do you mean? From the liquor?"

"Yeah, that," I said. "And from Roman. How can men be so cruel? It doesn't make any sense to me."

I started crying. A drunk cry. A hysterical cry.

"Girl, don't start that," she said, trying to sound firm. "I thought you had this under control."

I went on crying hysterically. Without shame. Like a baby. Way beyond the call of duty.

"*MISTY!*" Reesy screamed at me. "*Knock this shit off! It's not worth all that!*"

"*But he left me!*" I wailed. "*He left me like I was nothing! All I ever did was be nice to him!*"

Reesy tried to drive and watch me at the same time. While trying to watch me, she veered slightly off the road and hit the curb.

I felt the contents of my stomach bubble, churn, gurgle, and begin the quick ascension up my esophagus.

"Uh-oh," I moaned.

"Uh-oh what?" she said, then saw the look on my face.

"*Oh no, Misty . . . ,*" she exclaimed.

Too late.

The contents of my belly poured up, out of my mouth, onto the seat, the floor . . .

And Reesy.

Then I slumped back on the seat, and lapsed off into a drunken, heavy sleep.

VENUS FLYGIRLS

$\int$o how you feelin'?"

I sat up in bed, my head slightly throbbing. Reesy handed me a glass of pineapple juice with ice in it. She knew I always liked my juice with ice. I took a sip. The cool sensation of the liquid coursing over my tongue with its acidy sweetness was invigorating.

"Better," I said.

"That's good. You look a lot better today than you have in the past few weeks. Your skin's got a little color to it."

I rolled my eyes up at her and snickered at this remark.

"What the hell is that supposed to mean?" I asked in exasperation. "Of course my skin has some color to it. I'm brown."

I continued to sip my pineapple juice.

Reesy looked surprised.

"You know what I meant, you mean heffah. You look like you've got a little bit of life to you today."

"You need to say what you mean," I mumbled.

"I thought I did," she replied.

"Well, it's not like I'm white or something. I'm always gonna have a little color to me. That was such a stupid thing to say."

I took another sip of juice.

Reesy just stared at me.

"So is *this* it?" Reesy asked.

"Is *what* it?" I didn't even look up. I just kept sipping my juice.

"This!" she snapped, waving her hand over me in a sweeping motion.

"I don't know exactly what you mean," I said dully.

"I mean, is *this* what you've become now? You crawled into your little cocoon three weeks ago, all beat-down and pitiful, and *this* is what emerged? A bitter bitch who doesn't have the sense of humor God gave a goat?"

I pretended to drink the juice. My lips lingered on the rim of the glass. I felt a little sheepish.

Reesy kept on.

"I've been your friend through all this. I sat here and listened to you cry day in and day out. You call me from work whining. You crawl into bed as soon as you get home. You won't have lunch with Cleotis. Do you know he called me? I don't even know how he got my phone number."

I looked up at her.

"What'd he want?"

"He wanted to know what the fuck was wrong with you!"

"What'd you tell him?" I asked with concern.

The last thing I wanted was everyone at work knowing about what happened.

"I told him not to worry. You'd be all right."

I looked back down into my glass of juice.

"People have been noticing what's going on with you at work. You're crazy if you think they haven't. You've lost weight. You half-fix your hair when you go to the office."

I played with my juice glass.

"Why do you think I've been staying over here with you like

142

this?" she asked. "I didn't say shit about Roman or do anything to make you hurt any more than you had to, because, hell, Misty, I've been feeling your hurt for you. You don't know what it's like to sit around and watch your friend fall into a hole right in front of your eyes."

"You could have gone," I muttered meanly. "You didn't have to watch."

She sighed deeply.

"Do you think I like seeing you laying around suffering like this? You're my girl. You're my role model. You've got more ambition in your thumbnail than I'll probably ever have in my whole lifetime."

I looked up at her sidelong, surprised to hear such a confession from her.

"You're the role model, Miss Shake Your Groove Thang," I said with bitter sarcasm.

It was a rotten thing to say. I didn't really mean it. I was actually somewhat jealous. Learning that your best friend was an exotic dancer was a giant pill to swallow.

When I saw her in action, I was surprised at what I saw. Reesy was good. *Damn good.* And men *loved* her. Something I seemed to have a problem getting them to do.

Yeah. I was jealous of her in a big way.

"Go ahead," she said. "Be nasty to me, if it'll make you feel any better. But you need to change your program, girl."

I listened, my demeanor morose.

"I see you meet these guys, and they're losers. You have so many things going for you in your life, but you keep meeting these lyin', schemin', punchin', cheatin', layin'-up-in-the-cut-ass niggas who make you think there's something wrong with you. It's not your fault. You've just got a big heart. But you need to find a way to tie your head into the whole equation."

"Anyway . . . ," I interrupted.

"Anyway," she continued, "it doesn't matter how many losers you meet, or whatever happens in your life. I'm always here for you. I always listen. Sometimes I say stupid stuff that

I'm really sorry for, but I've got a big mouth. I speak my mind. I'm frank and I'm harsh. But you've known that for twenty-three years. It comes with the package."

"So what's your point?" I said quietly, my lips nibbling around the edge of the glass.

Reesy had her hand on her hip, her finger pointed skyward.

"My point to you, my sistah, is this: I'm gon' be here for you. It's not fair for you to turn on me, 'cause I'm gon' be here to wipe your ass, fix your tea, change your sheets, comb your nappy ass head, and hold your hand when all them niggas don't call, show up, or run off to San Diego and get married."

That smarted. It smarted real bad.

Reesy knew it did. And I deserved it.

"I'm not saying this to hurt your feelings, Miss Divine. I'm not. I'm just hurt 'cause you're laying up here snappin' at me, and I'm not the one who did you wrong. We sistahs need to know how to properly direct our anger. If a man hurts you, get mad at the man. Not me."

"I'm sorry, Reesy. I didn't mean to snap at you like that," I said softly. "I appreciate you being here for me like this."

She plopped down on the bed.

"Well, I didn't mean to hurt your feelings either, Misty. I'm mad about what that asshole did. I'm really mad. And to have you sit here and be mean to me instead of him ain't right. I shouldn't be taking the stabs. He should be taking 'em. Right in the fucking nuts."

"I know," I said. "I'm coping, Reesy, all right? It's hard. I took a sharp blow to my ego. And my heart. That's a year out of my life I'll never get back."

She rubbed my back.

"Yeah, girl. I hear ya. But it's gon' be all right. You'll bounce back like it was nothin'. I know you."

She smiled into my face brightly, her perky yellow face all teeth and dimples.

"After months of therapy," I added. "Some Prozac maybe. A lobotomy."

We both laughed.

"Silly. Girl, you don't need no lobotomy, and you damn shole don't need no Prozac. All you need is a trip to the beauty parlor and the mall. Get your hair done, have them do your nails. Maybe get a pedicure. Then we'll do some major shopping. That's always good for a purge. Go to Lenox and hit the stores."

"I don't think I want to go to the mall for a while, Reesy. Especially not Lenox."

She put her hand on my tangled head.

"See there? Look at how you're misdirecting your anger. The Lenox Mall ain't got nothin' to do with what Roman did."

"Association," I said. "Right now I don't need the association."

"Just because we were in the mall when you found out what an ass he is, don't let that keep you from going back. That's crazy."

I put the empty glass on the nightstand.

"I know it's crazy, Reesy. The mind's a crazy thing. Right now, I think I need to stay as far away from the Lenox Mall as I possibly can."

She sighed helplessly.

"Whatever," she said.

She ran her fingers through the matted mass of hair on my head.

"So are you gonna stay in bed all day?" she asked.

I shrugged my shoulders.

She turned sideways, facing me, all smiles.

"Whatsay we get up, wash your hair, and I'll fix it up real cute. We can go for a drive, or ride out to Piedmont Park. Maybe even go down to Little Five Points, to that record store you love so much. The one where they have all that music from the seventies and eighties on CD for so cheap. What's the name of it?"

"Wax 'n' Facts," I droned dully.

145

"Yeah. That's the place. Maybe I can find those old Rufus and Chaka Khan albums I been looking for. I can't find *Ask Rufus* on CD to save my life."

I listened to her, but my mind was going a mile a minute. I'd already come to a decision about what I wanted to do. And it didn't include riding out to Piedmont Park or trolling record stores in Little Five Points.

"So what do you say?" Reesy asked, all animated.

"I want to leave Atlanta," I announced.

"What?" she asked, totally taken aback. "Where did *that* come from?"

"It's been there for a while. I've been thinking about it a lot lately, and it's what I decided I want to do."

Reesy was quiet for a moment. Her lips were pressed tightly together.

I slumped back deep into my pillows, waiting for the barrage of comments I knew was about to come flying out of her mouth. I could practically hear the wheels a-turning in that tightly braided-up head of hers. I knew it was a matter of seconds before it all came pouring out.

"You know, you shouldn't let some nigga run you out of town like that," she said softly.

I was stunned. I wasn't expecting her to come at me so strong.

"I'm *not* letting Roman run me out of town!" I snapped. "He doesn't even live here anymore, so what does *he* have to do with it?"

"Exactly!" Reesy said. "He doesn't even *live* here anymore. So why do you have to leave? Let me guess. Association, right?"

I didn't say anything. I found myself getting angry at Reesy again, but I checked it because I wanted to make sure I was directing my anger at the right source. She took my silence as defiance, and kept prattling on.

"That nigga wasn't *shit*, Misty. He damn shole ain't worth leaving Atlanta for. This city has so much to offer people of

146

color. I mean, we actually have the opportunity to own things here. We run government here. We're *the shit* here. These are the kinds of positive images we need as sistahs and as a people. That's what you said when you moved here, and that's what you said when you talked me into moving here, too, I might remind you."

I rolled my eyes at her. She knew damn well I didn't talk her into moving here. She came of her own, ain't-got-no-damn-direction accord.

She huffed indignantly.

"I can't believe you're letting that asshole make you move away from a city big enough to swallow a million assholes like him whole without anybody noticing it."

I watched her, sitting next to me pitching a fit. She acted like I said I was going to kill myself or something. All I wanted to do was make a fresh start. Atlanta was cool and all, but I needed to get away from it for a while. It was association like a mug, though I couldn't tell Reesy that right now.

"Roman isn't the reason I'm leaving Atlanta," I stated calmly.

It wasn't actually a lie. Just partially one.

"I thought you liked it here," Reesy argued.

"I do. But I think it's time for me to make a change."

She shook her head in disbelief.

"You've only lived here two years. You have a good job, a nice future, everybody likes you. Why the hell would you want to leave all that?"

"I did it when I moved before."

"Oh," Reesy mused. "So you're gonna spend your life just hoppin' around from place to place every time things don't go the way you want them to romantically?"

"I'm not gonna sit here and defend to you all the reasons I have for wanting a change in my life. You know I moved here because of my job."

"And to get away from crazy Stefan."

I sighed in frustration.

"I'm not gonna even have this verbal joust with you. You know why I moved here. I think Atlanta is great. I like it a lot. It has a lot of things going on for us as a people. And I've had a chance to learn a lot and move up the corporate ladder. I learned stuff that I can take with me anywhere."

I brought my knees up to my chest.

"So what's your beef?" she asked.

"I'm just ready to go."

Reesy was quiet.

"So what are you gonna do about your job?"

"Leave."

She looked at me like I was crazy.

"*Just like that*, you're gonna walk away from your job? After Rich Landey flew down to Fort Lauderdale, practically begged your ass to take it, then moved you up here for free? You don't get opportunities like that, or people flying *to you* to extend them, every day. And you're gonna just walk away?"

I nodded.

"I've never had a problem getting a job. I can get another one."

She shook her head in disbelief.

"Misty, you done lost your mind."

"I'm gonna give notice," I said. "Plus, I have some leave time."

Reesy got up from the bed. She wandered around the room. She went over to the window and peered out.

"Why is this miniblind bent back like this?" she asked.

"I'on know," I lied, remembering the many nights I had peeked out, waiting for Roman to drive up.

We were both silent for a long time. I sat in my bed playing with my fingernails. They were long and hard, probably the only thing about me that was still in admirable condition.

"It's a beautiful day outside," she said finally. "If you got out of this depressing apartment and let the sun hit you for a minute, you might come to your senses, you know."

I sighed loudly.

"Reesy, I *have* come to my senses. I'm leaving Atlanta. That's all there is to it."

I didn't even bother to look up from my nails as I said this.

She turned around and studied my face. The zillions of braids that had defined her hair for the last two decades were twisted into a bun piled high on her head. She stood there, giving me a quizzical look that was part concern, part resignation. Reesy knew me. She'd seen me move before. She knew that once I made a declaration like this, it was useless.

Mentally, she knew, I was already out of Atlanta.

"Damn, Misty! Here we go with *this* shit again!"

I looked up from picking my nails, taken aback by her comment.

"What do you mean, *this* shit?"

"I mean, here I go, gotta find me a new job in a new city. Just because my girl's got wanderlust and can't keep her hot little ass settled down in one place."

I scanned her face. This girl was dead serious. Inside of me, I smiled. I was elated. If I had really thought about it, I should have known Reesy was coming with me wherever I was going. She was my sistah.

Anybody else might have thought we had some kind of weird, kinky thing going on, with her picking up and going every time I did. But our relationship was so special to me.

No matter what, I knew Reesy wasn't going to let me be out there alone.

"So where we moving to *this* time?" she asked, matter-of-factly.

I smiled at her, my long-nailed hands now folded in my lap.

"New York?" I said. Part question, part statement.

"Godddddamm!" She laughed, shaking her head. "Heaven help us, heffah! Heaven help us!"

"Why do you want to resign, Misty?" Rich asked. "You've been with the company two years now. You're one of the best managers I've got. Look at how you've built up your portfolio. The guys are even jealous because I give most of the important accounts to you. There's definitely room for growth for you with us."

I listened to him talk to me with sincerity and warmth. He was the quintessential Corporate American vice president: a neatly trimmed, military haircut that was frosty only around the temples; politically correct in his tailored blue suit, yellow power tie, and crisp white cotton shirt. Rich jogged ten miles every day and was a strict vegetarian. He had two Miss America–looking daughters in college whom the sun rose and set upon, and an anorexic, way-too-tanned wife who spent her days doing the country club thing.

His small eyes peered at me out of a ruddy, post-fiftyish face. Rich Landey was a good-looking man, if older, white men was your thing. It wasn't mine. Even though he did flirt with me quite often, in an inoffensive kind of way.

"There's no way I can talk you into staying on here? There are going to be some fantastic opportunities coming up in the near future. We're buying properties and investing in real estate like crazy."

I looked at him, so earnest and tenacious in his efforts to get me to stay.

No dice. Atlanta had been officially stricken off my list.

I shook my head slowly.

"No, Rich. I don't think so. I've made up my mind. Atlanta's had an impact on me lately in a way that makes me believe it's not meant for me to be here. I need a life change. I think it's time for me to make my home in a place where I feel there's a better fit."

Rich nodded as if he understood. He rubbed his chin pensively.

"You know, Misty, I went through the same thing ten years ago. Everyone thought I was crazy, wanting a change like that at forty-five, especially my family. But I did it. Uprooted my wife and daughters, and it was the best thing I ever did for my career and my life."

This made me feel somewhat encouraged, although realistically I knew that uprootings were probably far easier for a successful, well-educated white man than for me.

"Do you know where you're going, Misty?" he asked. "Perhaps I can put out some feelers for you, give you a reference. Maybe call up some friends in the business. That is, if you're not considering changing careers as well as locales."

I should have known he would say something like this. I'd gotten to know him well, and he had turned out to be my second-best ally. After Reesy.

"I'm really flattered you would do that for me," I said and smiled shyly.

He casually waved his hand.

"Don't you know what kind of contribution you've made to this company?"

"Well . . . yeah," I grinned.

"I'm sorry I haven't been able to spend the kind of time with you I did during your first year," he said pensively. "I've been so busy chasing down deals and concentrating on corporate expansion. I think we lost touch with each other a little."

"It's okay, Rich. I always knew you were in my corner. You didn't have to always be in my face for me to know that."

"Good," he said. "I'm glad you know how I feel."

I casually looked away, out of the window behind him. It was a breathtaking view of the Atlanta skyline. In the distance, I swear I thought I could see Stone Mountain.

"Rich, can I ask you a frank question?"

"Sure," he said, his expression earnest and intense.

"I guess I need to tell you up front, it's a racial question."

"Shoot," he replied.

"I know I've done a great job for you, I mean, heck, that's why you moved me up here in the first place. I can only guess that's why you've given me such a big portfolio now."

"Right," he agreed.

I looked down at my nails, then up at him again.

"You'll probably think this is a crazy question."

"No, I won't, Misty. Go ahead."

I smiled.

"I'm only asking you this because I feel like I can talk to you. About almost anything."

"Almost anything?" he smiled.

"Yeah. Almost anything."

"So? What's your crazy question?"

"Why aren't there any black males in the company that are being given the opportunities I am?"

His brow shot up quizzically.

I quickly tried to clarify.

"I mean, I know there are some out there who are capable. I keep moving up, up, up, and believe me, I've got no complaints about that. But I've been here for two years and haven't seen any black men in this whole big company getting the breaks that I am. I just see people who look like Jeremy."

He nodded.

"You're right, Misty. But that's not by design. There aren't a lot of black men out there that we've found qualified to do the level of work you're doing."

"C'mon, Rich, really. I know I'm good, but I don't think I'm that unique. Are we doing the kind of recruiting that would even reach the black men that are qualified? Or is it all done in an inside way, like how you got me? From a management company."

He pressed his lips together.

"You know, I've never really thought about it."

"I guess there's no reason you would have," I said absently. "I just think it would be nice to see more African-Americans in companies like this, representing both genders. This has been such a wonderful place to work. It's a place where a person can really feel like they're making a contribution."

"Maybe I should pay more attention to it," he said.

I studied his face.

"I didn't say that to take a stab at you," I explained. "It's just something I've thought about. I mean, I see people in positions like Cleotis's all the time. But I know there are plenty of black males out there who are very capable managers as well."

"Thanks for saying that, Misty. I'll remember it. But even now, I could show you some places in this company where you'll find some of the examples you're talking about."

"Yeah," I said. "Oh well . . ."

We were both quiet for a moment.

"You never did answer me. Are you making a break from this business, or can I help you out in any way wherever you plan on going?"

I answered quickly.

"No, I don't plan on changing careers. Not at all. In fact, I'm hoping I have a pretty good chance of finding work in New York, especially since corporate asset management is such a big deal there."

Rich burst out laughing, abruptly changing the mood of the room. A deep, hearty, gut-busting laugh.

"You're moving to *New York*, Misty?" he laughed.

"Yes," I said, surprised at his laughter. "Why?"

"*New York City?*" he questioned again.

"Yes. New York City," I repeated, puzzled.

"So you think you'll have a better fit in New York than in Atlanta?" he asked, his face contorted in disbelief. "The people there are cretins, Misty! Absolute asses!"

"Then, for the most part, Rich, it should be a smooth transition," I stated.

He quieted his laughter and began to rub his chin, a smile still haunting his face.

"That's an interesting comment, Misty. I won't pry and ask its etymology."

"Don't. It's too time-consuming and pathetic for me to go into."

He rose from his chair and started walking around the huge office.

"You know what, Misty?" his eyes were twinkling, like he'd just had a vision.

153

"What, Rich?"

"How about a transfer?"

"We don't have an office in New York, do we?" I asked.

"Well, yes and no," Rich said. "Remember six months ago we bought out the Burch Financial Group?"

"*Y-y-yesss,*" I said slowly, picking my brain for details of that particular deal. "I remember you spent a lot of time going back and forth out of town negotiating it, but you spent most of your time in Canada, I thought."

"That's because their former parent company, Gulfstream World Enterprises, is based there."

"Oh," I said.

"Well, the Burch Group is ours. It's headquartered in downtown Manhattan. We're the parent company now, and it's given us a stronghold in cities like New York without having to go in and try to build a reputation from scratch."

"I understand," I nodded.

"In the past few months we've been turning over personnel and transitioning Burch's standards to fall in line with ours."

I kept nodding, seeing a potential positive development out of all this.

"Remember Bob Blanculowitz?" he asked.

"I think so. Didn't he come here once? You took him on a tour of the department?"

"*Yes!* Not long after we closed the deal."

"I remember that," I said. "He was a tall, stiff-looking kinda guy. Like he never laughed a day in his life."

Rich chuckled.

"That's Bob," he laughed. "I don't believe he's really as anal as he seems, though. He was just trying to impress the boss. That's me."

"I see," I said.

I wasn't sure I did.

"Let me cut to the chase, Misty. Bob used to be the VP of Diversification for Burch Financial. His job was pretty much the equivalent of mine here, so when we took over, he began to report to me. His title is now comptroller for Burch, even though he's still handling diversification. With my guidance and supervision, of course."

"Uh-huh," I said, trying to follow where he was heading.

"We're going to be adding more asset managers at Burch. Right now the load on the existing managers is way too heavy for the type of concentration they need to be doing on their portfolios. I'm also having Bob turn over some of the less productive managers. We need aggressive people in our company, not slough-offs."

I nodded, a slight smile forming on my lips.

"Obviously you see where I'm going with this," he said.

"Possibly," I said.

"Well, Misty, I'm offering you one of those positions, if you'll take it. But there's a catch: I'd like to make you a senior asset manager. With a possible chance to take over Bob's job in the near future."

"Are you serious, Rich?" I exclaimed. *"You're going to give me his job?"*

"It's yours if you want it," he replied. "I think you're more than ready to move on to the next level."

Shit!

My heart was pumping wildly. I was finally going to get a chance at what I'd been working so hard for.

The skin on my arms had raised up in a million little goose pimples.

"What about Bob?" I asked.

His expression was intense.

"Bob's too set in his ways. He's not very open to new ideas and that makes it hard for us to make any progress. I need someone with a fresh approach. You've got just what it takes to get in there and do the job."

"I'll do my best, that's for sure."

"I know you will," he said. "That's why I'm offering you the job."

I nodded, in a daze, already picturing myself in New York running things.

"So what do you think?" Rich asked. "Are you ready to take on the Big Apple?"

"Are you kidding?" I exclaimed. "When can I start?"

"Unbelievable!" Reesy cried. "Un-*fucking*-believable!"

"What?" I asked innocently, knowing full well what she was talking about.

Reesy paced around erratically in my living room that evening, shaking her head.

"I can't fucking believe how your love life *sucks* to high heaven, yet shit just *drops* into your lap when it comes to your career!"

I didn't know whether to be flattered or insulted by her comment.

"My love life doesn't suck, Reesy," I said shortly. "And I don't exactly see you in a Cinderella relationship right now either."

"*Black*arella, honey. Ain't nothin' *Cinder*ella 'bout me," she quipped.

Amazing how yellow negroes were always so militant.

"Well, you ain't no *Black*arella right now either, Miss Thang, so far as I can see."

"Yeah, but I'm running the shit I do have going on. Niggas know they can't play me for no dummy. They got to come hard when they're steppin' to the Reesy!"

She pat herself on the chest as she strutted around the room like a cocky little peahen. Talking that ghetto talk again.

"You'd stop doing that if you knew how foolish you looked," I laughed.

"You're just jealous, bitch. 'Cause you know I'm *all* that," she grinned.

"Of course you are, Reesy. Of course you are." I rolled my eyes as I said this. "But this ain't the Magic City. Ain't no stripping going to be going on in here."

"*Exotic dancing,*" she corrected.

"Whatever," I said.

She came over to the arm of the chair where I was sitting. She looked at me, shaking her zillions of braids vigorously.

"Now, don't try to change the subject, heffah," she said. "I want to know how you always manage to get great jobs to just fall in your lap, while the rest of us sistahs are out here scrugglin' like a muhfucka."

I looked up at her, amazed.

"I didn't try to change the subject, Reesy," I laughed.

"Yes you did, bitch. You're doing it now."

"You know, you curse way too much. No wonder men are scared of you."

She chuckled.

"They're not scared of me, honey. They *respect* me." She worked her head sharply. "There's a difference, you know."

"Who's changing the subject now?" I asked.

"Quit playing, Misty," she snapped anxiously. "Now, you tell me how it is your boss offers you a job taking over an office in Manhattan, *just like that?* You go in there to tell his ass good-bye, and come out a fucking CFO. That shit ain't normal."

"It's not a CFO," I protested. "It's a senior asset manager."

"What difference does it make?" she returned. "You're gonna be running the office eventually. You must have given him some pussy once or something, for him to be carving out your career the way he is."

I glared at her, then shoved her off the arm of the chair.

"Get away from me with your little nasty mouth!" I huffed. "What would even make you say some stupid shit like that?"

"I'on know, girl," she said apologetically, realizing I was serious. "I was just playin'. But why else would a white man give you such a prize job? They're not ones to give us shit. There's usually a catch. And most times with black women, it's pussy."

"Did it ever dawn on you that maybe I'm good at what I

do? That maybe he saw a fit for me with the position in New York?"

She shrugged.

"Whatever," she said.

She hesitated a moment, then said, "How come everything with you is all about a *fit*, Misty?"

"Because, if it doesn't feel right, I have to move on."

"Then how come you never got hip to Roman and his shit?" she asked.

I didn't say anything. I actually had to think about that for a moment.

"Don't tell me you thought that nigga was a fit for you?"

I stared off into the nothingness ahead of me.

"Huh?" she persisted.

"No, Reesy," I conceded. "Roman wasn't a fit. You know that. I don't know why you're asking me that stupid question."

She plopped down on the couch across from me.

"I just don't understand why you put up with that mess for a year."

She shook her head in amazement, as if I wasn't even there.

"As sharp and driven as you are, for the life of me, I just can't understand it, girl."

"Yeah," I said softly. "I can't either."

Suddenly her tone was upbeat.

"Oh well, it don't matter now. Looks like it worked out to your advantage. You're about to go off to a big ass, hotshot job in Noo Yawk Siddy. *Gon', girl! Do your thang!*"

"You're so silly, Reesy!!" I giggled.

"I'm for real. I'm proud of you, even though you ain't got no sense when it comes to men."

I threw a pillow from my armchair at her.

"Quit!" She laughed, ducking from the pillow. "You gon' need me in Noo Yawk, so you better not hurt me."

"Is that right?" I asked rhetorically.

She nodded, her head moving so swiftly, it made her look goofy.

"Well, if you know what's good for you," I said, "you better stop saying the first thing that comes out of your mouth to people. You'll get shot up for that mess in New York with a quickness."

Reesy clucked her tongue.

"Honey, please!" she exclaimed. "I'll be fine. I'll fit in perfectly with all those assholes in Noo Yawk!"

"You're right about that," I laughed.

"You're the one I'm worried about," she added. "What's gonna happen when Pollyanna Purebred hits the streets of Manhattan? The niggas are gonna be knee deep with numbers standing in line to take a crack at your naive ass."

I laughed at that. I was feeling so much better now that I knew I, thanks to Rich Landey, once again had the opportunity of a lifetime to look forward to.

One that would include a relocation package.

This was a good thing, I realized. It was helping considerably in diminishing my concentration on the legacy of pain and hurt Roman had left me with.

"But it's all right, girl," Reesy continued, still wrapped up in our conversation. "I got your back."

"Do you now?" I asked sarcastically.

"Yep," she said, jumping up from the sofa. She walked over to her big heavy shoulderbag, which she had parked by the front door.

"Which reminds me," she said brightly. "I bought you something today. I almost forgot about it."

I was suddenly filled with affection for her. Even though she cursed like a sailor, and was way too frank and harsh with me most times, Reesy was always thinking about me. She always had my best interests at heart.

She pulled a plastic bag from the purse. She walked over and stood just above me.

I looked up at her, warmth and the spirit of camaraderie rushing over me, oozing through my very pores.

"I love you, Reesy," I said matter-of-factly.

"I love you, too, girl," she returned.

She pulled a book from the plastic bag. I smiled. Reesy knew I loved to read. She knew books often replaced boyfriends in the empty space that I loosely called my love life. She handed it to me.

I reached for it, staring at the cover for a few seconds before I actually focused on the title. When I finally did, my eyes were like saucers.

Smart Women, Foolish Choices.

That damn Reesy. She just never, ever quit.

I was packing up my things, excited at the prospect of something new, someplace different. This would be the *third* time I had moved to a major city in less than ten years. When I told my parents about it, they were very supportive and congratulatory. Mama was worried about me living in New York, but she was glad to hear that Reesy was coming with me.

As I thought about things now, I realized that Cleotis was right. About me being naive enough to think that I could spot a cheating man a mile away.

Roman taught me a lesson. Lesson enough to make me want to move on, away from Atlanta with its well-packaged men and their well-packaged, build-to-suit romantic plans that included the girlfriend du jour. I was not willing to be a part of that scene.

The move to New York would be the best thing for me. I knew it. In a city with nine million people, I could lose myself, take my time and find a man who was right for me.

More than anything else, I could concentrate on my career and build a solid future for myself.

I smiled to myself as I wrapped up my dishes in newspaper. I couldn't wait to get to New York. Starting over again would be a wonderful feeling. Just the feeling I needed to make me forget the shame of what happened with Roman.

It still hurt real bad to think about it. But the hurt was more ego than anything. I couldn't accept that I could be stupid enough to love a man so desperately that I chose to ignore all the signs that he was never really mine.

I had to admit, I always knew something wasn't on the up-and-up. But I figured if I hung in there long enough, all the problems would go away and Roman would be all mine.

I guess God has a way of making us look stupidity in the face, no matter how much we try to run away from the truth. Too bad we can't pick the moment to be confronted with that stupidity.

It hadn't helped that I was squatting over the toilet with my panties in a bunch when the bomb was dropped on me.

I had begun to act as if the whole thing with Roman never happened at all. I knew this was not a good approach, and that one day the dam would break. Then I'd have to face the issue for what it was.

For right now, I chose to tuck it all away inside.

I had a new life to start in a big city far, far away.

"Girl, I at least need to find me a job before I go. I ain't like you with shit just dropping into my lap."

Reesy sat on my couch crosslegged, the *New York Times* classified section open across her lap. There were several ads boldly circled in black.

I was still packing, stowing books, pictures, and towels into boxes. I had already packed up my most important stuff: the African masks, the Senegalese collection of villagers, and my black art.

I alternated between sitting and kneeling on the floor as I stuffed everything away.

"What are you looking for?" I asked. "The same kinda job you have now?"

"Hell no," she snapped. "The last thing I want is to be talking to folks on the phone all day long about stocking their vending machines with more Ding-Dongs and Ho-Hos. That shit's for the fucking birds."

I laughed as I pressed towels down into a box.

"That's not exactly what you do all day, Reesy."

"It's pretty damn close to it," she said.

I closed the box and wrote "TOWELS" on the outside of it.

"I've earmarked some stuff here in the *Times*. I think I want me a change of venue," she said.

"What about your night job?" I asked. "You're just gonna give that up? There's good money in that business."

She waved her hand, dismissing it all.

"No more exotic dancing for me. That was just a fantasy gig. Something I always wanted to do. Now I can walk away and say *Been there, done that*."

I struggled to get up from the floor, a little sore from all the bending. When I finally stood, I pressed my hands against my lower back and arched into a deep stretch.

"What do you *think* you want to do *now*, Reesy?" I grunted. "You've done it all, from hamburgers to hair. You've done everything but be a hoe. A real one anyway."

She laughed.

"At least, I don't *think* you have," I amended.

"Shut up, wench," she laughed. "And you know damn well I ain't done no hamburgers, so I don't even know why you gon' go there."

I abruptly stopped stretching and looked at her.

"Reesy, pleez!" I said. "I can't believe you! You were the burger queen. Miss McDonald's herself. You even got me a job there. You used to make everybody sick bringing all them free, dried-out, day-old hamburgers to school every day. And I'm surprised you ain't get fired for giving away all that free food to your friends when they came through the drive-thru."

"I forgot about that," she said and smiled.

"Of course you did."

She clucked her tongue and waved her hand at me, stretching her legs out over the arm of the sofa.

"I must have blocked it out," she retorted. "Plus, it don't count anyway. That was when we was in high school. Work before or during college doesn't count in the scheme of what I've done in my life."

I grabbed an armful of knickknacks and some newspaper, and sat back on the floor again.

"Come again?" I said.

"Just what I said," Reesy replied. "What I did before and during college doesn't count."

I began wrapping the knickknacks in newspaper and placing them into a box. I looked up at her, sitting there on my couch with her legs cocked up.

"How is that?" I asked,

"Those weren't real jobs," she said.

I laughed, shaking my head.

"I'll bet the people who hired you to do them thought they were. And if I recall correctly, you got paid for them, which usually qualifies for what is defined as a job."

"But I didn't need the money to survive," Reesy said. "That's what makes the difference. When I worked in high school, I was living with my parents. When I worked in college, that was for extra money to go partying and shopping with."

"And you need the money now to survive?" I cynically asked.

"Yes, Miss Smarty, I do," Reesy said. "My parents haven't given me money since I got out of school."

I rolled my eyes at her. I knew it wasn't a lie. It was just a gross distortion of the truth.

"What about that quarterly stipend?" I asked.

She was holding the paper up to her face now, blocking my view of her expressions.

"You know that doesn't count," she said dryly. "I barely even get to see that money. I've never even used it."

"Umph," I grunted.

She pulled the paper down from her face.

"What does *that* mean?" she demanded. "You know I don't take money from them."

"Nothing," I said, the pitch of my voice unnaturally high.

She clucked her tongue at me.

"Heffah, I know what you're getting at," she said. "Just because I take stuff from them, that don't mean nothing. I make my own way, and they ain't giving me nothing that contributes to my day-to-day existence."

"Yeah, whatever," I replied.

That was a crock of shit. Those years of stipends out there accruing interest and generating dividends smelled like day-to-day eventual contributions to me.

I stuffed the last knickknack into the box and wrote "FRAGILE: GLASS" on the outside when I sealed it closed.

I stood up and walked into the kitchen.

"You want something to drink?" I asked her.

"Case in point," she kept on, ignoring my question, "this morning I told them I was moving to New York. They asked me if I had a job lined up, and I told them no. They had a fit. Mama tried to talk me out of moving, and when she saw it was futile, she offered me five thousand dollars to help with the move."

I was pouring myself a tumbler of water. When I heard her mention five thousand dollars for the move, my hand froze, the cup just inches from my mouth.

"And you said . . . ?"

"NO!" she shrieked, incredulous that I would even ask.

I put the tumbler down and leaned against the counter. I tried to fathom the thought of anyone, especially my parents, *ever* offering me five thousand dollars, *gratis*, and me turning it down. Stuff like this never happened to me.

I peered at her from the kitchen. I studied her closely, like she was an amoeba or some other weird microscopic thing worthy of scrutiny. She stared back at me, her indignation at the offer of money quite comic and ridiculous.

"Just because I've taken trips and furniture doesn't mean they can just throw money at me to make things easy. This move is my thing, not theirs," she said.

"Actually, it's *my* thing," I corrected.

"I know that, heffah, but I'm talking about from their perspective. This has nothing to do with them, so I don't need their money to jump-start me on getting settled in New York."

I picked up the tumbler and drank some water. I needed it.

"Why don't you just take the money as a loan?" I asked. "At least until you find a job. You don't have to use it all."

Reesy shook her head vehemently.

"No way, Miss Divine. I don't want to even get myself in the habit of taking money from my folks, 'cause then it'll be too easy for me to do it again. A lot of the bad habits I have now are because my parents made things too easy for me. I spent my twenties trying to break those habits. Now that I'm thirty, I don't want to spend another decade doing the same thing all over again."

"All right," I said.

I brought my tumbler into the living room and sat down on the chair across from her.

"Do you understand where I'm coming from, Misty?" she asked.

She looked really pained about all this. For the life of me, no, I couldn't understand. But I lied to her. Unlike Reesy, I didn't get my jollies out of being brutal and frank.

"Sort of. I didn't grow up with money and there are never any instances in my life where it's being offered to me in chunks of five thousand, so it's hard for me to feel sympathy for you."

"What about this job you're getting in New York? Your boss just handed it to you like it was nothing. People would kill for something like that."

"That's different, Reesy. I work hard for Rich. I've put in sixteen-hour days on many, many, many occasions. I've spent lonely nights in hotel rooms, I've done the O.J. thing, the *old* O.J. thing, not the new one, running through the airport and nearly breaking my neck hundreds of times trying to make connecting flights. Rich didn't just hand this job to me. I've earned it."

She sat there listening to me, but I don't think she could really relate.

"Well, Misty, in your own way, you have people in your life like my parents, making it easy for you whether you want them to or not. Rich Landey is one of those people."

"Rich Landey and your parents are two totally different issues!"

"I beg to differ, sweetie. Believe it or not, they're both the same."

I knew we weren't going to agree, so I steered the conversation back to its original subject.

"So what kind of jobs have you circled?"

She picked up the paper from her lap.

"Well, I figured I'd try something easy at first, like an office manager position. That way I can see what the best jobs in the company are, and target the one I really want to go for."

Why was I not surprised to hear she'd pick something easy?

"Are all those circles office manager positions?"

"Yep."

I stretched out my legs in front of me. They were sore from all the kneeling and sitting I had been doing on the floor.

"Have you done a résumé?"

"Yep."

"When are you going to send them out?"

"I already have," Reesy smiled. "I just brought the paper over here to show you I'm already on it tryna get a job."

"Good for you," I said. I was proud of her initiative. "So have you heard anything from any of them yet?"

"No," she said. "But in the cover letters I told them I would be in New York for one full day on the tenth. I figured I could do all the interviews that day, and we could still go apartment hunting the next day."

That Reesy, I tell you. Leave it to her to set the criteria for an interview. She didn't even know how quickly the people were looking to hire. I wondered how many of them would call her. I also wondered how it would be having her as my roommate.

"So you think you're ready for this, huh?" I asked.

"What, the move?"

"No, living together."

She smiled, waving her hand dismissively.

"Yeah, girl. The question is, are *you* ready?"

I had to stop and think about it. I hadn't lived with anyone since Stefan, with the exception of the bizarre little arrangement Roman and I had going on. I wondered if I was ready for the clashing of personalities, the sharing of space, the synchronizing of menstrual cycles, and the general envy of anything and everything that came when you lived with another woman.

"I guess so," I said contemplatively. "I mean, we've been best friends most of our lives. It shouldn't be that bad."

"But we've never lived together," she warned. "And you know how vocal I can be. Are you sure I won't get on your nerves?"

I chuckled at this. I knew it would be a problem. It had been a problem my entire life.

"You forget about my little stint at your place after I left Stefan. And this last episode with Roman."

"Oh yeah," she said. "But that's different. You know that wasn't a permanent deal. My big mouth on a regular basis might be too much for you."

"I've lived with it this long," I replied. "I guess it'll just be a little more common than I'm already used to. Just do me a favor."

"What?" Reesy asked suspiciously. "Tape my mouth shut?"

"No," I laughed, "but close. Just try to think before you speak sometimes. I've got a soft heart. Sometimes you shoot daggers at it and keep on going. That might get a little hard on me on a day-to-day basis."

"I'll do my best," she smiled, "if you'll do me a favor as well."

"Uh-oh," I asked. "What's that?"

She tossed the paper on the floor beside her and sat up straight on the couch.

"Try to make better choices in men. And don't have no makeshift niggas spending the night and leaving at the crack of dawn waking me up all the time."

That stung a little, but I shouldn't have been surprised she said it.

"I'll do my best," I mumbled.

"Good," she said. "Did you read that book I got you?"

"No," I snapped, pretending to be offended.

I wasn't really, but a funky kind of somber feeling, I don't know what it was, washed over me.

"Well," she said, "I hope you read it before we go."

"Maybe I will. Maybe I won't," I retorted. "Maybe I don't need to. I haven't made that many foolish choices in men in my life."

"I never said you did. But I know a pattern when I spot one," she laughed. "Reading that book could head it off at the pass."

"Yeah, yeah, yeah, whatever," I said. I was beginning to feel a little depressed.

"So we're still flying up this Friday?"

"Unh-huh."

"Did you order my ticket?" she asked.

"Yep," I replied.

Since the company was paying for me to go up and meet with Bob Blanculowitz, I'd decided to redeem frequent flyer miles to give Reesy a free ticket.

We were flying up for the weekend to play. On Monday I was meeting with Bob. On Tuesday Reesy and I were going to try to find an apartment.

Which Rich, by the way, had arranged for the company to pay for, along with the utilities, for one year as a part of a relocation benefit package.

The company was also paying completely for my move. All expenses, the apartment, the utilities, the movers, hell, even the gum we chewed on the way there, were being charged to Burch Financial.

"So the ticket'll be here by Friday? We can leave after I get off work?" Reesy asked.

"Yep," I said.

"Why are you so tight-lipped all of a sudden?" she asked. "Are you mad at me? I was just playing, sort of, about that book. Read it if you want to. I don't care."

"I'm not mad," I said. "I don't know, I just got kinda weird for a minute. I don't know why."

Reesy rolled her eyes skyward.

"*Oh lord*, a moody bitch," she sighed. "Is this what I have to look forward to?"

"Probably so," I smiled.

"Oh well, she said. "Forewarned is forearmed."

I nodded, still pensive for I didn't know why. Perhaps her allusion to Roman coming and going early in the morning did something to me. I knew the demon of what he had done was still possessing me in a big way. I had to exorcise that demon and confront it. Otherwise it was destined to haunt me for the rest of my life.

"Oh well," I said, rising from the chair. "You wanna go get something to eat? I can't cook, 'cause I've damn near packed up every pot in the place."

"That's fine with me, girl," Reesy said. "Let's go to the Underground. I feel like some Hooters."

"*Hooters?*" I laughed. "Where the *hell* did that come from? You wanna go man-watching or something? You know you can't tell who's straight and who's not in that place. The straight men come to see the women. The gay men come to see the men."

She leaned forward and felt around the floor for her shoes.

"No," she said, "I actually just want some wings and curly fries. Believe it or not, I really do like the food at Hooters."

"I do, too," I agreed, remembering it was the place where I'd first met Roman. "It's just a surprise coming from you."

Reesy looked up from fastening her sandals.

"Why is that?" she asked.

I shrugged.

"You're so hardcore and intolerant when it comes to men. I figured the last place you'd want to be is in a restaurant with men ogling girls gallivanting around in T-tops and butt-outs."

Reesy stood up from the couch and walked over to me.

"I'm not a man-hater, Misty. I love black men."

"Yeah, but do you *like* them?" I asked, slipping on my shoes and picking up my purse.

Reesy put her arm around my shoulders as we walked to the door.

"Not all the time, sistah-girl," she replied. "Not all the time."

I didn't know my ticket to New York was going to be first class. Rich handed it to me just before I left work early Friday afternoon and I was stunned.

"You may as well take your big step in style," he said and smiled.

I didn't know what to say. I took the ticket awkwardly, but I was so happy, I kissed Rich Landey on the cheek.

"Thanks for everything you're doing for me. You're the best mentor a girl could have."

He smiled broadly.

"That's funny, Misty," he said. "I feel the same way, too. Have fun in the Big Apple this weekend. And if there's anything you have a question about Monday after meeting with Bob, give me a call."

"I'll do that, Rich. I certainly will."

We stood in line at the Delta counter. I was trying to upgrade Reesy's ticket to first class.

"I *told* you that man wants to get in them panties," Reesy mumbled. "First class. Yeah, right!"

"Reesy, please! Why don't you just go over there and sit down," I told her. "Here, take my purse and this bag."

The ticket agent upgraded the ticket without a hitch,

although she did deduct an additional twenty-five hundred miles from my frequent flyer account.

I went over to Reesy and handed her the ticket. I sat down beside her.

"So how did you manage to get Monday and Tuesday off?" I asked. "Are you taking them as vacation days?"

Reesy had her long legs crossed seductively. Across from her, a brother all geared out in Karl Kani and Timberlands was sloping in his seat trying to take a sneak peek up her way-too-short dress.

"I told Olivia I had a family emergency," she said.

I think Reesy knew the brother was looking up her dress. She had a wry smile on her face. She eyed him on the sly while she talked to me. I looked over at him. He had a smile on his face, too.

I shook my head. She could rag me all she wanted about my bad choices in men. Maybe I wasn't that smart when it came to the heart, but at least I didn't go around scoping out and picking up bad boys the way she did. Reesy liked roughnecks. The harder the head, the stronger the attraction.

"Hardheads know how to fuck," she told me once. "They ain't worth a damn for a future, but they'll fuck the shit out of your ass."

I looked at her now, casually working her legs up and down, right there in the terminal like a little hoe.

"*Reesy!*" I hissed. "*Reesy!*"

"*What?*" she snapped, turning to look at me. "Why you calling my name all harsh like that?"

"'Cause," I said sharply. "Look at you. You may as well just go ahead and lift your dress up."

She clucked her tongue at me.

"You need to close your legs," I snapped. "This place is full of people and you're sitting here acting like a slut."

"Just because you're uptight sexually, Misty, don't try to transfer that shit to me," she hissed back.

She wasn't looking at me when she said it. She was busy making eyes at the brother.

171

I was getting pissed.

"If you're not gonna stop, Reesy, I'm going to sit somewhere else. You can make a public display of yourself if you want to. I'm not havin' it."

I stood up abruptly, my purse and bag in hand.

She snatched me down.

"You make me sick sometimes," she griped. "I'm just tryna have a little fun to get in the right mood for the weekend. I can't fuck him or nothing, so what's the big deal?"

I sat there, glaring at her. She made me so furious sometimes, especially when she acted like this.

"I think *you* need to read that book you gave me. Cocking your legs open in a full airport terminal is a foolish choice if there ever was one."

"That book is about foolish choices in love, honey, not sex," Reesy gloated. "I don't make foolish choices in love. And there's nothing wrong with a little adventure in sex."

She patted me on the leg.

"You should try it sometime, if you ever learn how to detach your heart."

I was fuming. I turned away from her to cool off. She was messing up the mood for me already, and we weren't even off the ground. What would it be like living with her, I wondered. Would this be such a good idea?

Reesy leaned over my shoulder.

"Don't be mad at me, Misty," she cooed, her voice barely a whisper. "I'm sorry. I'm a slut, I know it. I'll try to keep it down."

I turned and looked at her.

"You haven't even told your boss you're moving, have you?" I asked, matter-of-factly.

She leaned away from me, surprised.

"N-n-no," she stammered. "There's no point in it."

"So when do you plan on telling her?"

Reesy shrugged.

"Olivia 'Booger-Eater' Bachrodt will have no problem replacing me," she replied, very nonchalant.

"So what were you gonna do, just leave?" I asked.

"Yep."

"What about your night job?"

"They can always replace me. One less set of tits in the house."

"What if you need a reference?" This nonchalance was quite incredible to me.

"From the Magic City?" she asked.

"No, your day job."

"Then I'll get one," Reesy said. "I happen to have a superb recommendation from the head honcho of a big-time firm in downtown Manhattan. She can attest to my positive work ethic, commitment, and reliability."

She looked me squarely in the eyes.

I shook my head in disbelief.

"Where do you come from, Reesy?"

"Same place you do. Venus. 'Cept we come from the black side, where the trees are. Got to have shade where the colored folks live."

I looked at her long and hard. She made a face at me, her cheeks puffed out and her eyes bucked.

Unexpectedly, I began to laugh. Reesy was so damn silly.

"New York City, *here we come!*" she squealed, putting her arm around me. "We gon' bust it out, ain't we?"

She kept talking, not giving me a chance to answer.

"Yep," she nodded, looking around. "We gon' bust that shit out. We gon' take Manhattan like a couple of dicks. Just run up in it like it's one big coochie."

She grinned broadly, turning to me for confirmation.

"We'll have to see, Reesy. We'll have to see."

"*See* hell," she said. "New York is gon' be my thang, Miss Divine. Watch. I'ma turn that mutha out. It's gon' be one big party."

As she said this, I worried again about the roommate situation. I began to wonder, even after twenty-three years, just how well I knew Teresa Snowden.

Maybe she had some surprises in store for me that I wasn't quite ready for. Maybe she had some things going on underneath that crown of braids that were gonna shock me right back to Venus.

BREAKING THE GLASS FEELING

Reesy and I got settled into a gorgeous apartment in Manhattan.

It was a good thing that Burch was picking up the tab for the first year. Reesy and I were stunned when we found out what the rent was.

"Girl, you could make mortgage payments on *two houses* for this much a month!" she exclaimed.

"Not here you can't," I said.

"I'm talking about in Atlanta. You could get two big houses with lots of square footage and land. This place is ridiculous. I'm just glad it's for free."

I smirked at her comment.

"This place isn't free, Reesy. Burch will more than get their return by working me to death."

I was putting the last items away. We'd been unpacking and setting up for a week. I started my new job the next day, and I was exhausted and ready for bed.

I looked around at the apartment. It was spacious, with

hardwood floors and huge rooms. And an awesome view of Central Park.

"You know ain't no colored working girls supposed to be living in a place like this," Reesy kept on. "Folks are gonna think we're *working girls* for real."

I chuckled. I was wearing a pair of loose gray sweatpants, an oversized shirt, and slouch socks. I hardly looked the part of a high-class call girl.

"I doubt if anyone will ever make that mistake about me," I said. "Now you. *You're* another story. You look like a hoe."

I expected Reesy to laugh, but instead she just looked at me sidelong.

"What do you mean?" she asked, suddenly serious.

I was hanging one of the Frank Fraziers on the wall. I stopped what I was doing and looked over my shoulder at her.

"I was just playing, Reesy," I said.

"Oh."

I finished with the picture and turned around to her.

"What's the matter with you?" I asked.

She was on the couch with her legs tucked beneath her.

"I don't know," she replied. She seemed a little depressed.

I came over and sat down next to her.

"If you're worried about a job, just relax. You'll find one."

She nodded solemnly.

"I just thought for sure one of those interviews would produce something," she said glumly. "My presentation was excellent. I know it was."

Reesy had gone on a few interviews before we actually made the move, but none of them had panned out. I didn't know why she was worrying so much, though. She still had that healthy stipend coming in. A safety net. A big ass safety net.

I stroked her hair, playing with a handful of the ever-present braids.

"This city has nine million people in it, Reesy," I said. "That probably makes it kinda tough. You only went on four interviews."

She sighed. It was odd being the comforter for her. I was so used to her coddling me. But I guess we each had our fortes.

I knew that I was pretty fortunate when it came to getting work. Successful and upwardly mobile work.

On the other hand, Reesy didn't have any problems with men the way I did.

"Don't worry, honey," I said. "You'll get a job."

"But when?" she whined uncharacteristically.

"You'll get one," I said encouragingly. "I know you. You're the toughest little heffah around."

"Plus," I added lightheartedly, "what do you have to worry about? We got a nice crib to relax in, with a view that's gotta be the envy of everyone we know. You can take your time and find a job. The job you really want."

Reesy slumped back against the pillows on the couch.

"What am I gonna use for spending money in the meantime?" she asked.

"Use one of those stipends," I said without hesitation. "For goodness' sake, Reesy, it's free money."

"It's my parents' money," she snapped, "and I'm not gonna spend it no matter what."

"All right, all right," I said. "Don't spend it, Reesy."

"I'll just get out there and pound the pavement tomorrow," she said.

She actually smiled as she said this, returning to her usual lively self.

"Well," I added, "I'll keep my ears open at Burch. It's a huge company. Maybe there's a fit for you there."

Reesy chuckled.

"You and your damn *fits*. Everything just has to be a *fit* for you."

"Hey, if it don't fit, don't force it," I replied.

Reesy nodded.

"That's true," she agreed. "I just hope you remember your own advice and have sense enough to know when to take it."

"I don't think I'll be needing to, girly," I said and grinned. "Everything right now seems to be fitting like a glove."

I leapt off the couch and danced over to the window. In front of God and all of Manhattan, I opened my arms and spun around in a big circle, just like Diana Ross in *Mahogany*.

Reesy sat on the couch in amazement, and amusement.

"All right, Miss Divine," she said with a cynical twist in her voice. "I hope this *is* your fit. And if it ain't, maybe we can *force* it for at least a year." She laughed out loud. "Just until the rent runs out."

I awoke very early the next morning, eager to get started.

I had taken a shower the night before so I wouldn't have to worry about the steam ruining my hair.

I sat on the edge of the bed staring at my feet. My toenails were painted "Go-Getter Red." That's what it said on the bottle they used at the salon.

My fingernails were painted the same color.

I had treated myself to a manicure and a pedicure.

I already *felt* good about my new job.

I wanted to *look* good, too.

I had my hair in big rollers. They were uncomfortable to sleep in, but I wanted to make sure I had the kind of look that suited a Manhattan corporate manager.

I wanted my hair to have lots of body and movement. Not too much curl. I figured I'd wear it that way the first few days, then maybe settle into a reserved bun. I pulled the curlers out, one by one, and set them on the nightstand next to my bed.

I slipped into a pair of lace panties with a matching bra, spritzed myself with a light misting of Clinique Aromatics, and slid on a pair of silky, jet-black Sheer Energy pantyhose.

I hummed to myself as I stared in the mirror.

"Mmmm! Mmmmm!" I said to myself.

I looked yummy. Even with those big, stupid loose curls, not yet combed out, piled high on top of my head.

I walked over to the closet and pulled out the suit I planned to wear. A rich red, very tailored Donna Karan that came to the middle of my thighs. It was sexy, but it meant business.

And I looked good in red.

Damn good.

I went into the bathroom, brushed my teeth, and applied my makeup. I wanted a fresh look, not too heavy. Just a little liquid foundation that I applied with my fingertips, a quick dusting of Corn Silk powder, and some mascara.

I applied a coat of flesh-colored lipstick.

I checked out my beauty mark. It was looking good. The perfect accent to my fresh, flawless face.

I ran my fingers through my hair to loosen the curls even more, then went through it again with a big comb.

Then I took a brush and smoothed it into shape.

I couldn't help but smile at the results.

"Damn!" Reesy said when I exited the bedroom in my Evan Picone pumps, carrying my new Coach satchel.

"You gon' scare them white folks to death, girl!" she laughed.

"You think so?" I asked, spinning around like a runway model.

"Hell yeah. That suit is a statement if there ever was one."

I smiled as I headed for the door.

"Good luck, girl!" Reesy said.

"Thanks," I replied, holding up crossed fingers. "I'm gonna need it."

I arrived at the office at 8:00 A.M. sharp.

The people at Burch knew that my arrival heralded the beginning of many changes in the way that Burch had been doing things.

As I walked into the building, I was proud to be a part of all this change. I was so excited, my legs were shaking.

Bob Blanculowitz met me at the front desk.

"So, Armistice," Bob began, "are you all settled in?"

His teeth were bared like a frightened mule.

"Oh yes, I got situated with no problem," I said and smiled at him.

The poor man look terrified. I wondered what he had been told about my arrival.

"Well OK then!" he chirped. "So, Armistice, you've already had a tour of the building, how's about taking a look at your brand new office. We had it done last week."

He waved me toward the elevator.

"Great," I said.

He strutted along beside me like an accommodating bell-hop.

"You know, Bob, I really would prefer it if you called me Misty. I'm way more comfortable with that."

"Are you sure?" he skinned. "We want to make sure you're *absolutely* comfortable here."

"Totally sure," I smiled, stepping into the open elevator.

"Well OK then!" he shrieked. *"Misty it is!"*

As the elevator doors closed shut and I eyed Bob standing nervously next to me, I began to wonder just exactly what I was in for.

The office was beautiful. It was also twice the size of every-one else's. Even the other senior asset managers.

There were fourteen asset managers, housed on the twenty-third and the twenty-fourth floors. My office was on the twenty-fourth, right above Bob's office on the twenty-third.

My office was the same size as his. Something that I don't think went unnoticed by Bob or anyone else.

Some of the other asset managers were milling around a coffee station. They were a sharp array of women and men, all white, engaged in happy banter.

Until we came along. They turned to us like soldiers and smiled brightly, nervously, as I came through.

"Everybody," Bob grinned, "you remember Armistice."

He looked at me with a frightened, corrective expression.

"I mean *Misty*. Misty Fine. From the *Atlanta* office. She worked with *Rich Landey*."

I stared at him as he enunciated Atlanta and Rich Landey like they were buzz words that should send the staff into a terrified frenzy.

"She's going to be starting today," he continued. "We want to do our best to make sure she feels she's a part of the Burch team, so if she needs any help, *any at all*, I *implore* each and every one of you to avail yourself to her immediately."

Implore? I found that to be an interesting choice of words.

The managers nodded and grinned like a pack of wild orangutans. One of them, a handsome blond man with broad shoulders, approached me posthaste, his hand extended.

"Jeff Branniker," he said.

He shook my hand furiously. I could barely see his face for teeth.

"Good to meet you, Misty." He kept grinning. "My office is just a few doors down."

He gestured to where his office was.

"If there's anything I can do to help, my door is *always* open."

I nodded pleasantly.

"Thank you, Jeff. I certainly appreciate the offer."

Jeff nodded in return, glancing at Bob for approval. Bob was nodding as well. So were the other asset managers. The whole lot of them looked like a passel of dashboard dogs.

Then, without ceremony, Jeff jetted off, the contents of his steaming cup of coffee sloshing onto his pant leg.

"Oops," he grinned, still in flight, his expression sheepish.

He darted into his office and shut the door. Suddenly, the door opened again and he stuck his head out. Still grinning. I guess he remembered his commitment to one hundred percent availability.

One by one, the assets manager introduced themselves, then fled from me like I was the plague.

Inside of five minutes, Bob and I were standing alone, the shroud of nervousness that engulfed him as visible as the Empire State Building from my office window.

"Well OK then!" he announced. "Now that you've met some of the guys, and . . . and . . . and gals," he stammered, "I mean *ladies*, why don't you get yourself settled in?"

He waved wildly at a woman who sat at an island just outside my door. She was an older white woman with granny glasses, tightly bunned hair, and a face that looked like she'd spent years straining on the toilet.

"Millicent, this is Misty," Bob said.

Millicent nodded militarily.

"Misty, Millicent is the department's office manager. In addition, she's my administrative assistant. She'll be your administrative assistant as well."

I thought I saw a brief flicker of disapproval flit across Millicent's tightly pinched brow.

"I thought Gladys was going to be my admin assistant?" I asked, surprised.

"Actually, *no*," Bob sighed. "You see, prior to the takeover, each asset manager had their own assistant. We've since found that isn't very cost effective. Only the senior managers have their own assistants now. And there are only three of those, all housed on the twenty-third floor, where I am. The rest of the managers share an assistant. One assistant for every five managers. Gladys already has five managers assigned to her."

"I see."

Millicent said nothing, staring at me like I was some wretched piece of rotting meat. Her glare was making me uncomfortable.

I shifted my attention back to Bob.

"Why not assign me to another admin assistant like the rest of the mangers? Millicent probably has her hands full with running this office and doing your work as well. It'll probably be tough with her working for me and you with us on separate floors, don't you think?"

I had no problem speaking my mind when it came to work.

Millicent suddenly stood at attention, all stiff and stony like she had a prod up her ass. The only thing she was missing was a swastika on her arm.

I definitely didn't want her working for me. I wanted as little contact with her as possible.

From the glimmer in her eye, I could see Mean Millicent mirrored my sentiments completely.

"I can't assign you to another assistant. You're a senior manager," Bob said.

"Why not just do it temporarily, Bob?" I suggested. "It shouldn't be a big deal."

Softly, almost imperceptibly, I heard Millicent snort.

I ignored her.

"Have you started looking for an assistant for me yet?" I asked.

I could feel her there, just staring at me.

Already, I despised her.

"I figured I'd wait and let you and Millicent work on that together," Bob said happily. "Perhaps you could run an ad. Whatever you like. It's your call."

I looked at Millicent. Her eyes narrowed slightly.

"Great," I said without enthusiasm.

It was obvious Bob was ready to scoot back down to his office and get away from me and this perceptibly ugly Millicent scene.

"Why don't you go into your office and start getting a feel for the place? Millicent will get you some coffee."

Millicent's head snapped toward him in shock.

"*Go on*, Millicent," Bob urged, his teeth bared in a gritted-tooth smile.

He gave her a gentle, apologetic pat on the back.

She huffed off.

"I don't think she likes me, Bob," I said.

He shook his head wildly.

"*No, no, no, no, no!*" he protested. "That's just how she is.

Millicent is a lovable old battle-ax. Mondays are the worst for her. But she'll do great work for you. Just you wait and see!"

He seemed a little frightened. This was getting funnier and funnier by the second. And not funny ha-ha either.

He walked me into my office. I couldn't get over how gorgeous it was. It had a breathtaking view of the Manhattan skyline.

"Why don't you get settled in? You can get acquainted with your equipment, review your portfolio, and just kind of get to know the place. Today's not going to be a big workday for you."

I nodded in agreement.

Bob backed out toward the door. Before he left, he turned around and added weakly, "If you don't have any plans for lunch, give me a yell."

It was so hollow and poorly delivered, I felt sorry for the man.

"Thanks, Bob, but I'm meeting a friend."

His expression instantly brightened.

"Well OK then!" he squealed. "If I can be of help, I'm at extension 663."

"Great," I smiled. "Thanks for everything."

"No problem." He saluted, his hand launching off his forehead like a pale white missile. "Perhaps later you can meet the other senior asset managers on the twenty-third floor," he said. "I think you'll like them."

"That would be nice," I beamed, fake as fake could be.

"Well OK then!" he shrieked as he dashed away.

I think you'll like them. I wondered what that meant.

Just outside my door, I heard mumbling. I stood up and walked a little closer to the doorway.

"Be nice to her," the voice hissed. It was Bob. "We have to live with her whether we want to or not!!"

"Well, I don't have to *like* her," I heard Millicent hiss back. "There's no reason that *black bitch* should have an office as big as yours. And I *don't* want to work for her!"

"It won't be long," Bob said. "The quicker you help her

184

find someone, the better. I suggest you sit with her today and place an ad as soon as possible."

I heard feet shuffling, so I dashed back to my chair and sat down. My head was pounding. I couldn't believe it. I was here less than thirty minutes, and already I was a black bitch.

As I sat there, poring over the oddity of the morning, Mean Millicent walked in with my cup of coffee. I planted a smile on my face as acknowledgment for the gesture, thinking maybe I could win her over with kindness.

Millicent never looked at me.

She marched in, set the coffee on my desk, on a tidy little Burch Financial coaster, and marched right out.

I watched her broad back as it cleared the doorway and made a right turn.

I realized the bitch never even asked me how I took my coffee.

I pulled the mug toward me and peered down at its steamy contents. I tasted it.

Black. No cream. No sugar. No nothing.

I jumped when the phone rang.

I'd been sitting at the computer, playing around in WordPerfect.

On my screen I had typed in very large letters "MILLICENT MEETS MUTANT MURDERERS EVERY MIDNITE AT THE MORGUE."

I deleted it immediately.

I pressed the flashing button on my phone.

"You have a call on line two," Millicent barked.

"Who is it?" I asked, but before I could get a response, Reesy's voice poured in over the line.

That heffah Millicent just transferred her immediately, without ceremony or clearance.

"How's it going, girl?" Reesy asked.

"Girl, I don't know. I wasn't sure what to expect when I came in, but it wasn't this. These people are acting too weird for me!" I replied.

"What's up?"

"I don't know. They act like they're scared of me. A few minutes ago, I heard my temporary assistant call me a black bitch."

"Are you serious?" she asked, stunned.

"As a heart attack," I replied.

"Are there any black people?" Reesy asked.

"Not that I've seen."

"Umph," she grunted.

I watched people walk past my door, not daring to look in, as I talked to Reesy on the phone.

"They won't even look at me," I said. "It's like I'm contagious or something."

"Maybe they think you're a spy for Rich Landey," she said.

I leaned forward in my chair, elbows resting on my beautiful cherrywood desk.

"I don't know *what* they think, girl, but my office is enough to scare anybody. It's laid. I don't think anybody, except Bob, has an office like this."

"Are you for real?" she asked.

"Yep. It's almost *too* nice. And you should see the view. My parents wouldn't believe it. They probably never imagined I would ever have an office like this. I can see everything from here. It's a wonder I can't see you in the apartment. Stand at the window and wave."

"Girl, quit it!" she laughed. *"You're so damn crazy!"*

"I'm too serious," I laughed. "I can see all kinds of mess from here."

"See?" she said. "Look at you. They can't give us nothing, 'cause we don't know how to act. Already you're sitting there chillin' on the phone. You got this high-powered, mack-mama job, and you're sittin' there now wasting corporate dollars."

"Hey! What can I say? When you got it, you got it."

"Gon', girlfriend!" she laughed. "You just gon' with your bad self!"

My phone buzzed.

"What's that?" Reesy asked.

"You could hear it?"

"Hell yeah! It was loud as fuck!" she exclaimed. "They're probably tappin' your ass. Oh well, it was fun while it lasted."

"Quit, heffah," I said. "I think it's that bitch Millicent ringing me for something. I can't believe she wants to talk to me."

"Umph," Reesy grunted.

"Hold on," I said.

I put her on hold and pressed the flashing button.

"Yes?" I said.

"You have a call on line three," Millicent barked at me.

She was pissing me slam off.

"Who is it?" I snapped back.

"Rich Landey," she barked again.

"Could you hold him for one second?" I asked.

Without a response, Millicent's end of the line went dead.

I picked up the line with Reesy on it.

"Girl, I gotta go. That's Rich on the other line."

"Oh, hell yeah," she said. "You better go take that call. What are you doing for lunch?"

"I don't know. Why don't you call me back in an hour. I'll know what I'm doing by then. Maybe you can meet me somewhere."

"Okay. Do you have a direct line or an extension?"

"I'm sure I do, hold a sec."

The phone didn't have my number listed. I laid the receiver on my desk and looked around for something with the extension written on it.

My phone buzzed again. I put Reesy on hold.

It was Millicent.

"Are you ready for this call yet?" she barked.

"One second," I snarled back. "Millicent, what's my extension?"

"666," she barked loudly, then her end of the line went dead.

666? I couldn't freaking believe it.

"Reesy?"

"Yeah, girl?"

"Check this out," I laughed. "My extension is *666*."

"Are you for real?" she hollered.

"I sure am," I choked.

"Bitch, them folks think your ass is the devil. Satan done come in and set up shop."

"Apparently so. Look, let me go. Call me in an hour."

"All right, Lucifer," she said. "I'll talk to you later."

As soon as she hung up her line, my phone buzzed again. This time, I knew Millicent's trick. I was already ahead of her.

"Rich?" I cooed.

"Misty!" he cooed back.

"Boy!" I exclaimed. *"Do I need to talk to you!"*

I didn't know Rich was in town when he called me. He had flown in that morning, and was going to take me to lunch.

A hush fell over the floor when he walked through the department, into my office.

Millicent rushed in, all smiles, and asked him if he wanted some coffee. He said yes, just a half a cup. She asked him how he took it.

Inside of a minute, she was back with it, smiling. She asked him if he needed anything further, then she wagged her wide ass out of my office and around the corner.

"Unbelievable," I said under my breath.

Rich, always aware of everything I said and did, noted my comment.

He walked over to the door and pushed it shut.

"Millicent's been not-so-nice to you already, huh?"

"How'd you guess?" I smiled at him.

"Oh, I've heard talk of how she is. What has she done?"

Rich sat down in one of the armchairs, stretching his lithe body and long legs casually.

"It's more what she *hasn't* done than anything," I replied.

"For instance?"

I sighed, trying to assess the list of offenses Millicent had already launched against me.

"Well, for one, she didn't act too excited when Bob told her she'd be working for me."

He nodded.

"For another, she brought me coffee as if against her will, and never asked me how I took it. Not that I need someone running around bringing me coffee. But it was Bob who asked her to do it."

He played with his immaculately manicured nails, still nodding.

"She transfers calls to me without asking if I'm ready for them or getting any kind of clearance from me."

"Hmmm" was the only thing Rich said in response.

"I feel a little awkward about addressing this last issue, Rich, but I think I need to."

He looked up from his nails at me in anticipation of what I was going to say.

"You can tell me anything, Misty. Off the record or on."

"Well . . ." I paused for a moment, gathering up what I was going to say.

"Spit it out, Misty," he said, his attention completely focused on me.

"This morning I heard Millicent talking to Bob outside my door. They didn't think I could hear them, I don't guess. Rich, I don't know what they've been told about my coming here, but the reception has been really weird. Do they know about your plan to have me take over everything from Bob?"

"No. What did you hear them say?" he asked, concerned.

"Well, to be exact, Bob said, 'We have to live with her, whether we want to or not.' And as if that wasn't bad enough, Millicent called me a *black bitch* to boot."

"Did she really?" he chuckled.

He knew I probably found the comment more amusing than anything else. Our conversations over the time I had worked for him had been peppered with many a black and white epithet.

Rich, who was about as liberal as they came, mostly laughed

189

at them. The epithets were usually comic references that colored the stories I told.

But never once had I related an anecdote with me as the object of the epithet.

"She said it," I confirmed.

"What exactly did she say?" he asked.

I sat there and thought for a moment. I wanted to deliver the statement exactly as I heard it.

"If I'm not mistaken, I believe the comment was 'There's no reason that black bitch should have an office as big as yours, and I don't want to work for her.'"

He laughed heartily at that.

"Interesting," he said.

"Yeah. Tell me, Rich. Do they know this black bitch's credentials?"

He stood from the chair and walked around to the window.

"They soon will," he answered.

"What have they been told so far?" I asked. "It's obvious there is some sort of fear sweeping over them."

"I'll tell you, Misty. These rats can smell cheese. They know you're a part of the new regime. And they know the new regime will not tolerate slackers and slough-offs. There's going to be some accountability around here now. They probably think you're a spy."

"Obviously," I said. "Everyone is alarmed. They've done everything but lick my boots, with the exception of Millicent. She'd put firecrackers up my ass if she could, I'm sure."

Rich laughed at that. It was so easy to talk to him. He was such a cool guy.

"I don't like coming into a new environment where I'm suddenly the bad guy. Do you know what my extension is?"

He turned toward me, puzzled.

"Your extension?" he asked.

"Yes, Rich, my telephone extension."

His left brow raised.

"No. What is it?"

"666," I said.

"Are you kidding me?" he exclaimed.

"No, I'm not."

He roared with laughter.

I looked toward the door.

"You'd better stop laughing so loudly," I whispered. "They're probably milling around outside thinking I'm conspiring with the boss."

"You are," he laughed.

"Am I?" I asked.

He straightened his face up a little, as best as he could.

"Yes, Armistice Fine," he said. "You absolutely are. Feels good, doesn't it?"

I had to admit, it did.

"You could have at least called me back and told me you couldn't go to lunch, heffah," Reesy griped.

I went into my bedroom and changed, yelling out to her as I rifled through my closet for my favorite pair of jeans.

"I'm sorry, girl," I said. "Rich was in town. He stopped by the office and took me to lunch."

I slipped out of my suit and hose, and slid into the jeans. I pulled on an oversized T-shirt and padded into the living room.

"What'd you eat?" I asked, plopping down on the love seat.

"A dry ass turkey sandwich," she complained, "no thanks to you."

"I'm sorry, hon," I cooed. "But I might have some good news for you."

Reesy's face was twisted in a mean pout, like she could not be bought.

"What?" she said begrudgingly.

"It's about a job," I smiled.

I had her attention now.

"Okay," she said, sitting there in shorts and a crop top with her legs cocked up on the couch. She probably hadn't even considered job-hunting all day.

"If it's good enough, I might forgive you for this afternoon," she added.

If it's good enough? She'd better be happy I was looking out for her ass. No-jobbers can't be choosers.

I started to tell her that, but I figured she was kinda crabby because she wasn't working and I was.

"Rich wants me to spend the next ninety days learning everything about the department from the inside out. After that, Bob's out, and so is his gila monster assistant Millicent."

"So where do I come in? I get Millicent's job? That's not for ninety days yet," Reesy asked. "What am I supposed to do till then?"

"If you'd let me finish, I just might tell you," I stated.

"Oh."

"As a senior asset manager, I get an admin assistant. We were getting ready to run an ad for the job, but over lunch I asked Rich if it would be okay if I offered the job to you."

"For real?" she asked, surprised, and apparently pleased.

"For real," I replied.

"Wait. What does it pay?"

I couldn't believe this girl. She was a freaking trip.

"More than you're making right now," I answered, annoyed at her question.

"Yeah, I guess you're right. So what did Rich say?"

I let out a deep sigh. Her stupid detour had distracted me.

"He was concerned that you were overqualified, but I told him that you'd be great to slide into Millicent's position once it became available."

"Oh really?"

"Really."

She grinned broadly.

"He did have one more concern," I added.

Her grin lost a little of its intensity.

"What was that?"

"He asked that since you were my friend, did I think

there'd be a problem in getting you to take orders or perform up to the level of expectation without infringing on the friendship."

"And you said . . . ," she replied apprehensively.

"I said I was absolutely sure that wouldn't be a problem at all."

I looked at her, my eyes narrowed threateningly.

"Why are you looking at me like that?" she cried. "Since when have you known me to take off work or not be up to snuff? Shit, I was working two jobs in Atlanta!"

"Exactly," I snapped. "Just make sure you don't start doing it now. My ass is your ass, and vice versa. Make sure you keep that in mind if you think about doing anything funny."

"Girl, please," she said. "I can't believe you would even front me like that."

"I just want you to understand how this deal works," I stated. "Before you think about playing hooky or calling in sick, picture my face. Put yourself in my shoes. It won't be Olivia the Booger Bitch anymore. It'll be me. I'm putting myself out on a limb for you for this."

"All right, Misty, *damn*. What you gon' make me do, give you a pound of flesh for hooking me up with a job?"

"Something like that," I replied.

We were both quiet for a moment.

"I appreciate this, girl," Reesy said.

"Do you?"

"Yeah, heffah, damn!"

She threw a pillow at me. It hit me square in the face.

"I'm not gon' be your heffah anymore," I said, rearing up on the couch, my expression serious and stern. "I'll be your boss. The Head Negress in Charge. And don't you forget it."

"I won't," she said, serious and stern as well.

I leaned back on the couch.

"Um, Boss," she said, her voice firm and direct.

"Yes."

"Uh . . . you don't eat boogers, do you?"

I threw the pillow back at her. It whizzed past her head toward the outline of the Empire State Building behind her.

Before I could duck, another pillow hit me right in the mouth.

We both burst out laughing—crazy, silly, foolish—until we fell on the floor, our faces wet with tears.

I was glad she was going to be working with me.

I felt like, with my best friend Reesy beside me, the two of us could take Manhattan.

And any damn place else we wanted to.

CHASING TO THE CUT

When Reesy walked into the office for her first day of work, Millicent's eyes narrowed suspiciously. She immediately marked off her area so Reesy wouldn't be confused about where she was supposed to sit.

In fact, Millicent did everything but piss in a big square around her own workstation to keep Reesy (and me, I'm sure) away.

Reesy strutted in that morning in a purple wool pantsuit with a fuchsia silk scarf tucked inside the collar.

She looked very sophisticated and corporate, but also very ethnic with her headful of braids twisted into a formal chignon.

I introduced her to Bob as soon as he appeared.

"Bob, this is Teresa Snowden. She's my new administrative assistant."

"Call me Reesy," she corrected, extending her hand.

She smiled with a seriousness that impressed even me.

Bob shook Reesy's hand limply. His expression was one of mild surprise.

I don't suppose he, like Millicent, expected me to be so blatant as to hire a black assistant.

Having Reesy there made me feel a little more secure. Like I was building my own team.

And with her looking as professional as she did, I felt like she reflected exactly the kind of image I wanted to present.

Reesy proceeded right away to get her workstation in order.

She even took the initiative to go around the office and pleasantly introduce herself to the rest of the staff, even the ones on the twenty-third floor.

By 9:30 A.M., Reesy had made the rounds. She came into my office and sat down with me to discuss my agenda.

She had a Daytimer in hand.

"I think I'm gonna like this," she said with a smile. "This is a pretty nice office. The people seem kinda friendly."

"What'd you think about Millicent?" I asked.

"That bitch," she responded quickly.

I chuckled.

"And what's up with Bob?" she added. "His hand felt like a piece of melba toast. That handshake he gave me was pathetic, all limp and dry."

"Bob's nervous. He has no clue what's going on around him," I said.

"That's obvious."

She opened up the Daytimer.

"All right, Misty. Let's get serious: give me your schedule for the next few weeks. That way I have an account of your whereabouts and plans."

"You know, I'm really impressed with you," I said and grinned.

"I know," she grinned back. "See? You didn't know I had this side, did you? Just shows you, you never know about a person."

"Now, you know I believe that, if I don't ever believe anything else you say."

Reesy forced her face into a serious expression.

"We're wasting time," she chastised. "Let's get to work."

Reesy was ripping through the work I gave her.

She was the model assistant: she came in early, riding to work by cab with me. She undertook monumental amounts of paperwork, and stayed late with me to go over line item after line item in not only my portfolio, but the other asset managers' as well.

Not once did it seem too much for her. She had an eagle eye, catching a lot of things that I missed. Inaccurate calculations, managers whose portfolios were underperforming—none of these things were lost on her.

I felt like I had Rain Man working for me.

By the end of the first week, she had gone through all the lateral files that I accessed on a regular basis and reorganized them.

She put a typed tab on every one of them and put them in color-coded folders. She sorted them by year, area, and profitability.

I couldn't believe my great luck. How could I have *not* known that she would be *this* competent?

I would have tried to hire her long before.

Reesy was completing the projects I gave her with lightning speed.

Even though I was cranking out the work, I couldn't keep up with her. Every time I gave her something to do, she'd whip through it, then sit there, hands folded, and wait for me to give her more. I couldn't tell her to take the initiative and do something else around the office.

She'd already done *everything* there was that needed reorganizing.

She couldn't offer to help Millicent.

No explanation necessary.

She definitely couldn't offer help to anyone else. They would have thought she was a spy.

So she sat there, hands immaculate and dainty on the desk, and except for the phone ringing and the squall of the fax machine, I could damn near hear crickets chirping in the background because it was so quiet around her desk.

In a way, it made me nervous. For the first time, I felt like my productivity wasn't up to par. If it were, I wouldn't be worrying about Reesy sitting out there with nothing to do.

But slowly it began to dawn on me: there was nothing wrong with my level of productivity. Rich was happy, and changes were taking place on a positive level all around the office.

What I did realize was something more important. About Reesy.

The girl just wasn't normal.

She was a freaking machine.

"Misty, can I tell you something?" Reesy asked late one rainy night.

We had been going over numbers and Reesy was entering them on a spreadsheet on my laptop computer. Half-empty boxes of Chinese food covered the coffee table.

I was lying on my stomach on the floor, disheveled and intense in my sweats, with a Sharpie pen tucked behind my ear.

Reesy was sitting on the couch plugging in the data I fed her.

"What?" I replied absently.

I was trying to figure out how one of the properties in Jeff Branniker's portfolio could make a three-hundred-thousand-dollar profit for six months straight, then drop by seven-tenths of a percent.

To someone else, it might have seemed negligible. A three-hundred-thousand-dollar profit on a property in a depressed part of Philadelphia was damn good.

I knew that was true. But I felt that a two-thousand-dollar difference needed to be accounted for as well.

I went through line item after line item hunting for the reason. Was it some onetime purchase for the property? A semi-annual expense?

My eyes were beginning to get crossed.

"You promise you won't get mad?" Reesy pressed.

"*No!*" I snapped, still really ignoring her, but annoyed at the distraction.

It was bothering me that I couldn't find the line item difference. I searched and searched, but there was no major obvious expense to account for it.

"Do you have the abstract for this?" I asked.

"Which site is it?"

"Bavarian Bridge."

"Yeah, it's here in this pile."

She sifted through the stack of folders on the sofa beside her.

"I just don't get it," I mumbled. "Where'd that two thousand dollars go? I can't find anything to explain it."

"You want me to dial in to the system in the office and check the history?" Reesy asked.

"Would you do that?" I said. "And could you print it out for me?"

"Sure."

I kept burrowing deeper into my paperwork.

She got up and grabbed the phone cord for the computer. Since it was a long cord, she plugged it into the back of the laptop and plopped back down on the couch.

I heard her sigh.

"Misty, I'm bored," she announced.

"Mmm-hmm," I responded.

"You're not even listening to me," she complained.

I rifled through a few of the pages, hoping some blatant error would jump out and announce itself.

"Are you?" Reesy asked.

"What?" I said, frowning, finally looking up at her.

"I'm bored," she repeated, her voice uncharacteristically whiny.

The squall of the modem connecting to the office file server gave what she was saying a surreal weirdness.

I was confused. What the hell was she talking about?

My brows knitted up. I didn't have time for bullshit chitchat. I didn't want to be up all night working on Bavarian Bridge's numbers.

I was tired and cranky, plus the Chinese food had given me gas.

"Bored with what?" I asked.

She was pissing me off. She had told me she would help me go through this stuff, and now she was announcing that she was bored. As if *I* was excited about sifting through this shit.

"You can go to bed if you want," I said irritably. "I don't know how long I'm going to be up."

She picked up the file on Bavarian Bridge and opened it, reading through it as she talked to me.

"I'm not bored with what we're doing right now," she said.

"Then what are you talking about?"

She sighed again.

"Reesy," I snapped, "why don't you just cut to the chase? *Jesus!*"

She twisted her face into a foolish grimace, like she had something crazy to say, but was hesitant about it.

"I'm bored at Burch," she finally admitted.

I just sat there, glaring at her. I was stewing inside.

I couldn't believe that this *bitch* had the nerve to tell me she was bored, when I was the only one in all of Manhattan who would even hire her ass.

"So what, you wanna quit now?" I replied with sarcasm.

Reesy put the file down and began pecking away on the laptop.

"No. I don't wanna quit. But I finish the stuff you give me as soon as you give it to me. Then I just sit there. I feel stupid."

"So?" I quipped. "Pace yourself."

"Misty, this *is* my pace. I can't slow down what I'm doing. It would feel forced, and it would piss me off."

She kept typing on the computer.

"Here's the file. I'll download it," she said.

"No. It's probably too big. Just print it."

"Okay."

She pressed a few more keys, and the printer on the coffee table began to whir.

She picked up the file on Bavarian Bridge again and began to look through it while the history printed out.

"Reesy," I began, "if you're so bored, what do you propose to do? I mean, I know you didn't just tell me this for no reason."

She sat over there, pretending to peruse the Bavarian file.

Shit. I really didn't need this right now. I had way too many things to be concentrating on.

"I don't wanna leave the company," she said. "But I need to do something more. Something to add a little excitement to my life."

Inside, I was so mad at her, I could have spit.

"Misty, I know you get off on this shit. Paper trails and power lunches. But I need something else. This is all fine and dandy, but it don't move me in the slightest."

"*Move* you?" I repeated. "I didn't know you expected this to be a party."

"Why are you gettin' mad?" she asked. "I'm just tryna be honest with you."

The report had finished printing. She leaned over and picked it up off the printer.

"So what do you want to do? Start dancing again?"

I was kidding, of course.

"Maybe," she said.

I looked at her closely.

This fool was dead serious.

"Girl, you done *lost* your mind!" I exclaimed. "This ain't Atlanta, Reesy. You can't just go out there and shake your naked ass at the world and expect to walk away. New Yorkers don't play that shit."

"Like you've done this before."

"Don't you watch TV?" I said with indignation. "The violence stats in this city are through the roof. New York makes Atlanta look like Oz!"

"Whatever," she said.

She read through the paperwork.

"So when did this bright idea come up?" I asked. "Knowing your ass, I'll bet you've already been out there looking around."

"Mmm-hmm," she mumbled, going through the file's history.

"Are you out of your mind?" I screamed. "Huh? I thought we were through with this chapter of your life!"

Reesy didn't even glance at me when she responded.

"I was never embarrassed about this chapter in my life. Apparently you were. Dancing is something I actually enjoy doing."

I had forgotten all about the Bavarian dilemma at this point.

"So you found a job already?"

"Mmm-hmm. I'm going to be starting this weekend."

No fucking way!

"What about Burch?" I asked. "Suppose someone at work learns about this?"

"Then I'd have something to hold over them, now wouldn't I?" She chuckled. "They'd have to be there to know I was working."

"This isn't funny."

"Well, yeah, it is. All I'm going to be doing is dancing and showing my cut. So what? I'll be another naked dancer in New York. The world's not gonna end."

I couldn't even respond. And she knew I hated that word *cut*. It was so vulgar. Pussy was bad enough. Then some smart ass nigga had to reduce it to *cut*, like it was one big long slice between a woman's legs.

"It's not as big a deal as you make it out to be. I'll be fine."

"Yeah," I said flatly, and turned away from her.

"Really. Nudity's accepted here. People ain't as uptight as they are in the South. Haven't you ever heard of that play *Oh Calcutta!*? The whole show was performed in the nude."

"But those were a bunch of people nobody gave a shit about seeing naked."

"*Anyway* . . . ," she said, dismissively.

I could practically feel steam rising from my skin. If she didn't care enough about herself than to risk her life dancing naked in New York, so be it.

But to put *my* fucking job on the line for some shit like this let me know she didn't give a damn about me.

"It's not as big a deal as you make it out to be," Reesy said, still looking through the report.

I tried to ignore her. I was sulking.

"And I *do* give a damn about your job," she added, "despite what you think. Misty, no one's gonna ever find out."

"Yeah."

Neither of us said a word. After a few awkward seconds, Reesy spoke up again.

"Bavarian Bridge is short because the property is smaller. I don't see anything showing a sale taking place, but the acreage is definitely down a quarter in size."

"What?" I said, turning around toward her.

"Apparently the company sold off a piece of the property," she repeated. "Didn't you know that?"

"No, I didn't," I responded.

I sat there, confused. There hadn't been any sales of property since I came on board. Only acquisitions.

"Well, there's nothing here showing the company was credited any money with the actual sale of property," Reesy said. "But the land itself has definitely been adjusted."

Something wasn't right about this. I'd check it out tomorrow.

Reesy put the report down and stood up.

"I'm sleepy," she stated. "If you don't need me anymore, I'm going to bed."

"Fine," I said, perplexed by the whole evening. "I'm going to bed, too."

An hour later, I was lying in the dark, still wide awake.

I had just gotten off the phone with Mama. It was one of those rare moments where I just felt like hearing her voice. At first, she thought something was wrong, but I quickly reassured her. I tried to keep the conversation as brief as possible, especially before she had a chance to ask me if I'd met any nice, mannerable men here yet. I had enough on my mind as it was.

I was mulling over Reesy's decision to dance again. And tripping over the fact that a portion of property was inexplicably missing.

That damn Reesy.

I don't know how she caught it, but she did. She had an eagle eye.

What a shame it was wasted on dumb shit like shaking her naked ass.

QUARTER ACRE AND A FOOL

Reesy started her new job that weekend.

She worked from seven to midnight. I really couldn't complain because the hours didn't conflict with her day job.

Still, I didn't like it.

All I knew was that four days a week, Wednesday through Saturday, she caught a cab down to Times Square and went to work at a place called the One Trick Pony.

Her boss was some greasy guy named Marco Polo.

It was Tuesday evening. Her night off. We were watching *Frasier*, and she was eating a bag of Cheese Doodles damn near bigger than the couch.

"He's one of those dark Italians," she explained. "Sicilian. You know, the one's with nigga in 'em. Real tall and fine, with this long ponytail hanging down his back. That motherfucka's got it goin' on!"

"You better watch yourself," I warned, "before you catch some of that *goin' on*, and your ass ends up *goin' off* to the hospital."

"Child, please," she replied, waving a big fat Cheese Doodle at me. "Ain't nobody tryna fuck Marco."

"I hope not. You better make sure you don't get into bed with one of those Mafia types. And I mean that literally *and* figuratively. They'll own your ass."

"You watch too much TV," she laughed. "Besides, I got my eye on this fine motherfucka who's been coming in every night since I started."

"I don't want to hear about it," I said, cutting her off. "Just make sure none of this spills over to Burch. You got that?"

"Ain't nobody studyin' Burch," she said, clucking her tongue.

She saw the flicker of anger in my eyes.

"Girl, I'm just playin'," she said with a smile. "I'll keep them both separate. I promise. Okay?"

"Yeah," I said, still mad at her.

We both watched TV in silence.

I guess I'd just have to wait and see.

After thoroughly reviewing the Bavarian file, I realized that Jeff, the asset manager for the property, had somehow sold off a piece of the land that had a freestanding building on it.

It was a tiny drive-thru Philly cheese steak stand that had been paying two thousand dollars in rent for over a year. The property had been sold in just the last month.

The interesting thing was, we could find no records of the sale anywhere in Burch Financial.

So I sent Reesy to the courthouse to go through public records regarding the transaction.

The records revealed that there was indeed a new owner.

Jeff Branniker.

Rich Landey had flown into town posthaste after I told him about the Branniker file. The door to my office was shut.

He paced the floor.

"God, Misty. How could something as small as two thousand dollars tip you off to something as big as this?"

Reesy sat in a chair across the desk from me, a wry smile on her face.

"I don't know, Rich. It just didn't make any sense to me that a property like that would be *losing* money. Even if it was just a little. It had been constant for such a long time."

"No one's said anything to him yet, I hope?" he asked.

He looked from me to Reesy.

Reesy shook her head.

"We're keeping this close to the hip," I confirmed.

"Good," he muttered. "I want to see just how much our man's been up to. I'm inclined to believe he's done this a time or two before."

I nodded.

"Legal should have caught it," he said. "This transaction should have never been able to take place without them."

Reesy sat across from me saying nothing.

I wondered why she didn't jump in. Then I realized why.

"Rich," I said, "I can't take full credit for this discovery. Reesy noticed the difference in property size. She pulled it out of a report that would have probably taken me hours to sift through."

He stopped pacing.

"Good deal."

"Thank you," she said in a quiet voice.

"She's also the one who dug up the information at the courthouse," I added.

"I appreciate your hard work, Reesy," he said.

"You're welcome."

It was only noon, but already I was tired.

"Why don't we go grab some lunch?" I suggested. "We can pick up the subject over at Gleason's Deli."

"Good idea," Rich said. "I want this matter resolved as quickly as possible."

I spent the next day holed up with Legal in the conference room poring over Jeff's portfolio with a fine-toothed comb.

As it turned out, he had sold the property in Philadelphia to another holdings company, Becton-Wrye. Becton-Wrye was based out of Denver. They had purchased all the land adjacent to the steak stand that wasn't owned by Burch. They wanted the property with the steak stand as well.

Since that portion of the property brought in such a small amount of money, Jeff was stupid enough to have done up a deed on Burch's behalf showing the sale of the property to himself.

It had been easy to get a copy of the deed. It was a matter of public record.

There weren't many other tip-offs to the transfer. The contract for the management company that handled the property stayed the same. The only difference was there was just a quarter of an acre less property to manage. Someone had whited-out the part in the contract with the original size of the property and changed it to the new size.

The records showed that Burch sold Jeff the land for three hundred thousand dollars. Jeff, in turn, sold the property to Becton-Wrye for eight hundred thousand dollars.

We also discovered this deal was not the first one he had done.

He had sold tiny portions of land from properties in Reston, Virginia, and Gaithersburg, Maryland. In areas where he knew he could press the buyer to pay top dollar for a small piece of land.

Rich and I were back in my office going over the file one last time. Everyone had already left for the day.

"Why don't you go home?" Rich said. "No point in both of us sitting here going through this again."

"Are you sure?"

"Yes, go on. I've got to make a decision. I'll give you a call a little later and let you know what I'm going to do."

"All right," I said with a yawn.

"I won't call too late. Looks like you need a good sleep after all this."

He was right.

I was exhausted.

It was dark when I got home that night.

"Good evening, Miss Fine," the doorman said in greeting.

"Hey, Len," I moaned.

"Working late again?"

"Always, Len, always."

I rode the elevator up in silence, the dull thud of my heart the only sound reverberating off the walls.

All I wanted to do was crawl into my bed, pull the covers up over my head, and go to sleep.

I put my key in the lock, determined to do just that.

The living room was dark, but the TV was on when I opened the door.

Reesy was balled up on the couch, a blanket over her, clutching the remote.

"What are you doing home?"

"Girl, I don't feel so good," she moaned. "My stomach's tor' up. I've been in the bathroom all night."

"You're probably not eating right. The only time I ever really see you eat is lunch. You rush right from Burch to home to that other job."

She just lay there on the couch looking weak and pale.

"Have you had any soup?" I inquired.

"Uh-huh. I can't keep nothin' in. I'm shittin' like crazy."

"Get up," I said, helping her off the couch. "Go get in the bed. I'll bring you some hot tea."

She let me guide her down the hall.

"Misty," she whined, leaning against me as we walked into her bedroom, "I know I said I wouldn't take advantage of you as my boss, but can I have tomorrow off? I think I need to get whatever this is out of my system."

"Sure, girl!" I exclaimed. "You know I wouldn't be mean enough to make you come in when you're sick like this!"

"I appreciate it," she moaned.

She climbed into the bed. She looked so innocent and piti-ful, balled up under the covers like that. Her teeth were chat-tering.

"I've got chills," she said.

"I'll go put the tea on," I said, feeling like her mother. "Just lie there and try to get warm."

I went into the kitchen and put on the pot.

I stood over the stove, deep in thought.

When the teapot began to whistle, I heaved a heavy sigh of my own, relieved to have made it through the events of the day.

Later that night, I was balled up under my own covers, unable to get to sleep, when the phone rang.

"Hello?"

"Misty, it's Rich."

I could hear pieces of paper being shuffled on his end.

"Sorry to call you so late. I've reached a decision."

"What are you going to do?"

"I want him arrested in the morning."

"At the office?"

"At the office," he replied. "Think everyone else will get the message?"

"Oh yeah," I said. "They certainly will."

"I want you to be there when it happens. This was your baby. You'll get all the credit for catching this," Rich said. "You *and* Reesy," he corrected.

Great. That was *all* I needed.

Even though Jeff was the bad guy, I knew what the percep-tion around the office would be.

Once again, that black bitch of a boss and her trusty black ass sidekick had managed to mess things up for everybody else.

FREAKIN' DOWN HANGUP ALLEY WAY

Reesy's case of the flu made her miss Jeff's arrest, which caused a real scene around the office.

The police didn't come until 8:30 that morning to pick up Jeff. Rich wanted to make sure everyone witnessed what happened to an embezzler.

Jeff was beet-red, his head down, as the police led him away. He didn't deny, protest, or proclaim his innocence.

He just went away quietly.

What he had been doing was way out of his league. How he'd gotten the idea to ever do it was beyond me. I guess the environment at Burch had gotten so lax, he pretty much figured he could get away with anything.

Millicent's eyes shot daggers at me the whole day. I knew she hated me now more than ever.

Reesy was back to work inside of a week.

She was also back to work at the One Trick Pony. I know, because I took a call from Marco at home that Tuesday night after she returned to Burch.

Reesy was in the shower when the phone rang.

"Hello?"

"*Heyyyy!* Reese!" the voice exclaimed.

"This is Misty," I said drily.

"Misty? Hmmm, do you dance, too?" he asked.

This bastard didn't know me from Adam, and was asking me a stupid ass question like that. For all he knew, I might not even know Reesy was a stripper, and here he was busting her.

"No, I don't.'

My tone was flat.

"Too bad" was his abrupt reply. "Do me a favor: tell her I got her message. Seven o'clock tomorrow night is fine. Everybody else will be back on schedule."

"Sure," I said, my tone curt.

His voice gave me the creeps in the worst way.

The worm hung up without even saying good-bye.

When Reesy got out of the shower, I was sitting on the sofa with my mouth stuck out.

"So you're going to work tomorrow night?" I said accusingly.

She sat down on the couch, rubbing her wet hair with a towel.

"Yeah. Why?"

"You shouldn't have washed your hair," I said. "You just got over a cold."

"Thank you, Tyrene," was her flippant reply. "I'll be just fine."

"Fine. That's you if you get sick again." I rose from the couch. "I'm not gon' nurse you back to health again."

I walked toward the kitchen. I turned back around, pissed, before I even cleared the doorway.

"How can you be crazy enough to go out and dance naked again, when you're just getting over the flu?"

"Misty, stop being so dramatic! I'm fine! Shit. My *cat* didn't catch the flu."

"Fine," I said. "Whatever."

I turned on the faucet and ran some water into the teapot.

212

"Make me a cup?" she asked.

"Make your own," I snapped.

"There was the weirdest guy at the club," Reesy said one night after coming in late.

I was still up, going through cash flow statements. The hours just after midnight were turning into the most productive time of the day for me.

"What?"

"This guy," she said, slopping down on the couch.

Reesy had on a pair of tight-fitting jeans and an oversized sweater.

"He kept buying lap dances from me. I lap danced for him five times."

I looked up from my paperwork.

"I made a lot of money," she added, like that was supposed to make it all right.

"So what's the big deal? You like lap dancing, don't you?"

My question was part sincerity, part sarcasm.

Reesy bent down and pulled off her shoes. She began to massage her feet.

"He kept getting hard-ons. And, what's worse, the motherfucka would cum in his pants."

"You're used to that, aren't' you?"

"Yeah," she said. "But there was just something nasty about this guy. I mean, he was really getting off on this shit."

I listened to her.

"He kept saying 'I wanna suck your titties. Can I suck your titties? I wanna fuck your black ass so bad.'"

She grimaced as she recounted this.

"He was butt-ugly. His face was full of crags and craters."

"Was he black?" I asked.

"Naw," she said, wrinkling her face. "It was some Italian guy. He was setting that money out, though. That's for sure."

She picked up her shoes and went into her bedroom. After five minutes, she returned to the living room.

213

"Are you going to be up for a while?" she asked.

"Yeah."

"Well, I'm going to bed. Good night."

"Good night."

It was an empty response.

I was disgusted with her. I needed to sit down and tell her how much this job of hers bothered me.

I couldn't live with Reesy under these circumstances. Pretty soon, I knew, my resentment of her job would begin to manifest itself in other areas of our friendship if I didn't address it now.

I tried to return my attention to what I was doing.

I had a headache.

I'd talk to her about it tomorrow. Between worrying about her job and my job as well, my own resistance was beginning to wear thin.

I actually went home early the next day so I could talk to Reesy.

It was five-thirty when the cab let me out in front of the building.

"Evening, Miss Fine," Len smiled, holding open the door. "This is early for you, isn't it?"

"Yeah," I replied.

"Between you and Miss Snowden, you two are always coming and going," he said. "She just dashed out of here on her way to work."

I turned toward him, surprised.

"Is that what she said?"

"Yes, ma'am."

"Umph!" was my only reply.

Oh well.

I guess I'd just have to talk to her when she got off work later that night.

It was late and I was asleep on the couch when Reesy came in. The phone began ringing the same time she opened the door.

214

She was frantic. Tears were streaming down her face.

"What's the matter?" I cried. *"Oh, my God, Reesy, what happened to you?"*

Her clothes were torn and her face was bruised.

"That motherfucka tried to rape me!" she exclaimed, out of breath.

"Who?" I asked.

I knew this was going to happen. I knew it. It was just a matter of time. She was lucky she wasn't dead.

The phone was ringing like crazy.

"The guy from last night. The one who kept buying all the lap dances."

"He tried to rape you right there in the club?"

"No!" she screamed. "He was waiting outside for me when I got off. Before I could even hail a cab, he pushed me into an alley. That greasy motherfucka ripped my shirt and stuck his hand inside my jeans!"

The phone stopped ringing.

"What happened to your face?"

"He hit me. He slapped me hard."

"Did anybody see this? I'm going to call the police."

I started for the phone.

"No!" she cried. *"Don't call anybody! I'm okay!"*

Reesy sat there on the couch shaking violently.

I came and sat down beside her.

As soon as I put my arm around her, she burst into tears.

"I can't believe that motherfucka! People just fuckin' walked by and watched him hold me down! Nobody tried to help or anything!"

"I'm sorry, sweetie," I said softly, rubbing her back.

I felt terrible about this. I had been afraid of something happening to her, but lately my major concerns had been for me and my own job.

"Marco saw it," she sobbed. "I saw him come to the edge of the ally and stand right there watching. He didn't think I saw him. That son of a bitch!"

"He *saw* you?" I exclaimed. "I'm calling the police!"

She put her hand on my leg, gripping it firmly.

"Just leave it alone, Misty, okay?"

She looked up at me, her braids hanging wildly around her tear-streaked face.

I sighed heavily, frustrated about what to do.

Someone rang the doorbell.

Reesy jumped.

"Don't open it!" she hissed.

I turned to her, alarmed.

"He doesn't know where we live, does he?"

"I don't know," she whined softly.

"Did he follow you here?"

"I took a cab," she said.

"Then he probably didn't," I assured her, hoping the guy hadn't followed her tonight, or any other night before.

I got up and went to the door. I looked through the peep-hole.

It was Len, the doorman.

I opened the door a crack.

"Yes?" I said, sticking my head through.

"Is Miss Snowden all right?" he asked, a look of concern on his face.

"She's fine," I said.

"She came in and her clothes were torn. Was she mugged? I tried to call up here, but no one answered the phone."

I tried to relax my face so he would go away.

"She's okay, Len. Thanks for checking on us, though."

"Do I need to call the cops?" he pressed.

"No. Just don't let anyone in for either of us without calling up here first."

He nodded.

"Of course, Miss Fine! I would never do that anyway!"

"Thanks, Len," I said. "We appreciate it."

I closed the door.

• • •

"Are you going back?" I asked Reesy.

She was drinking a cup of tea.

"No."

I sat next to her, saying nothing.

"I know this is what you wanted," she mumbled. "You were right, okay?"

"I didn't want this to happen to you, Reesy" was all I could say.

"I know," she said.

We were both quiet.

"Are you going to try to work somewhere else?" I asked after a while.

"Exotic dancing? I don't think so," Reesy sighed. "Once bitten, twice shy."

Thank God.

"That oughta make you happy," she added. "Now you don't have to worry about my being seen by anybody at Burch."

"What are you going to do about your face?" I asked. "You can't go to work tomorrow like that."

"I can put some makeup on it," she said.

My eyebrows shot up.

"Have you looked at yourself? There's a huge purple hand-print covering the whole left side. You can't go in looking like that."

"I can't take off again," Reesy said. "They already think you show me too much favoritism at the office anyway."

"Don't worry about that," I said. "There's only two days left in the week. I'll deal with what they say in the office. That's the least of your worries."

Reesy sat there, biting her lip.

"It was crazy for me to try to dance in New York, wasn't it?"

I didn't say anything. She knew the answer to that already.

"I guess I'm stuck with just working at Burch for a while."

"You make it sound like a form of damnation," I said.

"No, it's not," she protested. "I just get the work done too fast. Maybe I can find a way to keep myself busy."

I glanced at her. I wished I could find a way to get her more involved with my work, but I knew she didn't have the level of interest in it that I did.

I just wanted everything to get back to normal.

And I wanted to put this whole exotic dancing thing behind us as far as it could possibly go.

CHICK AND STRIPS

Reesy was *always* on the phone.

I don't know whom she was talking to, but she was always talking.

She was no longer bored. She had managed to fill up the holes in her day at Burch with gossip and idle chitchat.

It was amazing. Really. I mean, don't get me wrong. She was still incredibly productive. She still managed the work she did for me extremely well. I delegated tasks to her and they were done with almost zero turnaround.

And even though the other asset managers and their assistants were afraid for their jobs, they still liked her. They even preferred dealing with her over me, whom they hadn't yet quite figured out.

After the incident with Jeff, they were more terrified of me than ever. How Reesy managed to escape being the object of that fear as well was beyond me.

Of course, Millicent hated Reesy with a passion. But with the exception of Millicent's undisguised venom, Reesy was practically the new darling of the department.

She had become particularly good friends with Mary, one of the administrative assistants on the twenty-third floor.

What was interesting about Mary was that she worked for Rick Hodges, a black senior asset manager on the twenty-third floor.

I realized when I first met Rick that it must have been him that Rich Landey had been referring to when he said there were black males in the company.

Okay. One.

Bob Blanculowitz had even once said that he really wanted me to meet the senior managers on the twenty-third floor because he thought "I'd like them."

Well, he was partly right.

Rick was very attractive, albeit a little aloof. I kept my distance from him for the most part, for the obvious reasons.

The last thing I needed was to congregate with the only other black manager. Nor did I need to complicate work in any unrelated way.

I really didn't have to spend that much time with him anyhow, other than for introductory purposes. Rick had excellent control of his portfolio, and Rich and Bob had nothing but high praise for him.

Reesy got to know Rick a little better than I did because she went down quite a bit to shuttle papers and talk to Mary.

"Mary said Rick supported you in that situation about Jeff," Reesy told me one day.

"Good for him," I said. "Why didn't he come to me and publicly show his support?"

She shrugged. Knowing her, she probably told Mary what I said. She sure as hell went down to Mary's floor enough.

That didn't bother me a great deal. She was never gone from her station for very long.

But it did bother me that she was *always* on the phone.

Theoretically, I wouldn't have minded so much, because she always did work while she talked. But from an appearance standpoint, it looked terrible.

I could hear her fingers typing away on the computer. The printer was always roaring, and the fax machine stayed busy.

But I couldn't begin to count how many times I heard her say "hold on" to someone on the phone while she dashed off for a minute to make some copies or pick up some paperwork.

I didn't know who she was talking to. It had to be long distance, because other than me and the people in the building, she didn't have anyone in New York with whom she could have the kind of conversations she was having.

I wondered if whomever she was talking to called her, or if she was the one placing the calls. Perhaps it was one of her stripper friends from the Magic City. Sometimes, I knew, it was Mary.

It annoyed the hell out of me.

Reesy was embodying virtually every stereotype that white people expected of us when they put us in the workplace.

You see, even though she was productive and meticulous as hell, that's not what most people saw.

What most people saw when they passed her station or came up to her for assistance was Reesy chatting away casually on the phone. And it was plainly obvious these calls had no relevance whatsoever to Burch or to business.

She would sit there, smacking on gum, talking a mile a minute. I could hear everything from my office. She wore a headset. That way, she could keep her hands free to do actual work. The content of what I heard was typically

"No, girl!"

"For real?"

"Stop!"

"Get the fuck outta here!"

"It was THAT big?"

This tormented me terribly, for Reesy sat in the most conspicuous area on the floor.

One station over sat Millicent, who scowled and fumed on a daily basis.

Sometimes I caught Millicent just glaring at Reesy, her expression so indignant, I thought she was going to spontaneously combust—white skin, gray hair, and portions of pinched nose scattering all over the place.

The twist of the knife for Millicent was that Reesy was not just *any* black bitch. She was a black bitch who sat in plain view of God and everybody and talked the day away. Millicent knew that *she* could never, ever get away with the same thing.

One day I accidentally rounded a corner, just near the water cooler, while Millicent was in the midst of a vicious chat-off with Gladys, one of the other admin assistants.

It was a Tuesday, and I was rushing to my office to place a call to one of the companies who fee-managed a property we owned in Virginia. I could hear voices clearly as I rushed forward, but I didn't pay them any mind.

As I got closer, what they were saying became plainly audible, and I was stopped dead in my tracks.

"That black goon sits there all day hooting on the phone, and does her boss say anything about it? *No!*"

It was Millicent.

"Can you hear what she's saying?" Gladys asked.

"Can I?" she hissed. "It's scandalous! She talks about sex and all matter of filth, right there in the middle of the floor! She's so vulgar, the way she chews her gum while she blathers away. Never before has Burch been defined by such garbage. The company's going to hell in a handbasket!"

"Why don't you say something?"

"Whom am I going to say it to?" Millicent barked. "It's obvious that spider-headed witch has been given carte blanche to do as she pleases. Her boss, *Misty,*" she uttered my name like it was poison, "is probably going to fire everybody one by one until the place is filled with niggers."

"Sssshh, Millicent," Gladys whispered. *"Suppose someone hears you?"*

"I don't *care* who hears me," Millicent announced. "It's a sad state of affairs around here, Gladys. The place has com-

222

pletely lost its professionalism. And poor Bob. He's practically suicidal. He knows he's going to be out of here soon. I *hate* those two black wenches! I'll bet Rich Landey is screwing them both!"

"You think so?" Gladys gasped.

"I *know* so!" Millicent said. "He comes to town all the time. He never did that before. And he calls every five minutes. I know, because I always get the calls. *Reesy* is usually tied up on another line chatting away."

"So do you pass the calls on to Misty?"

"*Are you kidding?* She hired Reesy to take her calls, so, dammit, I let her do it. I forward them right over to Reesy's special line. The one she thinks no one knows about. She still hasn't figured out how Rich Landey keeps buzzing through to that line, the dumb nigger."

They both laughed viciously.

"I just wish I could catch her doing something, *anything*, that was remotely unethical," Millicent snapped.

"What could you do?"

"I'd go to someone at the parent company. Someone higher than Rich Landey."

I could hear the determination in her voice.

"You would?" Gladys asked incredulously.

"*Yes I would!*" Millicent said with indignation. "I have a moral obligation to the history of Burch. I may go down, but I won't go down without the powers-that-be getting an earful. I'll bet they don't know what's happening here. They can't. It's *shameful!*"

"I'd stay out of it if I were you, Millicent," Gladys warned.

"I will not," she replied. "Just you watch. They're niggers, for goodness' sake. They'll make a mistake. And when they do, Gladys, you can bet I'll be right there to see it. And I'm going to set off a twelve-alarm fire!"

I stood there, mortified.

I slunk away, before either of them could see me, and slipped into the bathroom.

I turned on the cold water and let it course over my hands, which were shaking violently. I was a bundle of nerves.

Partially because I was surprised that Gladys, who was always so pleasant to me, was a part of the hateful and bitter cesspool that Millicent swam so comfortably in.

I wondered how many of the others were smiling in my face and behind my back calling me a black bitch who was screwing the boss.

Mostly, I was mortified because of Reesy. Because for all Millicent's bitterness, everything she said about the way Reesy sat there smacking her gum and talking trash all day was true.

Reesy was taking Burch's image down a notch.

And she was taking mine right down with it.

"We need to talk," I announced after work, walking into the living room in sweatpants and a T-shirt.

Reesy was crunching on a saucer of carrot sticks, her eyes glued to *Jeopardy!*

"Hold up," she said, her finger raised. "I think I'm about to get this one."

I glanced at the tube. Alex Trebek's perfect enunciation fired the answer in expectation of the question.

"While this Muse represented heroic poetry, she was also the Chief of all Muses," he said.

"Who is Calliope?" I answered, or rather, questioned, matter-of-factly.

"Who is Terpsichore?" the matronly contestant responded, unsure of herself.

"No, I'm sorry," Alex said pityingly. "The question is Who is . . . Calliope? Terpsichore was the Muse of dancing and choral song."

"Bitch," Reesy said and smiled, looking up at me. "You need to get on this damn show."

She crunched another carrot stick.

"Yeah, right," I sighed, flopping down on the couch.

"No, really. I want someone to get on that show and smoke

the shit out of Alex *Whiteass* Trebek. He can't just give you the answer and tell you you're wrong. He has to show you what was wrong about your answer. Always gotta be so damn right."

"He hosts the show," I retorted, "he's *always* gonna be right."

You idiot, I thought.

"Yeah," she continued, "but he has this way of making you feel so *stupid*. Like he's the fucking smartest person in the world."

"Then maybe you should quit watching the show," I said, annoyed at her now more than I was when I initially walked into the room.

She glanced over at me, alarmed.

"*What's the matter with you?* That job's kicking your ass, ain't it? I can tell."

"Oh really?" I asked with sarcasm. "You actually took the time to notice something other than the telephone?"

"Huh?" she asked, surprised. "What are you talking about?"

I stopped for a moment, not wanting this to turn into an "it's-your-fault, shame-on-you" finger-pointing match. I knew Reesy could get really ballistic if I confronted her. She'd outshout me and get the upper hand, and I'd end up feeling like the bad guy. I didn't want that to happen.

Plus, you can get more flies with sugar than salt, my mama always said.

"Nothing, girl," I sighed. "I'm just a little stressed. I don't know if you noticed, but today was a particularly bad day for me.

"And I still can't get used to this cab business," I contin-ued. "They drive like maniacs. The one that drove me home this afternoon scared the hell out of me, turning corners and switching lanes without looking. I think I'm gonna just start walking to work and back. It's only a few blocks."

"*Are you crazy, girl?*" she shrieked. "You work past dark

every night. You can't be walking in no midtown Manhattan at night by yourself. I'on care how bad you think you are. You'll get jacked up somewhere. Look at what happened to me!"

"I just can't see taking a cab every night," I said. "And it seems like a waste of money to ride just a few blocks."

I was successfully diverting the subject so I could come back around to it from the back way. She was becoming sympathetic.

Perfect.

"Girl, you better take them cabs," she snapped, crunching down on another carrot stick. "Money is the last thing you got to worry about. Those cabs ain't but a drop in the bucket for what you're making now."

"That doesn't mean I should just throw money away. I have to plan for a lot of things. I can't guarantee I'll have that job forever. They may decide they don't like the work I'm doing."

I was working my segue precisely.

"Why wouldn't they? You've been hustling around that office like a fiend. People jump when you appear. Mare says they have nothing but respect for you downstairs. None of those guys ever really liked Bob to begin with."

"Who the hell is Mare?" I asked.

"*Mary*. You know, that guy Rick's assistant."

"Oh. Since when did you start calling her Mare?"

Reesy kicked her legs up on the couch, another carrot stick disappearing in her mouth.

"Since she asked me to," she smacked.

She paused for a moment.

"When you first walked in here, you said you wanted to talk." She studied her carrot stick. "Talk about what?"

Bingo! She brought it up on her own. I went into my mode, like I was really pained about what I had to say. Actually, I kinda was.

But truth be known, I really wanted to just rip into her for being unprofessional enough for me to even have to talk to her like this.

I was quiet for a minute, angling the best way to go into this thing.

"How do you think things are going so far?" I asked her. "You talk to a lot of the people in the department. What kind of feel are you getting?"

"Hmmm," she muttered, thinking out loud.

She looked up toward the ceiling, her legs thrown over the arm of the chair, and crunched rudely on the carrot stick.

"From what they're telling me, everybody seems to like you."

"Yeah, right!" I exclaimed.

"No, really," she said. "A lot of them were just as surprised about what Jeff was doing as you were. They thought he kissed way too much ass. Bob's especially."

I couldn't help but smile at that.

"'Course, that bitch Millicent can't stand the sight of either of our black asses, but you know that."

"Yeah, I do," I replied.

"That hoe spends most of her damn day watching everything I do. She sits there with her face scrunched up, all mad and shit."

Reesy grimaced as she said this, imitating Millicent, I suppose.

"I just look at her sometimes and cross my eyes, just to fuck with her."

She laughed, her feet swinging in the air over the side of the chair as she kept looking up at the ceiling.

I just watched her. She didn't have a clue.

"Yeah . . . ," she kept on, "other than her crazy ass, everything is cool. I don't think people are as scared about what's gonna happen to them as they were when you first came. Now that they all know Bob is eventually going to be out, everybody's getting back into their own little groove. They're hustling, though. All of 'em."

"What do you think about Gladys?" I probed.

"Oh, Gladys is cool," she chirped, looking over at me. "She comes by all the time. Sometimes I see her on the floor just watching me. I'll look up from the phone, and she's there. But she's real friendly. I think she's just kinda nosey."

"Is that right?"

"Yeah," she nodded. "Why? How do *you* think things are going?"

She looked over at me.

I figured I'd just burst out with it. Just put it out there and see what she said.

"Well, Reesy," I said, leaning forward, "to tell the truth, I'm kinda worried."

She stopped chewing on the carrots and focused her attention on me.

Finally. Those little orange sticks were getting on my last damn nerve.

"What are you worried about?"

"I don't know, girl," I sighed, going into my girlfriend mode. "People are talking. They're saying the department's not as professional as it used to be."

"What?" she cried. "What the *hell* does that mean, 'not as professional'?"

I rested my elbows on my knees and shrugged my shoulders.

"I've been overhearing people talking. They say we're bringing the department down. I heard in a roundabout way a complaint that I haven't been spending enough time with the managers. That's there's an air of coldness on the floor that wasn't there before."

"Really?"

She was totally surprised.

"Yeah."

"Who'd you hear it from?" Reesy asked. "No one's said anything to me."

"They wouldn't. They're not gonna talk about the problem to the problem."

"What do you mean, 'to the problem'?" she asked, her eyes narrowing. "I thought we were talking about you."

I didn't say anything for a moment.

"Huh?" she prodded.

"Well," I said, very slow and deliberate, "I'm hearing complaints about you, too."

"Fuck no!" Reesy exclaimed, jumping up from the chair. "From whom?"

"Apparently a number of people."

"Get the *motherfuck* outta here, Misty!"

Oh boy. Now she was *really* in her ghetto mode.

She stormed around the living room, hot.

"Ain't nobody said shit to me 'bout that job since I started! Probably ain't nobody but that old dried-up bitch sitting across from me every day!"

I didn't say anything. I was going to let her pull it out of me. She kept racing around the room, ranting.

"That ratty ass heffah'll do anything to keep me from getting her job. But she can forget that shit! Her ass is out the door, and ain't nothing she can do about it!"

I was quiet.

Reesy came and stood directly in front of me, her hands on her hips.

"What'd they say to you about me? What did you hear?"

"There's a lot of talk about how much time you spend on the phone."

"For real? Why the fuck do they care about that? I'm doing ten times the work as the other assistants around there. Probably half the managers, too."

"I thought you said they were hustling," I replied.

"They ain't hustling *that* damn much," she snapped. "Outside of you, I'm the busiest bitch around there."

"But people don't care about that Reesy. They don't care how much work you've been passing across my desk. They don't care that you're excellent at meeting deadlines. They don't even care if you've made their workload easier. All they care about is that every time they walk by, you're sitting there on personal calls. Something they'd get written up for if any of them were caught doing the same thing."

I didn't look up at her as I said this. I could feel her eyes boring holes in my head.

"Whose idea was this?"

Now I looked up.

"What?"

She stamped her foot like she was about to have a fit.

"Just what I said! Who said something to you about me being on the phone all the time?"

She spun around, talking to herself.

"Those fake motherfuckas! Ain't nobody had the nerve to say *shit* to me!"

This was incredible. It didn't even dawn on her that I sat in my office, day in and day out, and listened to her run her mouth on the phone, and that possibly it bothered me. Like this *couldn't* have been my idea. Like if it were up to me, she could talk on the phone all she wanted.

Actually, this was a good thing. This way, I could get my point across without being the fall guy.

"Where'd you get this from?" she demanded. "Is someone tapping my phone? How the hell would they know I'm talking on personal calls?"

"It's all over both floors, Reesy. But I didn't get it from anyone there."

She stopped cold at that.

"Where'd you get it from then?" she hissed.

Reesy was furious. Her eyes were glazed. She was seething. This whole thing had come as a total shock to her.

"Huh?" she persisted.

I sighed deeply. Thought about my next breath. Then let it fly.

"Rich Landey," I lied.

"Rich Landey?" she screamed.

She stared at me, stunned.

I stared back at her for as long as I could. I felt a little guilty for lying. But I was walking a precarious line. Reesy was my best friend. Reesy worked for me. As her employer, I needed to counsel her. But damn. I didn't know how to be straight up and do it.

I was beginning to realize it was probably the stupidest move on the planet to hire her to work for me.

She finally loosened her glazed lock on my face. She collapsed on the couch beside me, sinking back deep into the covers. When she spoke again, her voice was a whine.

"I can't believe this shit," she whimpered. "I talk to Rich every day. He's never said anything to me. He's always laughing and bullshittin' on the phone like I'm his best fucking buddy. *Crackers.* You can't trust none of 'em."

"He wouldn't say anything to you, Reesy," I said. "*I'm* your boss. He'd leave that to me."

She didn't respond back. She just sat there, staring off ahead of her. Her eyes looked a little moist.

I felt like a creep. Her feelings were crushed. I mean, I should have gloated, because she was always doing this kind of thing to me when it came to men. But I felt so bad. As sharp as Reesy was, she didn't have a clue about what was appropriate in the workplace.

Maybe this was why she always had static, dead-end jobs. No one wanted to promote a public slough-off up the ladder to publicly slough off at an even higher level.

We both sat there, silent. I know a good five minutes must have passed before either of us said anything.

"I wouldn't worry about it too much if I were you, Reesy," I said. "Just don't spend so much time on the phone. People are watching you. Especially Millicent. The last thing you need is to have a negative reputation with the company. We've only been there two months."

Reesy wasn't saying anything. I glanced over at her to see if she was crying. Her eyes were now bone dry.

"Don't sweat it," I kept on. "Just keep in mind they're watching everything we do. It's like I told you before. My ass is your ass, and vice versa. If Rich is questioning you, in no time at all he's gonna be questioning me."

"Mother*fuck* them *white* motherfuckas! All of them!" she screamed, jumping up from the couch and stalking away. *"I don't need this shit!"*

She snatched her jacket off the coatrack in the hallway, snatched open the front door, and slammed it so hard I thought it was gonna snap off the hinges.

I could hear her block heels clacking on the tile in the corridor as she stormed off toward the elevator. I got up and went to the door. Just as I opened it, I saw her enter the elevator.

As the doors closed, I could hear her mumbling angrily to herself.

I felt bad about the whole scene. I really did. But how else was I going to tell her? She was going to be mad any way you look at it.

Oh well.

Reesy stayed out for several hours. I was worried sick, with her being alone in New York out on the streets. Especially after the incident with that weirdo at the club.

Reesy was too much of a hot-tempered, fly-off-the-handle person. I was afraid that, in her rage, she would tell some person on the street to kiss off and end up getting the shit slapped, knocked, raped, or shot out of her.

By midnight, I had gone into my bedroom with the intention of going over paperwork and keeping myself awake until she came home. By 2:00 A.M., I had submitted to sleep.

At 3:00 A.M., I was awakened by the sounds of moaning. I was in a deep slumber, and for a brief moment I kept sleeping, thinking that I was dreaming the sounds.

A particularly loud moan made me snap wide awake. I sat up, rubbing my eyes. I looked around, papers strewn all over my bed, black permanent ink all over my pillow from the open Sharpie felt tip pen I had tucked behind my ear. For a second, I was unaware of anything.

Then I heard the moaning again.

Suddenly, I remembered Reesy. She was home.

Oh God, I thought.

I found the living room dark, except for the floor lamp I had dimmed before I'd gone into the bedroom earlier.

There was no sign of Reesy or blood.

I heard the moans again. They sounded deep and pained. I glanced toward Reesy's room. The door was pulled together, almost shut, but a sliver of light peeked through.

The moans got louder. I wondered if Reesy was crying or hurt. Maybe that guy from the club had gotten ahold of her.

God, I felt terrible. I should have never said anything to her about that telephone business.

Fuck Millicent and Gladys. Reesy was doing an excellent job for me. How much time she spent on the phone had nothing to do with how great the work was she produced. It was all about appearances, and those crackers just didn't like it.

I could still hear her in there crying.

Shit.

I walked up to the door, my eyes filling up with tears. I should have never done that to her. For all her tough exterior, Reesy was just as soft on the inside as I was.

I put my hand on the knob. I was going to just push it open, confess what I had done, and tell her I was sorry. I'd ask her straight up to just stay off the phone. I'd explain about overhearing Gladys and Millicent. I'd tell her it was just them, not the whole department, especially not Rich Landey, talking about her.

I pushed the door softly, my eyes clouded by tears.

I could smell the sex as it rushed over me like a shroud. The moaning was loud and feverish. As the tears cleared from my eyes, my focus became sharp and direct.

I followed the line of clothes, beginning with a pair of over-sized jeans, on the floor. A huge pair of sneakers was kicked off at the foot of the bed. Beside them was one of those neon see-through pagers.

And a pair of Joe Boxers with smiley faces all over them.

My eyes scanned upward to the bed. I saw the blue-black butt pumping up and down furiously, with Reesy's yellow legs wrapped around the back. The bed was singing in high C, and Reesy's moans were wild and unrestrained.

I stood there, stunned, blood rising in my irises like mercury in a tube.

After a few seconds of sheer shock and utter rage, I turned around and fled from the room.

Reesy sat at her desk the next morning, her outgoing box completely full, her incoming box completely empty.

She had finished all the tasks I had given her for the entire week, and was already ahead on new projects I wanted her to handle.

As soon as I gave her something to do, Reesy did it, handed it to me without a word, and returned silently to her military post at her desk.

The headset she always wore lay on the desk beside her keyboard, untouched and unattached.

I stepped out of the office and went to the coffee station. I glanced over at her sidelong as I poured myself a hot cup of java.

She busied herself with her Rolodex file, completely ignoring me.

The phone rang. She picked up the handset. The headset had obviously been retired. Her voice was cold and monotone as she answered the line.

"Burch Financial," she droned. "This is Teresa."

She listened to the voice on the other end, her expression nebulous, her intonation detached.

"I'm fine. She's right here," she responded, not even looking at me. "Please hold while I transfer your call."

This was awful.

"Who is it?" I asked.

I didn't know how to act with her. I was still shocked from

the inexplicable sex scene from last night. I wanted to scream at her and call her a fool for picking up a stranger, but she had turned the tables on me and wasn't even talking.

I made the mistake of letting her set the tone for the day, but I had no choice. I couldn't let it be known that Reesy and I were having problems. It would not bode well in the office. They would see it as a weak link in our program. They'd be on it like ducks on a June bug.

"Rich Landey," she replied, still not looking at me.

My heart skipped. I hoped she wouldn't get bold enough to say something to him. That would put me in a fix for real. I also hoped he didn't notice anything in her tone. She was always so bubbly when she talked to him.

"Give me a second to get into my office, then transfer it," I said.

Exactly a second later, long before I cleared the doorway of my office, my phone was buzzing with the call.

This scenario, and equally icy variations thereof, went on for a couple of days. I struggled to make eye contact with Reesy, but she acted like my face was the last thing she wanted to be looking into. In the office, she was the Snow Queen—cold, efficient, and entirely unapproachable—freezing the hearts of all who dared near her. By the time I arrived home from work, she was either noticeably absent or locked up in her room.

By Thursday, I'd had enough. I couldn't stand the strain any longer. I decided that Reesy and I really needed to talk. Maybe I'd take her somewhere nice, like the Russian Tea Room, for lunch. She'd mentioned she wanted to go there when we first moved to the city, but we hadn't got around to doing it.

I walked out of my office with my purse on my shoulder, prepared to take her to lunch, make amends for my lie, and confront her for bringing whatever hoodlum that was the night before into our place for loud, unscrupulous sex.

Mary, rather *Mare*, from the twenty-third floor was standing at Reesy's station. They leaned toward each other, whispering animatedly.

Mare stood there with her long brown hair and her perfect little Barbie body, a tiny purse slung across her shoulder.

I really didn't like her.

She was the kind of white girl brothers lusted after and cheated on sistahs for. I was surprised she and Reesy had even become friends.

I figured Mare had access to something Reesy wanted. Men, information, contacts, *something*. It wasn't like Reesy to be hanging with no white girl just for the hell of it.

When I appeared, they both stopped talking.

It was painfully obvious, and my feelings were slightly hurt. Reesy leaned back like an automaton. Mare just stood there looking dense and obvious.

I ignored this blatant interruption and walked over to Reesy.

"Do you have any plans for lunch?" I asked with indifference.

"Mare and I are having lunch," was her flat reply.

"Fine," I said. "How long will you be gone?"

"From noon to one," she said. "No more, no less."

"Fine," I said, searching her face for a hint of emotion.

I found nothing.

I was now totally hurt.

Reesy bent down and pulled her desk drawer open. She took out her purse and pushed back her chair.

"You ready, girl?" she asked Mare, like they were the best of friends.

"Yeah, chica," Mare ginned. "I'm all set."

"Let's go then," Reesy smiled.

"I'm heading out, too," I said. "I'll walk out with you guys."

Part of me was hoping they'd invite me to come.

Neither of them said anything.

We walked down the hall to the elevators in total silence. I felt like a third wheel. Like I was the last person either of them wanted to be riding down the elevator with.

I wanted to smack Reesy for making me feel this way. She had completely frozen me out in front of a white girl. We had a friendship that spanned more than twenty-three years, and she had opted to side with a white girl whom she had known for little more than sixty days.

Just to make me feel bad.

My hurt was rapidly turning to anger.

When we got downstairs, the three of us headed out through the revolving glass doors.

An extremely attractive brother was coming in as we were exiting. He stopped and spoke to Mare. Apparently she knew him.

"Hi, Dandre," she said. "Rick's up there waiting for you."

"What's up, Mary-Mary," he replied, smiling at her and nodding at me.

He turned to Reesy and appraised her. A broad grin covered his face as apparent recognition washed over him.

"Hey!" he exclaimed. *"I know you!"*

Reesy smiled uncomfortably and gave me a skittish glance that I immediately recognized as fear.

"I don't think so," she replied in a rushed tone. *"Let's go, Mare!"* she snapped. "I only have an hour to eat."

Mare and I watched this exchange. Mare seemed fascinated that Reesy would know him. I was fascinated by the fact that something was obviously wrong.

Then I realized what it probably was.

This guy had recognized Reesy from her stripping days.

Holy shit!

"We've met before," Dandre continued. "I don't forget a face. It'll come back to me, give me a minute."

Reesy was now beet red. She grabbed Mary by the hand, and the two of them rushed from the building. I stood in the lobby for another half second. The guy looked at me, shrugged his shoulders, and headed off to the elevator.

I began to worry, hoping I was wrong about where he knew Reesy from. I thought, since she'd quit her job at the One Trick Pony, those troubles were behind us, and we didn't have to worry about the dancing thing anymore.

With the climate at the office being the way it was, there was no way the employees at Burch could find out about *that*.

Reesy would be out the door quicker than you could say *Tupac*.

And my black ass would be right behind her.

I got back from lunch way later than expected. I made several stops in the city. I met Bob at Chemical Bank to discuss one of the joint ventures they had pending with Burch. I did a ride-by at one of the properties to check out the curb appeal. I ran a few errands while I was out.

When I got back to the office, all hell had broken loose.

Reesy was at her desk, screaming hysterically. Millicent was in her face, screaming back.

"It's not true! It's not fucking true!" Reesy cried.

She was livid, but her face was streaked with tears.

"It *is* true, you filthy whore!" Millicent sneered.

A crowd had nervously gathered around the two women. People from other floors were spilling out of the elevators to get a look-see.

I raced over to them, mortified. My heart was thumping like a beaver tail.

"What the hell is going on here?!" I demanded.

"This bitch is spreading lies about me! I'm about to kill her, Misty. *I swear to God I am!"*

"They're not lies! And they didn't come from my mouth," Millicent shouted back. "They came from one of your own people!"

I pushed between the two of them, panicked and desperate to figure out what the hell was going on. Part of me was afraid because I already had an idea.

"I want both of you to go into my office," I stated.

Neither of them moved.

"NOW!" I bellowed.

Reesy and Millicent reluctantly shuffled into my office.

I turned around to the crowd, who had done everything but pull up chairs and break out popcorn and Cokes.

"You all need to go back to what you're doing," I said, waving them away. "Everything's under control. Go back to your workstations."

They looked at me as if to say, *Bitch please! We wouldn't miss this shit for the world!*

"Go on!" I repeated. "The show is over."

One by one, they turned away, glancing over their shoulders in case the fireworks erupted once again.

Mare and Gladys were among the last two to leave.

I turned to them.

"Did either of you witness what went on here?" I asked.

They both nodded.

"I was with Reesy the whole time," Mare said. "I know exactly what started it."

"Well, I was with Millicent, and I saw it, too," Gladys said defensively.

"Go into my office," I told them. "Shut the door behind you," I added.

They both trotted in, willing witnesses to the ugly fray.

I stood outside the door for a few moments, taking a deep breath.

This was going to be a spitting match. I knew it. I didn't know how I would handle it. If it was about the stripping, what could I say? Reesy *did* used to strip. There was *no way* for me to get her out of this one.

I clasped my hand over my brow and shook my forehead. This shit was for the fucking birds.

Reesy was rapidly becoming my career nightmare.

I took a deep breath again, let it out, and grabbed hold of my office doorknob.

Chin up, resigned to whatever, I charged in.

• • •

"Okay," I started. "Who's going to tell me what went on out there?"

Reesy and Millicent started at the same time, both of them shouting.

I held up my hand, stopping them.

"Let me tell the both of you something," I snapped. "I will *not* have you in here making the same ridiculous display of behavior you just showed out there!"

I pointed toward my door.

"Now *someone* here is going to tell me what happened, and dammit, they better tell me quick!"

I was furious.

Reesy and Millicent started again.

I held up my finger in warning again.

"And they're going to do it without raising all this hell!" I added.

My expression was firm. My eyes were narrowed and my hands were on my hips.

"I think I can help," Mare said weakly.

"Good, Mary. Then you start," I said, walking around to the chair behind my desk and taking a seat.

"And I don't want any interjections from either of you until I hear the story from her," I warned. "The whole story. Not just a piece of it."

My head was pounding.

"Well, Misty," Mary began, "when we got back, Dandre was still here. He and Rick were on their way downstairs, but they had come up here to bring me something because Rick thought maybe I was up here talking to Reesy."

Of course, I thought. Already folks knew Reesy's desk was the freaking company watering hole.

I nodded, not commenting.

"We weren't back from lunch yet, so Rick was standing there talking to Millicent."

Mary pointed toward Millicent, like none of us knew who the hell Millicent was.

"Before he got a chance to ask her anything, Reesy and I rode up on the elevator."

I kept listening.

"Rick saw us walking up," she continued. "When we got to Reesy's desk, he introduced Reesy to Dandre. Dandre was looking at her like he thought he knew her."

I saw Reesy squirm uncomfortably at this.

Millicent, in turn, looked on the verge of a happy discovery. Her expression said everything but *nyah-nyah-nyah-nyah-nyah*.

I cut my eyes at Reesy, trying to send her a surreptitious signal.

"Keep on," I told Mary.

"Well, while Rick was talking to me, handing me some paperwork to do, Dandre said he remembered where he knew Reesy from."

"And where was that?" I asked.

Mary looked a little awkward.

"Well, I don't know the place myself," she stammered.

"What place?" I pressed.

Mary was quiet for a second.

"What place, Mary?" I demanded, my voice just shy of shouting.

"The Magic City," she spat out.

"The Magic City?" I asked, my voice constant, indicating no recognition whatsoever. "What is that?"

I looked over at Reesy, silently telling her to just follow my lead. Right now, we needed solidarity. And hell, I was more than willing to lie.

Instead, Reesy looked off from me, averting her eyes.

"It's a strip joint," Millicent declared. "In *Atlanta*, where you came from."

Millicent spat the word Atlanta out like it burned her tongue to say it.

"Millicent, let Mary speak please!" I admonished.

She clucked her teeth and shut up.

Reesy was watching the walls, her facial muscles working furiously.

"So what was this guy's point?" I asked Mary.

I didn't want to have to go into this, but I had to at least *act* legitimate to appear to be objective about the whole thing.

"What was the big deal?" I continued.

"Dandre said Reesy was one of the best strippers in Atlanta," Mare said. "He said her stripping name was Peanut Butter."

Millicent laughed bitterly.

Shit. There was nothing I could say.

I searched all of their faces. Gladys was saying nothing. She looked completely uncomfortable, like she didn't want to be in the room at all.

Millicent was about to burst. She sat there, evil incarnate, too giddy to speak.

Mary looked sad and pitiful, like she wished none of this had ever happened at all.

And Reesy sat there, a vibe of anger shooting off her and bouncing all around the room.

"All right," I sighed. "Somebody tell me something. I'm not getting it obviously. Again, what's the big deal about all of this?"

I looked at Mary.

She hesitated, glancing over at Reesy like she was sorry for having to tell.

"Dandre said she was one of the best at the Magic City. He said he used to pay top dollar to get table dances from her. He wanted to know how long she'd been with Burch . . ."

Mary paused shyly.

". . . And he wanted to know if she still did a little *work* on the side."

My head was spinning. I couldn't believe that asshole would go out on Reesy like that. In front of all these damn white folks. He deserved to die for that shit.

He'd broken every racial code of ethics in the book.

"Reesy?" I whimpered softly. "Reesy?"

She didn't answer.

I put my head in my hands.

"That's right!" Millicent hissed. "What can you say? Your precious little blabbermouth assistant is nothing more than a two-dollar stripper! I knew I'd find something on her dirty black ass! I just got it way quicker than I thought! You were so quick to expose Jeff Brannike! Here! *Expose this!*"

Before I could say anything to Millicent, Reesy jumped up from the chair and stood over her.

Millicent's face was triumphant and proud. Reesy reached back, clear to Kansas, and slapped the living shit out of the woman.

Millicent gasped as she fell out of the chair, her glasses flying across the room, ricocheting against the window and landing on the floor.

Mary and Gladys sat there in pure shock.

I was delighted. Millicent deserved it, the evil bitch. Reesy didn't warrant being humiliated like this, which she obviously was.

Before I could get a chance to sympathetically try to discuss the matter with Reesy, she turned away from the crumpled heap of Millicent on the floor, and violently snatched open my office door.

When she opened the door, people scattered away like errant roaches. The hall cleared inside of seconds.

She stormed over to her workstation, snatched her purse from her desk, and raced away.

"Reesy!" I called. *"Reesy!"*

I ran part of the way down the hall after her, damn near breaking my neck in the process. I tripped momentarily, recovered, and raced after her again.

Back at Reesy's desk, the phone began ringing.

Millicent, Mary, and Gladys politely sat in my office listening to the ringing phone. Like it had absolutely nothing to do with them.

I stopped running and turned back, anxious, wondering if one of them was going to answer it.

It kept ringing.

I glanced toward the elevators, watching Reesy disappear behind the closing doors.

The phone rang on.

I raced toward the phone and picked it up, glaring at the three women, who could plainly see me from my office.

"Burch Financial," I panted.

"Misty?"

It was Rich Landey.

"Yeah, Rich," I breathed.

"What's going on?"

"We have a problem, Rich," I confessed.

"What kind of problem?"

I sighed a heavy sigh, my breath escaping me like air from a burst balloon.

"Give me a minute. I'm gonna put you on hold, then transfer you to my office."

"That's fine," he said.

I put the line on hold and went back in. Mary, Millicent, and Gladys were just sitting there looking stupid.

"You all can go back to work."

They got up. Millicent was visibly steaming. She rubbed her cheek, unable to hide the bright red print from Reesy's hand.

"Pull my door shut, Mary," I said, slumping down into my chair. "And could you transfer the call at Reesy's desk to my phone?"

"Sure," Mary said softly, closing the door.

She seemed to be the only considerate one in this whole mess. For a brief second, I started to like her.

Until I realized that if she hadn't known that guy Dandre, he might never have stopped and recognized Reesy.

My phone was ringing now. I looked at it for a moment, postponing the inevitable. On the third ring, I picked it up.

"Misty?" came the voice.

"Yeah, Rich."

"Now, tell me what this is all about," he demanded.

"Okay," I replied.

I took a deep breath, and began my descent into one of the most embarrassing experiences I ever had in my life.

OUT! OUT! DAMNED SPOT!

I had the biggest, most explosive headache I had ever had in my life.

I remembered how bad my head hurt after Stefan clocked me in the eye that time.

Right now, that didn't even come *close* to what I was feeling.

When I got home from work, I was a wreck.

My nerves were rattled and my future seemed shaky as I sat on the couch going over what had happened at work that day.

I thought about how Rich sounded when I told him about what happened.

Well, I figured I could kiss my job good-bye. With this discovery, I knew everything was fucked. Reesy's ruin was, in effect, my own.

Rich had handled the fiasco at the office with aplomb. Said he'd seen worse. Told me to just roll with the punches and not let it get me down.

But he expected it to be resolved by the next morning, which was Friday. And by "resolved" he meant that he didn't want another trace of this incident with Reesy to rear its head again.

He said he would handle Millicent's exit. It was best her termination come from him, rather than look like some bitter repercussion on my part because of Reesy.

I think I knew what he meant by "resolved." It didn't take a rocket scientist to know Reesy's ass was history. And I guess it would be a matter of time for me.

When I walked into the apartment that night, I was determined to tell her she was fired from Burch, but also determined to comfort her and reaffirm our friendship in the face of this obviously humiliating development.

I needed to apologize to her anyway. For lying and telling her Rich was the one complaining about her talking on the phone so much.

The lights were off in the apartment. I turned on the ones in the foyer and the living room.

"Reesy," I called. "Reesy, I'm home."

The apartment was like a ghost town.

I went to her bedroom, suddenly reminded of the awkward scene the night when I saw her and the guy going at it. I imagined I could still sense the smell of sex hanging in the air. The door was closed. I knocked three times, and walked in.

It was empty. No sigh of her.

I stood there like a zombie. My face was tight and my head was pounding.

I walked back into the living room and flopped down on the couch. I put my head in my hands, still unable to digest the trauma of the day.

I needed some Aleve. It was the only thing short of a gun that would make a headache like this go away.

Just think, Tuesday I had been plotting how I was going to tell Reesy she spent too much time on the phone. Now here it was, Thursday, and everybody in the office knew Reesy used to strip.

And she had practically vanished from existence, like she was Jimmy Hoffa.

I picked up my head, in desperate need of a drink to go with those Aleve. Knowing Reesy like I did, I knew she had proba-bly gone out somewhere to get trashed. She'd crawl in some-time tonight, perhaps with another roughneck, and screw this whole incident out of her system.

Not so easy for me. I had to figure out how to tell her she was fired.

I definitely needed a drink. Or three.

When Reesy finally came home, she was straight as an arrow.

I, however, was toasted.

I had found a bottle of Raynal in the kitchen cabinet. I hit that puppy.

And it hit me back.

Reesy walked in and sat on the couch beside me.

I was ready for the confrontation with her. I didn't need to lie or blame it on anyone else.

Drunk, I could deal with Reesy's hotheadedness. I could deal with that fiery, in-your-face temper with no problem.

I could fire her without regret.

. . . As long as I was full of liquor.

I leaned forward.

She took one look at me and burst out laughing.

"What you laughin' at?" I slurred.

"*You*, you drunk bitch!"

She picked up the half-empty bottle of Raynal from the cof-fee table.

"What are you doing drinking this stuff? You know the hardest you get is a beer or an Amaretto Sour."

I slumped back on the couch.

"Obviously, I needed something harder."

"Obviously," she chuckled.

I sat there, my stomach churning from the sudden move I'd made when I leaned back.

"This isn't funny, Reesy," I said sourly. "This isn't funny at all."

She pressed her lips together, nodding seriously.

"So you mean to tell me the way I slapped Millicent upside the head wasn't righteous? You know your ass wanted to laugh. Tell me you didn't. I saw you crack a smile before I stalked out of your office."

I couldn't help giving up a giggle.

"But she deserved that," I said. "I wanted to hit her my damn self."

My stomach made strange bubbling and gurgling sounds.

"So what happens next?" she asked.

"I think you already know," I said.

We both sat there in silence. Except for the sound of toil and trouble in my belly.

"You sound like you're in for a case of the shits," Reesy said as she glanced down at the source of the gurgles.

"I think so," I half-said, half-moaned.

"So you gotta fire me, huh?" she asked.

I didn't say anything.

"Huh?" she repeated.

"Yeah. I do."

She was quiet for a second.

"Did Rich tell you to do this?"

"He told me to handle it," I replied.

I clutched my stomach. My bowels were in a rage.

She pressed her lips tightly together.

"What's going to happen to that bitch Millicent?" she demanded.

"She's outta there, too," I said. "Rich is going to fire her personally."

"I wish I could be a fly on the wall to see that," she said.

"So do I."

I clutched at my middle as it churned and fizzled.

"My stomach is tor' up," I moaned.

"I don't know why you even tried to drink that stuff. You know damn well you can't handle hard liquor, Miss Divine."

I lay back against the couch, thinking.

"I guess I'll be outta there shortly."

Her head snapped toward me.

"Why do you say that?"

I shrugged.

"I don't know. I can't imagine Rich is going to let this go unnoticed. Millicent made a really big deal of it all."

"*Fuck* her!" she snapped. "And you know damn well Rich Landey ain't gon' fire you!"

"Why not?" I asked.

"I just know. Even though he obviously can't stand me, he's crazy about you. You're his little black protégée. Trust me, girl. Your job is secure."

I felt a pang of guilt at her comment about Rich not being able to stand her. I knew I should go ahead and tell her.

What the hell? *In Raynal veritas.*

"Yo, Reese."

"What?" she answered. "Stop worrying about your job."

"No, that's not it," I said, feeling sheepish.

"What then?"

"I lied to you," I said point-blank.

Her eyes narrowed.

"About . . . ?"

"The phone calls. Rich didn't say anything to me about you being on the phone so much."

"Oh yeah?" she said. "I'm listening."

"Yeah. I was the one upset about you being on the phone so much. Everybody was talking about it, and I didn't know how to discuss it with you."

I paused, sighing.

"So you blamed it on Rich?"

"Yeah. That was fucked up, I know."

"*Very* fucked up, Misty." She rubbed her leg. "I knew it was you, though."

I looked at her.

"What do you mean?" I asked in surprise.

"I know you, Misty. You're way too nonconfrontational in

your personal relationships. So you'd rather blame something that upset you on somebody else than tell me flat-out how you feel. You knew I'd get mad. And look at what ended up happening."

"What?" I asked, puzzled.

Reesy chewed on her lip.

"I still got mad at you anyway," she said. "That's why I've been mad at you all week. I knew that was bullshit you was talkin' the other night. You couldn't even be straight enough with me to tell me the truth. That hurt me. Especially after we've been friends for so damn long."

Now I felt terrible. Drunk and terrible. Like I wanted to cry.

"Who was that guy you brought here the other night?"

"He's the fine motherfucka I told you about that used to come in the club when I first started working there."

"The crazy one?" I asked, alarmed.

"No! That guy was butt-ugly. Plus, he was Italian. This brother is a straight-up, roughneck stud."

"Oh," I said.

She didn't respond.

"So you brought him home just like that? And had sex with him?"

She nodded, shrugging her shoulders like it was no big deal.

"I needed a fuck," Reesy said. "I was mad, and drunk, and horny. I needed me a nice, hard, no-strings-attached fuck."

She chuckled.

"Something you've probably never had in your life."

She was right about that.

I opened my mouth to say something, but she cut me off.

"Don't worry. I used a condom."

I closed my mouth abruptly. That wasn't what I was going to ask her.

We both sat there in silence.

"So what are you going to do for work?" I asked after a while.

"I'on know," Reesy replied. "I've had a few interesting thoughts."

"Like what?"

"Well," she smiled, "I am a dancer. And this is New York."

My brows raised at this.

"Exotic dancing?"

"No, Misty," she chuckled, "not exotic dancing. I thought maybe I'd go to some auditions."

"Don't you have to have been in the business awhile to make it as a dancer here? You're thirty, Reesy."

She rolled her eyes at me.

"I see liquor makes you frank."

I laughed.

"No, seriously. Won't it be tough for you to try to break in here?"

"Tough ain't never scared me."

"I guess not," I agreed.

"Who knows," she added, "maybe I'll even try my hand at some acting auditions. There's lots of amateur theater groups around."

I laughed out loud.

"You, Reesy? Act?"

She couldn't believe I was giving it to her so straight.

"Misty," she said. "Do me a favor, okay?"

"Anything," I smiled.

"Stay away from this stuff," she said, grabbing the bottle of Raynal from the table. "I can't take you when you're fucked up. It's like talking to myself."

"Not a pretty thang, is it?" I asked.

"No. It's actually very ugly."

We both started laughing.

Reesy exhaled deeply, rubbing her forehead.

"Well, I guess I can go in tomorrow and get my stuff," she said.

"I can get it if you want me to."

"No," Reesy replied. "I'll get it. I don't want any of those motherfuckas to think I'm too ashamed to come into that office."

"Then why did you get so mad about it today?" I asked. "Why did it turn into a fight?"

"Because. That bitch Millicent wanted to try to act like she was all high and mighty and shit. Like I was supposed to be embarrassed. What I got mad about was her tryin' to front me."

She worked her neck back and forth.

"And that punk ass nigga who tried to bust me in front of everybody."

"Yeah!" I exclaimed, my stomach lurching as I did so. "That was fucked up!"

She waved her finger in the air.

"That's all right," she said. "I'll see his ass again."

She said that with conviction.

"I will see his black ass again."

Rich Landey was at Burch Financial first thing the next morning. When I came in, he was already there.

"Hi," he said. I couldn't gauge his tone. "How are you today?"

I was unsure of how to talk to him. I didn't know if we were still business buddies. Mentor and protégée.

Or if he now thought I was someone who had turned out to be a bad mistake.

I knew that was a stupid thought to have after working for him for more than two years, but still I was worried. You just never knew with white people.

It was a coin toss as far as I was concerned. Really.

"Fine," I answered, my voice weak despite my attempt to sound self-assured.

"I've already let Millicent go," he said. "I had her and Bob meet me here before the office opened. I felt it was important that Bob be present. Especially since he's managed her for all these years. Her departure will be announced as a resignation."

Oh Lord. Rich wasn't wasting any time. I guess I'd be next.

"I'm paying her a sizeable severance, Misty." He made this statement with a slightly accusatory tone. "I want her to go away quietly. The last thing we need is a legal issue to come out of this."

"I understand," I said.

"Bob and I talked at length afterward. He spoke very frankly about the way he's been feeling the past few months."

"Oh really?" I asked with surprise.

"Yes," Rich nodded. "I wasn't expecting him to be so open about his resistance to the changes that have taken place around here. He recognizes that much of Millicent's anger was fueled by her loyalty to him, and his own negativity."

That was a shocker. Ol' mousy Bob must have grown himself some balls. Or borrowed Millicent's.

"I offered him a severance package."

"What did he say?" I asked.

"He accepted it without hesitation. He's ready to go. I think he would have quit soon enough, with or without the severance, but I felt like it was the right thing to do. Burch is progressing and Bob isn't. The time has come for us to part ways."

I stood there, silently studying him. There was such a sense of purpose in his voice. I could see he meant business about letting nothing get in the way of the success of Burch.

"But I see this as a good thing," Rich kept on. "I think we need to eliminate as much negative influence from around here as possible."

He stood there, all neat and crisp, almost machine-like. He had accomplished so much, and it was only seven in the morning. What time had he met with Bob and Millicent? The crack of dawn?

Had I been feeling like my old confident self around him, I would have asked him about it.

Right now, however, I felt like I was the next one in line to be talked to. He was getting ready to do it.

"Let's go into your office," he said.

Aw, hell.

Rich was going to fire me.

Before we had a chance to go into my office, Reesy appeared, coming in to clear out her workstation.

Rich noticed her immediately.

Reesy's greeting to him was curt and abrupt.

"Good morning, Rich," she said. "I'll be out of here in a little bit."

"Good morning, Reesy," he returned. "I'm about to sit down and talk with Misty. Can you come in here for a moment and join us?"

Oh shit. He was going to fire both of us together. I guess when it got down to it, we were just a couple of disposable employees.

An experiment that had failed miserably.

"Sure," Reesy consented.

He stood in my doorway, waving us both into the room.

"So, Reesy," Rich began, "Misty tells me you were an exotic dancer."

Reesy's eyes narrowed in the defensive. I prayed to God she wasn't going to go off on him.

I just wanted us to make our exit with dignity. Not some ugly episode that would go down in Burch's history and forever fuck it up for another sistah, or brother, who tried to get their foot inside the door.

"Yes, I was," she said flatly.

Rich nodded.

"Heard you were the best," he kept on. "And you know, Reesy, I believe if you're going to do something, you damn well ought to strive to be the best."

What the hell? Was Rich playing with her? Because if so, he definitely picked the wrong sistah to play with.

Reesy would eat him up alive right there in that office.

"What are you saying?" Reesy asked. "You think my being an exotic dancer was a good thing?"

"I'm not discussing *what* it was you did," he said. "If it was a legal profession, who am I to judge it?"

He rubbed his chin contemplatively.

"I'm just saying that if you chose to do it to the best of your ability, then that's a testament to your hard work and commitment."

I saw a faint smile form on Reesy's lips.

I was completely confused at this point.

"So am I fired or not?" she asked, in pure, direct Reesy fashion.

"Reesy, I think you need to look at the bigger picture of all this," Rich began.

She was fired. I could tell by his tone.

"And what's that?" Reesy asked with sarcasm.

"A lot of what comes out of yesterday's little fracas will have to do with perceptions," he said.

I didn't say a word. I just sat there listening.

"Burch is in a very volatile phase right now. I'm trying to establish a climate here in keeping with the way I run things, and Misty is playing a huge role in helping me to do that."

He glanced over at me as he said this. I looked into his eyes briefly, unsure, then looked away.

"I'm going to be honest with both of you," he said. "I have an agenda here. It's a self-serving one, but it can benefit Misty as well. I need somebody on the inside I can trust to do the job. Misty is that person. On the flip side, she gets an opportunity that not too many women have a chance at."

Reesy was watching him closely.

"I think I can be frank and say you both know this is an opportunity not very many African-American women have. I'm not trying to pat myself on the back for this," he said and looked over at me. "I think you deserve this opportunity, Misty. You're definitely the best person for the job."

"Thank you," I said quietly.

"Do you understand what I'm saying to you, Reesy?" he asked.

"I hear you, but I don't think I know what you're trying to say."

He sighed, rubbing his chin.

"It means the three of us have to come to a decision in this room," he said. "We have to decide what's most important here: your keeping this job and having Misty continue to be viewed as a Teflon manger, or your resigning and allowing us to add a little human touch to the place."

A Teflon manager? I guess that thing with Jeff really fucked my corporate image.

"My resignation would do that?" Reesy asked. Her brows were knitted tightly. "So you're saying my staying here makes the place a little inhuman?"

"No, that's not what I'm saying, Reesy," Rich replied, his brow knitted as well. "Bob and Millicent are both going to be gone as a result of this. Possibly you, if that's the decision you make. If the employees see equity in how yesterday's fight was handled, I think they'll be more inclined to trust that they can expect fairness in exchange for hard work."

"What if I decide not to resign?" Reesy asked smugly.

"Then I'll accept that," he answered. "I'm willing to live with that decision on Misty's behalf because you're her friend. I'll allow her this one leniency, because, remember, I have an agenda.

"But the environment around here won't improve. And I don't think Misty will be able to earn the confidence of the staff. You'll be closely watched."

Reesy started at that statement, and looked directly at me.

"And not just by the people here," he added. "By me personally."

Reesy sat there, chewing her lip. I didn't know how to react to any of this.

Out of all of this, I realized that Rich wasn't going to fire me, which was a relief.

But I was puzzled that he would give Reesy the choice of what to do about her job. Especially when his preference about what she should do was so clear.

Reesy needed to go for the sake of him and the company. And me.

But what if she, just to be evil, elected to stay?

Things wouldn't be the same between Rich and me.

And if there was ever anything out of line from that point forward, he would find a way to get rid of both of us.

That was something I knew for sure.

"Sounds like the decision's been made for me already," Reesy returned.

"No, it hasn't," he said. "I'm going to let you make the call. I know you need a job. But I also think you understand the importance of what's happening here with your friend. No one could predict that things would turn out the way they did. But the die's been cast, and I think the two of you need to consider what is best for this whole situation overall."

He turned toward me.

"I'm going to leave you two alone to work this out," he said. "You can let me know in an hour what it is you're going to do."

He pushed his chair back and stood.

"That's not necessary," Reesy announced.

I sat there, ny heart beating with a dull thump.

"I'll resign," she said, her tone flat and unemotional. "I know what's best for my friend. She deserves this job, and I'm not gonna be the cause of her losing it."

Inside, I breathed a quiet sigh of relief.

Rich nodded. His brow relaxed.

"Good deal," he said. "I think you're doing the right thing, Reesy. For everybody."

"Whatever," she said.

He stood over her, starting to resemble the old Rich I felt was my boss and my friend.

"Millicent and Bob are getting severance packages. We'll

258

put together something that can keep you going for about six months. At least until you can get on your feet again."

I shot a faint smile her way. To make sure she realized how generous he was being.

Especially when he didn't have to be.

"Thanks," she said in a dry voice.

"It's the right thing to do," he said. "You helped us catch Jeff, after all."

Reesy stood from her chair.

"Well, I better get out of here," she said. "I need to get my stuff out of that desk. I don't want to be the cause of negative vibes around here any more than I have been."

She walked toward the door and pulled it open.

"Reesy?" Rich called after her.

She turned and stared at him, her expression dry and unreadable.

"Thank you," he said.

"Whatever," she returned, and pulled the door shut behind her.

BUBBLING BROWN SUGAR

orry about your friend," Rick said.

He stood in front of my desk, appearing out of nowhere, looking all chocolate and fine.

Making it clear to me why I stayed away as much as possible from the floor where he worked and only had conferences with him when necessary.

I had run into Rick Hodges several times since I'd arrived at Burch. He was usually as abrupt with me as I was with him. I knew why I stayed out of his way. Mainly because he was as fine as he was, and the last thing I needed was to be caught up in a romantic relationship with a coworker. A subordinate, at that.

I also didn't want to align myself with the only other black manager in the company. It seemed too obvious and expected. I didn't want him to think I'd show him any favoritism just because we happened to be the same color.

But I was never quite sure why he kept his distance from me. I partly believed it was because he despised me, like the rest of the staff. I studied him as he stood in front of me now.

He probably just came to gloat because the black bitch in charge had lost her right-hand girl and had her pride taken down a notch.

"Is she going to be okay?" he asked with what seemed like sincere concern.

"Reesy will be all right," I returned, trying to keep a straight face.

No way was I going to even entertain any thoughts about Rick Hodges. He was taboo. We worked together. He worked *for* me.

I looked back down at the paperwork I was reviewing. An attempt to encourage him to take his fine ass somewhere else.

"What Dandre did was very uncool," he offered, still hanging around.

"I'm glad *you* said it," I said, head still down.

"Oh, I know it was," he chimed, apparently happy to be having dialogue with me. "I told him what happened after he left, and he acted like he didn't even realize what the problem was."

"Are you serious?" I exclaimed, finally looking up.

He nodded.

"That's Dandre. He's a typical spoiled rich kid. As long as it isn't affecting him, he doesn't give a shit."

I opened my mouth to say something, then, thinking better of it, I abruptly closed it.

"What?" he asked.

"Nothing."

"Really?" he encouraged. "What? You can say it."

I sighed in frustration.

"Didn't he realize what he was doing to her? There aren't enough of us around here for us to be breaking on each other like that!"

He shrugged.

"That's Dandre," he said again.

"That's fucked up," I replied.

He grinned.

"It's good to see you've got a soul sistah side. I was beginning to get worried that maybe you were too serious and stiff. That's why I stayed out of your way so much."

"If you thought I was so serious, what made you come around today?" I asked.

He shrugged his shoulders, smiling.

"I don't know. I guess I felt like I needed to come say something to you. And apologize on Dandre's behalf somehow. Sort of a show of solidarity."

I didn't smile back.

"You're not the one who needs to be apologizing."

"I know," Rick said. "I know. I don't think Dandre really meant any harm. He's a pretty cool guy, under the right circumstances."

"I'm sure," I said.

"You know, I supported what you did on the thing with Jeff."

"I heard."

He chuckled.

"I guess I don't have to ask you from where," he said. "Mare's got a pretty big mouth."

I didn't respond.

He stood there awkwardly.

"Well," he said after a while, backing away toward the door. "I'm not going to keep you."

"Okay," I said.

My expression was plain.

I watched him walk out of my office, his handsome physique holding my attention.

I sighed heavily, shook my head, and dove back into my paperwork.

"Maybe we can go to lunch sometime," a voice blurted.

I looked up to find him standing in my doorway again.

"What?"

He looked a little unsure of himself. It seemed completely sincere.

"Maybe we can go to lunch sometime?" he repeated, this time couching it as a question.

"I don't think so," I smiled wanly. "I don't think that would be too wise."

"*No, no no!*" he protested. "I don't mean it like that!"

I didn't know if I liked that comment any better.

He seemed to be aware of my thought.

"I didn't mean *that* the way it sounded either."

"Sure," I replied in a dry voice.

His forehead was wrinkled in a futile attempt to read my response.

"Forget it," he said, waving his hand. "Forget I even said anything. I can't seem to get this right."

He disappeared out of my doorway.

"*Rick!*" I called after him.

But he was gone.

Oh well.

When I got home from work that night, Reesy was just coming in.

She had a large duffel bag thrown across her shoulder.

"How's it going, girl?" I asked. "How's the acting auditions?"

She cut her eyes at me, searching for some hint of sarcasm on my part.

There was none.

"The acting auditions suck," she said finally. "There's only a handful of casting calls I've seen for black people. And at the ones I go to, a million of us show up."

I sat down on the couch and kicked off my heels.

"Don't sound so bitter," I said. "You're just getting started at this. I understand the acting business requires a shitload of commitment."

Reesy sat down next to me.

"I don't know if I'm going to keep pursuing the acting thing anyway," she said.

I should have known. Reesy didn't stick with anything for too long.

"So what are you going to do?"

"Well," she began, reaching into her duffel bag, "I picked up this flyer from one of the auditions today."

She handed it to me.

Dancers Wanted. Bubbling Brown Sugar.

"What do you think?" she asked.

"Reesy, this is a serious show. I've seen *Bubbling Brown Sugar* before. Are you sure you're ready for something this big?"

"I feel like I am. What about all the years of formal training I've had? That should account for something."

"Yeah," I agreed, "you've had lots of training, that's for sure. And you're pretty damn good, from what I saw."

Reesy studied my face, her eyes narrowing.

"Are you being serious, or are you just making fun of me?"

I handed the flyer back to her, my expression fixed.

"No, Reesy, I'm being very serious. If you want to dance, I say go ahead and do it. One thing I've learned about you is that when you get something in your head, the best thing to do is support you, 'cause when it comes down to it, you're gonna go for it, no matter what anybody says. That's one thing I admire about you."

"Really?" she asked with surprise.

"Really. Sometimes I'm too afraid to step outside of the box. You not only step out of the box, you break it down and shred up the paper."

She giggled.

"So you think I'm crazy for doing this, don't you?" she asked.

"Yes. But there's nothing wrong with being crazy. Many a successful career was born from a crazy, risky move. Look at me. Who knows? Maybe dancing is your thing. It seems to be what you have the most passion about doing."

"Yeah. It's like I get off on it. I love seeing the effect I have on people when I dance. It's like a whole 'nother language.

Seems like I communicate better with my body than I do when I speak."

"I won't *even* get into what you mean by that," I laughed, cutting my eyes at her.

"You know what I mean, heffah," she laughed. "All right, then. I'm gonna try it. All they can tell me is no."

"That's right," I said. "You go to that audition, and you work that body until it's speaking Chinese!"

She shoved me lightly on the arm.

"You're crazy, Misty. Certifiably nuts. But it's good to see you relaxed for a change. You've been so uptight since we moved here. We hardly ever joke around like we used to."

"I know," I replied apologetically. "I think it was the strain of working in the same place and being your boss. It got too messy for our friendship. I couldn't keep things separate. I guess I learned a valuable lesson."

"I guess we both did," Reesy replied. "I don't ever wanna work for you no more. You're a terrible boss."

I glanced over at her. For a second, her expression was serious. Then she flashed me a radiant, toothy grin.

"Very funny," I smirked, then added, "Guess who had the nerve to come up and talk to me today?"

"Rick Hodges," she said without hesitation.

I stared at her.

"How did you know that?" I asked, perplexed.

She sighed heavily.

"Mare told me she thought he had taken a liking to you. She said he mentions you a lot. For no reason. Dumb stuff."

"Like what?" I asked, trying to be nonchalant.

Reesy shrugged.

"I'on know. Stupid shit. Like asking her if you ever say anything about him. If you date anybody. High school shit. He was tryna do it on the sly, like she wasn't gon' come back and ask me."

Now that Reesy was out of Burch, her ghetto talk popped up with more frequency.

"What'd you tell her when she asked if I was dating any-body?"

"I told her to have him ask you himself," she said. "He's a grown man. He's got a mouth. He don't need to have two women refereeing for him like that."

I leaned back against the couch beside her.

"How come I never knew this?" I asked her.

"Because," Reesy replied, "you were so busy getting people arrested and tryna find ways to tell me to stay off the phone that you didn't even know what was going on right under-neath your nose."

I guess she was right. I had no idea Rick had the slightest interest in me.

Damn.

"Would you go out with him?" she asked.

Before I could get a chance to answer, she said, "'Cause it would be stupid if you did."

This made me mad. It's not like I said I would go out with him anyway.

"People already talk about you around the office as it is," she kept on. "They'll talk about you like a dog if you start going out with the only other black person there. Plus, you're his boss. They'll holler favoritism with a quickness."

"I don't want to go out with him," I protested, leaning for-ward again. "He came to my office. I didn't go to his."

"You're considering it, though," she said in a soft voice. "Otherwise you wouldn't be asking me no dumb questions about what he's been saying."

I sat beside her, stewing.

I didn't want to go out with him. I mean, he was fine and all, but even I knew that going out with an employee was a stupid move. Reesy didn't have to talk to me like I was a two-year-old.

"Don't get mad," she cooed, rubbing me on the back. "It's been a long time since you had some dick. That man's proba-bly looking like a piece of candy to you right now."

I stood up from the couch. Just like that, she had changed my mood.

"Fuck you, Reesy," I snapped.

I went into my bedroom and slammed the door.

The next day, Saturday, I brought a huge pile of laundry into the living room and began sorting through it.

Reesy had gone to the audition for *Bubbling Brown Sugar.* She left at dawn, determined to get a spot in the show.

I didn't have the heart to discourage her. But I knew the odds were definitely *not* in her favor

I divided the clothes into whites, jeans, towels, sheets. As I did so, I began to picture Rick's face as he stood beside my desk the day before.

He had such gentle eyes. And his voice was *sooo* sexy. I wondered what he was like in bed.

I quickly banished the thought. The last thing I needed to be doing was thinking about black dick. Especially when I hadn't had none in so long.

I felt my panties getting warm in the seat.

Damn.

I stood and went into the kitchen for some bottled water. I opened the refrigerator door and looked inside.

I heard the front door open.

"Misty! Misty!"

"I'm in the kitchen," I called.

She burst into the kitchen, her face bright and excited. She was breathing hard.

"Did you get it?" I asked, stunned.

"No," she exclaimed, "but the guy liked the way I danced and said he wanted me to audition for another show he's involved in!"

"Oh, Reesy, that's wonderful!" I exclaimed.

She stood there in front of me, her face beaming like a bright yellow sun, the braids snaking out like crazy rays. I felt so glad for her, I reached out and embraced her in a big, congratulatory hug.

"I'm proud of you," I added.

"Can I have some water?" she panted.

I handed her the bottle of Evian intended for me.

"What'd you do? Run up the stairs?"

She took a sip, then caught her breath.

"I ran down the hallway," Reesy said.

She walked into the living room, stepped over the piles of clothing, and flopped down on the couch.

"You gonna do mine?" she asked, referring to the laundry.

"Why not?" I said, reaching in for another bottle of water. "Go get your stuff and sort it into piles."

"Are you gonna wash 'em for me?" she asked.

"Yeah."

"Thanks, Miss Divine. This must be my lucky day."

"Silly," I said, rolling my eyes at her.

It was the least I could do. In honor of something positive coming out of her audition attempt.

Reesy got up and went into her room. She went through her clothes and gathered them together.

"Are you sure you don't mind doing this?" she yelled from the room. "I got a lot of dirty shit."

"Bring it on," I called out in return.

I picked up one of the piles of clothes that were already sorted on the floor.

I went to the washer, opened the lid, and dropped them in. I turned on the machine, and reached for the detergent.

The box was empty.

Reesy's fucking ass. She had to be the one who would be lazy enough to leave an empty box of detergent.

I stormed out of the laundry room.

"What's wrong?"

She was sitting there looking so happy and innocent.

I straightened up my face. I didn't want to ruin her good mood by letting her know I was mad.

"Nothing," I said. "I'll be right back."

"Where you going?"

"To the store. I gotta get some washing powder."

When I went outside, the sun was shining brightly and the wind was a gentle breeze that washed over my skin.

It was such a pretty day, I decided to take a drive instead of walking to the store on the corner.

I went to the parking garage and got my car.

I turned on the engine, drove slowly out of the garage, and pulled off down the street.

It felt good to be driving. I spent so much of my day taking taxicabs or walking, I had begun to forget what it felt like to have a steering wheel in my hand.

I was lucky enough to find a parking space in front of a store across town, so I stopped and went in to pick up some Tide.

I also bought a bagful of apples and some grapes, some Gatorade, and a big bottle of bleach.

I was taking the long way home, eating grapes, when I realized I needed to stop by the office and pick up a file.

I turned the car around and swung by Burch. I parked out front instead of going into the garage. I jumped out of the car and ran inside the building.

I rushed into the elevator, hoping not to run into anyone, even the security guard. He wasn't sitting at his station. Perhaps he was making the rounds checking the building.

I wore a pair of sweats and sneakers, and my hair was pulled back into a ponytail. I didn't look too bad, but I looked nothing like I usually did when I entered the doors of Burch Financial.

I got off on the twenty-fourth floor, dashed into my office, grabbed the file, and zipped back into the elevator.

The security guard was at his station when I emerged.

"Good afternoon, Miss Fine," he said. "It's too pretty a day for you to be here."

I held up the file.

"Had to make a pickup," I smiled. "Se ya later, Carl."

I rushed out of the revolving door and back onto the side-walk.

I opened the car door and tossed the file on the passenger seat.

When I stuck the key into the ignition and turned, the car made a groaning sound, a clunk, a thud, and a hiss.

When I tried to crank it again, it wouldn't turn over.

"Fuck!" I exclaimed.

I sat there, alternately pumping the accelerator and turning the key.

I had no idea what pumping the accelerator did. It was something Stefan had taught me a long time ago, but he'd never bothered to explain the reason.

After going through that exercise for some ten minutes or more, I dropped my head against the wheel and banged it gently in disgust.

"Shit, shit, shit!"

"Need some help?" a voice close to my ear boomed.

I jumped clear out of my seat, I was so scared.

I leaned far away from the offending sound, and looked into a pair of dark, sexy eyes.

Rick Hodges stood there smiling at me.

"You scared me!" I frowned.

"I'm sorry," he said, backing up, raising his hands. "Didn't mean you any harm."

"Yeah, right!" I snapped.

"Car problems?"

I nodded.

"What are you doing here anyway?"

"Stupid reason," he said and grinned.

Jeesus, this man was fine.

"Is it a reason you can tell me?"

"You're the boss," he said. "I don't know."

"It's Saturday," I returned. "Pretend, for just a moment, that I'm not the boss."

He chuckled softly.

"That's easier said than done, Miss Fine."

"Go on, hurry," I said. "I need to get my car fixed."

"All right, all right. Why don't you slide over and let me see if I can fix this. I'll tell you why I'm here while I do it."

This was a harmless enough suggestion. No one could read anything into it.

I picked up the file off the passenger seat and tossed it into the back.

Rick got in and slid my car seat back. He glanced over at me.

"You think you sit close enough? As tall as you are?"

I giggled.

"Don't even go there," I warned.

He reached for the ignition, but stopped before he turned it.

"Did you pump the gas?" he asked.

What was with men? Was pumping the gas some universal thing they all knew the meaning of?

"Yeah."

He pumped the accelerator hard a few times, then turned the key.

The car started right up.

"I guess all it needed was a man's touch," he smiled.

"I guess I had already done all that pumping, and you just happened to make the lucky turn that started the car," I replied.

"Could be. Could be."

I turned toward him.

"So what are you doing here?" I asked. "I didn't see your car when I pulled up."

"I parked in the garage. I was just driving away when I saw you stranded here on the side of the road. I pulled up right behind you."

I looked out the back window. There was his shiny black Benz.

"If I were you, I wouldn't leave my car on the street like that," he said. "Somebody might strip it. Or worse yet, it'll be gone when you come out."

"Thanks, Dad," I smiled.

"You're welcome. Anytime."

I was silent, waiting for an answer to why he was at the office on a Saturday. I raised my eyebrows in anticipation as a not-so-subtle reminder.

"Oh," he laughed, "I came by to get my Prince CD. I play it in the office. You *do* know I play CDs in my office, don't you? Ever since we got those new computers last year with CD-ROM, it's been hard to resist."

I listened to him without commenting.

"I don't play them loud," he continued nervously. "I wasn't sure whether playing music was in violation of some sort of new office policy. Things have changed a lot in the past few months."

I cut my eyes at him.

"For the better," he added. "Definitely for the better."

"Yeah, right," I laughed. "Well, nobody cares if you play your CDs. Certainly not me. I play them all the time. It relaxes me, especially when I'm here working late."

It was his turn to raise his brow.

"You listen to music? You mean you're actually human after all?"

I dropped my head, embarrassed at the comment. When I looked up at him again, his teeth were gleaming, bared in a wide grin.

"I guess everyone does think I'm Medusa, huh?"

"Not everybody," he chuckled. "You're all right."

"Well, if it's any consolation, I happen to like Prince."

"Do you really?" he said with surprise. "What, just certain cuts?"

"No. I like everything. Okay, he has a weird song here and there, but for the most part, I love all of his stuff."

"Interesting" was his reply.

He was looking at the floor of the car, nodding his head. I detected a smile at the corner of his lips.

"The only thing I hate is that he changed his name," I said,

"I don't know what to call him now. I guess it was right in keeping with his personality, though. Only Prince can change his name to a symbol and get away with it."

"Tafkap."

I didn't think I understood him.

"What?" I said.

"Tafkap."

"What is that?" I asked, getting lost in those sexy dark brown eyes.

"That's what I call him."

"Who?"

"Prince, Misty," he laughed. "Isn't that what we're talking about?"

"Yeah." I giggled like a kid. "Why do you call him that?"

"It stands for The Artist Formerly Known As Prince," he said.

"Oh. That's clever."

"I thought so," he replied. "At least I can pronounce it."

I laughed.

"Well," I sighed, "I guess you better get going. I don't want to hold you up. Anyway, you're burning up my gas."

He laughed.

"I'm not in any rush," Rick said. "But I guess I am burning up your gas."

He opened the door and got out of the car.

I slid over. He leaned in on the edge of the window.

"It was nice talking to you, Misty," he said. "You're turning out to be a really nice person."

I couldn't help smiling at that.

"I guess you're off to a busy Saturday afternoon?" he probed.

"Just laundry," I sighed. "Nothing major."

He hesitated a moment.

"I probably shouldn't ask you this, but, would you like to go get a sandwich? There's a deli down the street I like. Gleason's."

I didn't answer right away.

"I probably shouldn't have asked you that," he added quickly. "Just forget it. Take it easy, Misty."

He stood up and walked away.

I stuck my head out of the window.

"Rick!" I yelled.

I was not about to let him walk away again.

Fuck what Reesy and anybody else said. He seemed like just a regular nice guy.

A regular *fine ass* nice guy.

He turned toward me.

"Yeah?"

"I like Gleason's. It's one of my favorites. But I do have to get back and do laundry."

He responded with a weak, embarrassed smile, like he thought that I was trying to be polite but reject him all the same.

"All right," he said. "I guess I'll see you around at the office." He quickly turned away again.

"I don't have any plans for dinner," I blurted, surprising myself.

"Yeah?" he grinned, turning around.

"Yeah," I grinned back.

"Would you like to have dinner with me this evening, Miss Fine?" he asked. A happy light danced and twinkled in his eyes.

"I'd love to."

"Is seven o'clock okay? Maybe we can take in dinner and a movie? Catch that new Spike Lee flick everyone's been talking about? That is, if you like Spike Lee."

I smiled.

"I like Spike Lee just fine."

I grabbed my purse, pulled out a card, and jotted my number down on the back.

"Give me a call later. We can finalize everything then."

I handed him the card.

"But it's definitely a date, right?" he asked, clearly nervous and excited. "You're not going to change your mind?"

"It's definitely a date. I'm not going to change my mind."

"Hot damn!" He beamed. He stood there a moment, stunned at his good luck. Still grinning, he turned and walked toward his car.

I watched him from my rearview mirror.

He opened the door of his Benz and started the engine. He pulled up alongside me and let the window down.

"Think your car's gonna make it?" he joked.

"I think so. Just don't drive too far ahead for the next mile or so."

"You got it, lady," he smiled.

As he pulled off, I checked my face in the rearview mirror, realizing I didn't have any makeup on.

Fuck it, I thought. I was tired of being slicked-up and oiled-down just to get a man to look at me.

Rick didn't even say anything about how I looked. He didn't seem to mind.

Not that it mattered anyway. This was as good as it was going to get.

I wasn't going to put on any airs for a man anymore.

As I pulled off behind him, I smiled to myself.

I made one more stop before heading home. Pascal's carried a select reserve of limited merlots. My spirits were so high, I felt the occasion merited a taste of the grape.

I may have had a merlot in mind when I entered, but once inside, I took leave of my senses and spent far more than I'd intended.

There was a song on my lips and a bubble in my head and heart as I slid back behind the wheel of the car. I was a lot broker than when I started out, but I was happy as hell.

When I got back to the apartment, Reesy was sitting in the middle of the floor, separating the clothes into piles.

"What are you doing?" I asked. "I told you I'd take care of that."

She looked up at me as I walked in.

"You said you would wash them, not sort them," she said sarcastically. "Besides, you were gone so long, I didn't think you were ever coming back."

I carried my bags into the kitchen and set them down on the counter.

"Put that stuff down for a minute and come in here," I said.

"Uh-oh," Reesy laughed. "Sounds like I'm in trouble about something again."

I opened a slender white bag and pulled out the bottle. I played around with the top, taking care to aim it away from my face, until I managed to pop the cork.

Foam was spewing over the counter when Reesy finally walked into the kitchen.

"What's that?" she asked with surprise.

"Perrier Jouet."

"I can see that, fool," she laughed. "What's the occasion?"

I opened the cabinet and grabbed two champagne flutes. I poured generously until the bubbles spilled over the sides.

"You're only supposed to fill the glasses halfway," she remarked. "That's proper etiquette and convention."

"The hell with etiquette and convention. You kill me with your selective manners. One minute you're Hoodrat Helen. The next, you're the black Emily Post."

She couldn't help but grin.

"Here," I said, offering her one of the glasses. "Take it. It'll be our secret how full they are."

"When did you buy this?" she said, examining the bottle.

"Just now. On my way back."

I raised my glass in a toast. I waited for her, but she just stood there, looking at me like I was crazy.

"Would you please raise your glass, Teresa Snowden?"

"I still don't know the occasion," she said stubbornly.

I sighed. This was like pulling teeth.

"Didn't you say the man at the audition liked the way you danced and asked you to audition for another one of his shows?"

"Yeah," she grinned.

"Don't you think that's worth celebrating?" I asked.

"Damn right it is!" She clinked her glass against mine and was about to take a drink.

"Wait a minute!" I exclaimed, stopping her hand. Some of the champagne splashed out of the glass onto her blouse.

"There! Now your glass is half-full!" I laughed.

Reesy laughed, shaking her head.

"Why did you stop me?" she asked.

"Because," I grinned, "I've got news, too."

Her eyes studied my face for some sort of clue.

"What is it?"

I breathed in deeply, and then let it fly. I looked her squarely in the eyes as I spoke.

"I have a date tonight at seven. With Rick Hodges."

I waited for her cries of protest, but I wasn't going to let them make me change my mind. I was going out with Rick tonight, dammit, whether Reesy approved of it or not.

A smile crept slowly across her lips.

"I'm surprised it took this long," she said. "You must be like a camel. What do you do? Store fucks in a hump? I guess that's why your breasts are so big, huh?"

I burst out laughing, surprised and relieved that she didn't raise hell like I expected.

"He seems to be a pretty nice guy," Reesy mused. "I've talked to him a few times. Seems kinda shy. But maybe that's more your speed. Just make sure he doesn't pee in the bed, and that his weekends are free."

"Today's Saturday," I reminded her, "and we're going out tonight, so he's obviously free."

"Well, just make sure he doesn't pee in the bed. Or go to titty bars. Those places are evil, you know."

Her eyes twinkled wickedly.

I help up my glass. She followed my lead and held up hers. Before I could open my mouth to say a toast, she began one of her own.

"To good friends. No, to *best* friends."

"Yes," I repeated. "To best friends."

"To keeping our heads up and trying again, even if I don't get picked to dance or if your date is a bomb."

"To keeping our heads up and trying again," I repeated.

She rubbed her chin, then added,

"To life, liberty, and the pursuit of good fucks."

We paused for a moment. The toast still felt unfinished. Suddenly, we both came to the same realization.

"To life, liberty, and the pursuit of *great* fucks!" we squealed in unison, amending the toast.

Complete, we lifted our glasses heavenward. Then, like two giggling schoolgirls, we proceeded to drain them dry.

This was turning out to be a really beautiful day. The two of us hadn't had this much fun in a very long time.

I watched Reesy refill my glass, this time halfway, with the giddy rush of champagne and bubbles. I stood there grinning, bubbling over with the joy of the moment. For no reason at all, I thought of Mama and smiled. Pretty soon, I might even be able to tell her about the nice, mannerable man I was going out with tonight.

I happily downed my second flute of champagne.

Maybe, just maybe, things were going to be all right after all.